Totally Spies!™

PAPERCUTZ™

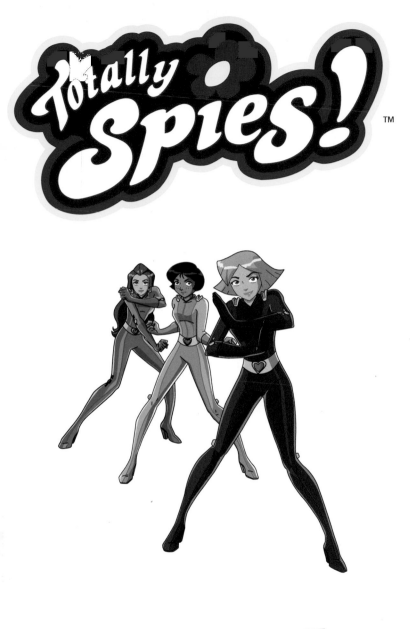

Totally Spies! ™

#1

The OP and Futureshock

PAPERCUTZ ™

NEW YORK

The OP and
Futureshock
MARK LERER — Letterer
JIM SALICRUP
Editor-in-Chief

ISBN-10: 1-59707-043-2 paperback edition
ISBN-13: 978-1-59707-043-0 paperback edition
ISBN-10 1-59707-044-0 hardcover edition
ISBN-13 978-1-59707-044-7 hardcover edition

Printed in China.

Distributed by Holtzbrinck Publishers

10 9 8 7 6 5 4 3 2 1

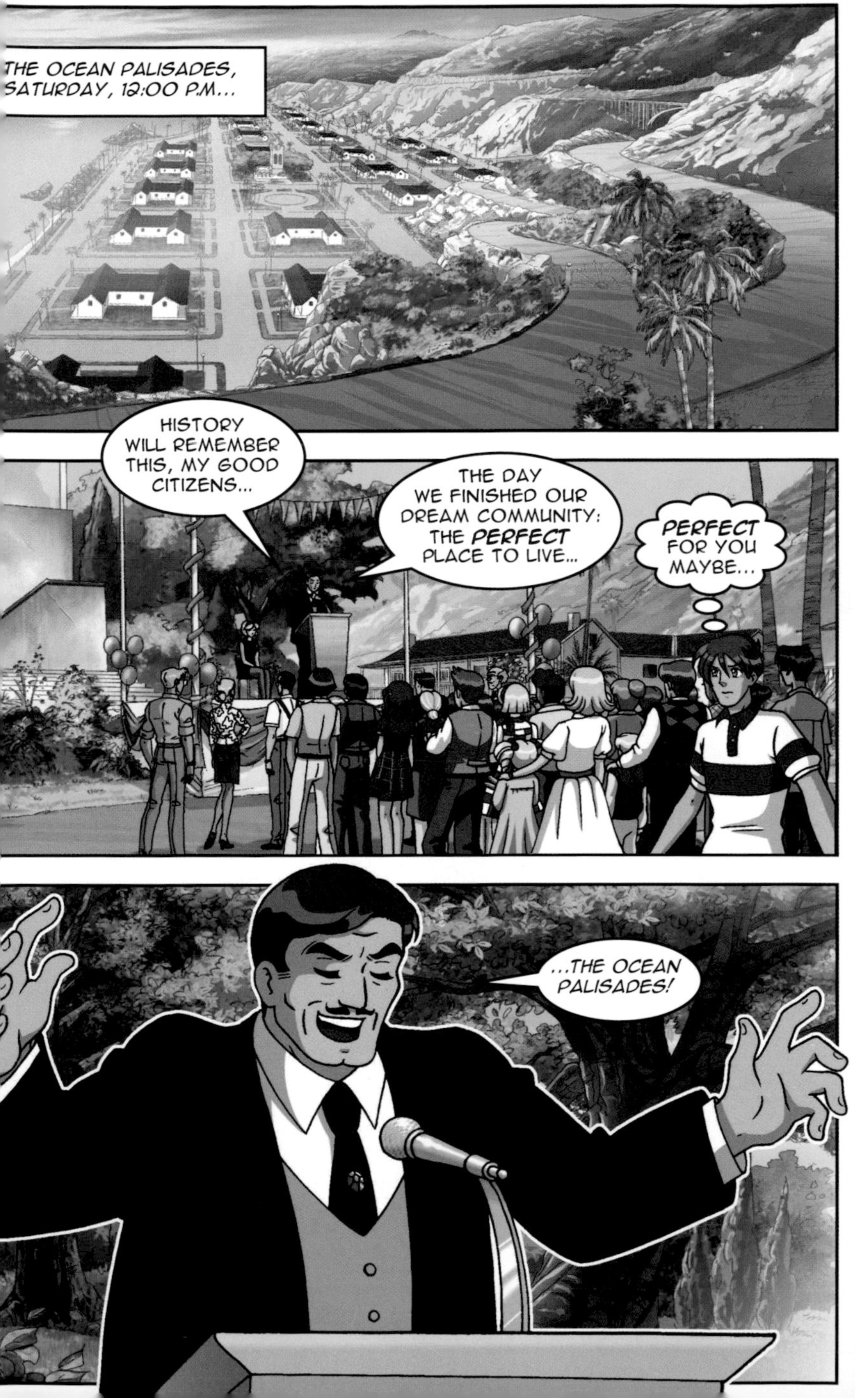
THE OCEAN PALISADES, SATURDAY, 12:00 P.M...
HISTORY WILL REMEMBER THIS, MY GOOD CITIZENS...
THE DAY WE FINISHED OUR DREAM COMMUNITY: THE *PERFECT* PLACE TO LIVE...
PERFECT FOR YOU MAYBE...
...THE OCEAN PALISADES!

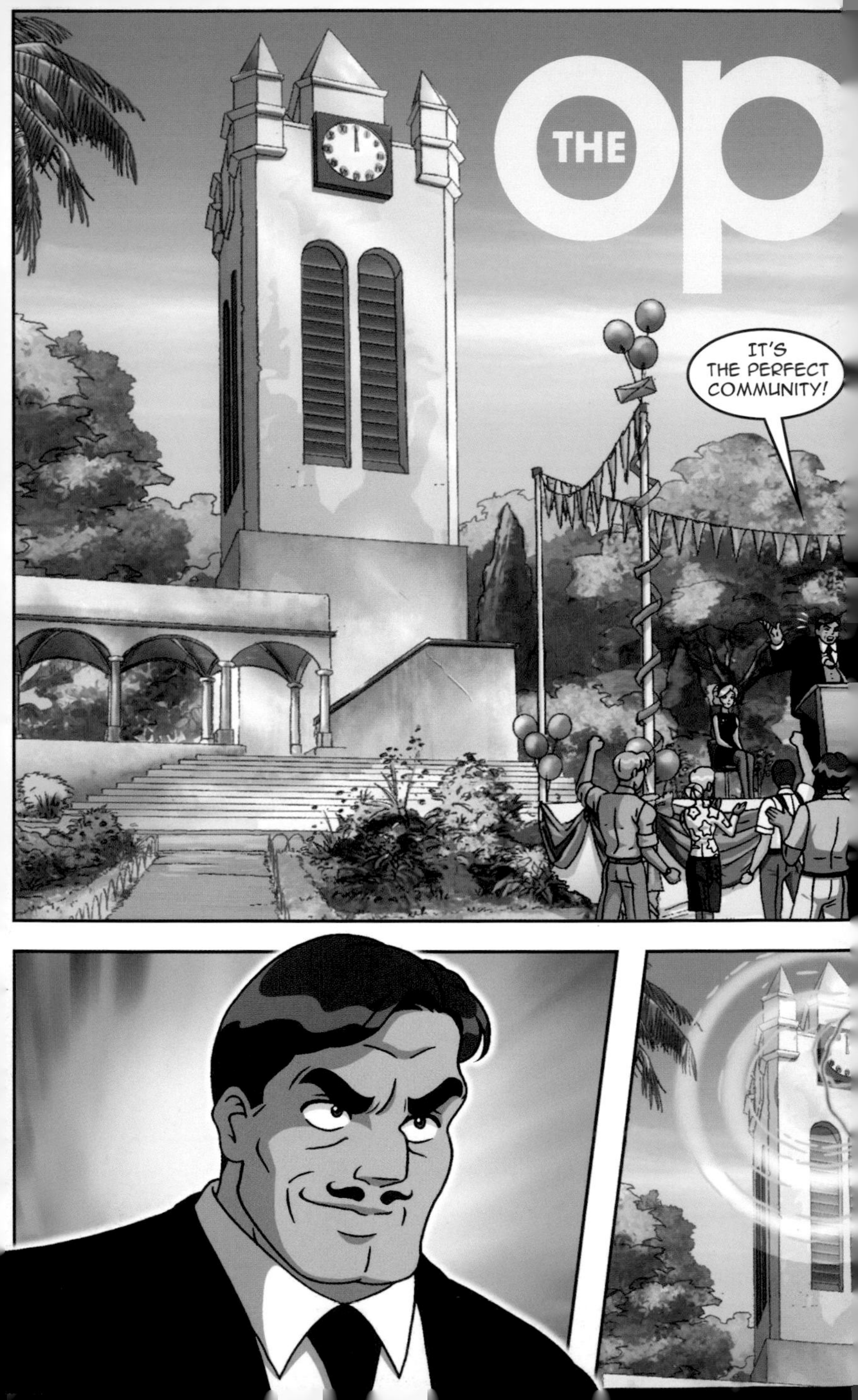
THE op
IT'S THE PERFECT COMMUNITY!

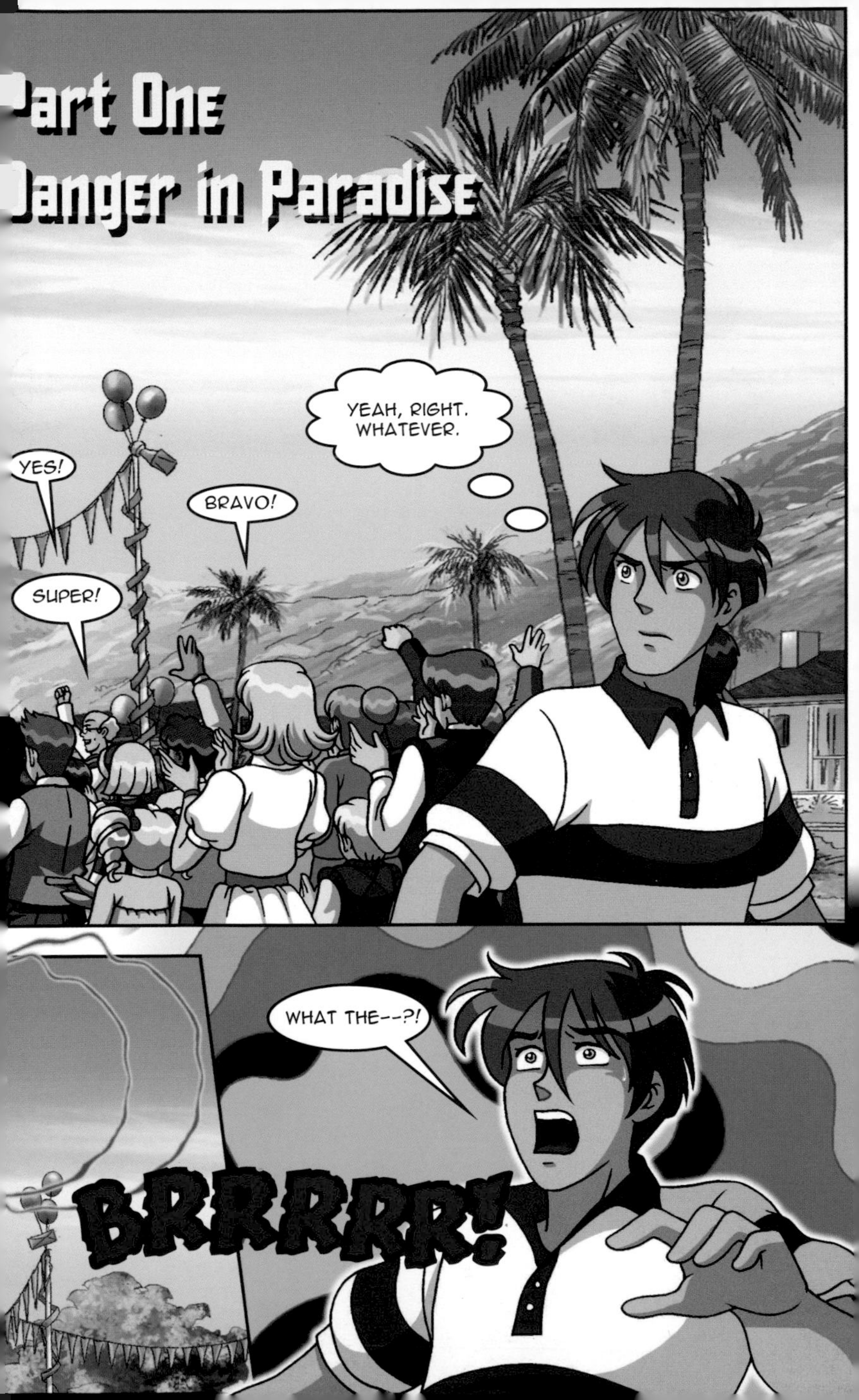
Part One
Danger in Paradise
YES!
SUPER!
BRAVO!
YEAH, RIGHT. WHATEVER.
WHAT THE--?!
BRRRRRR!

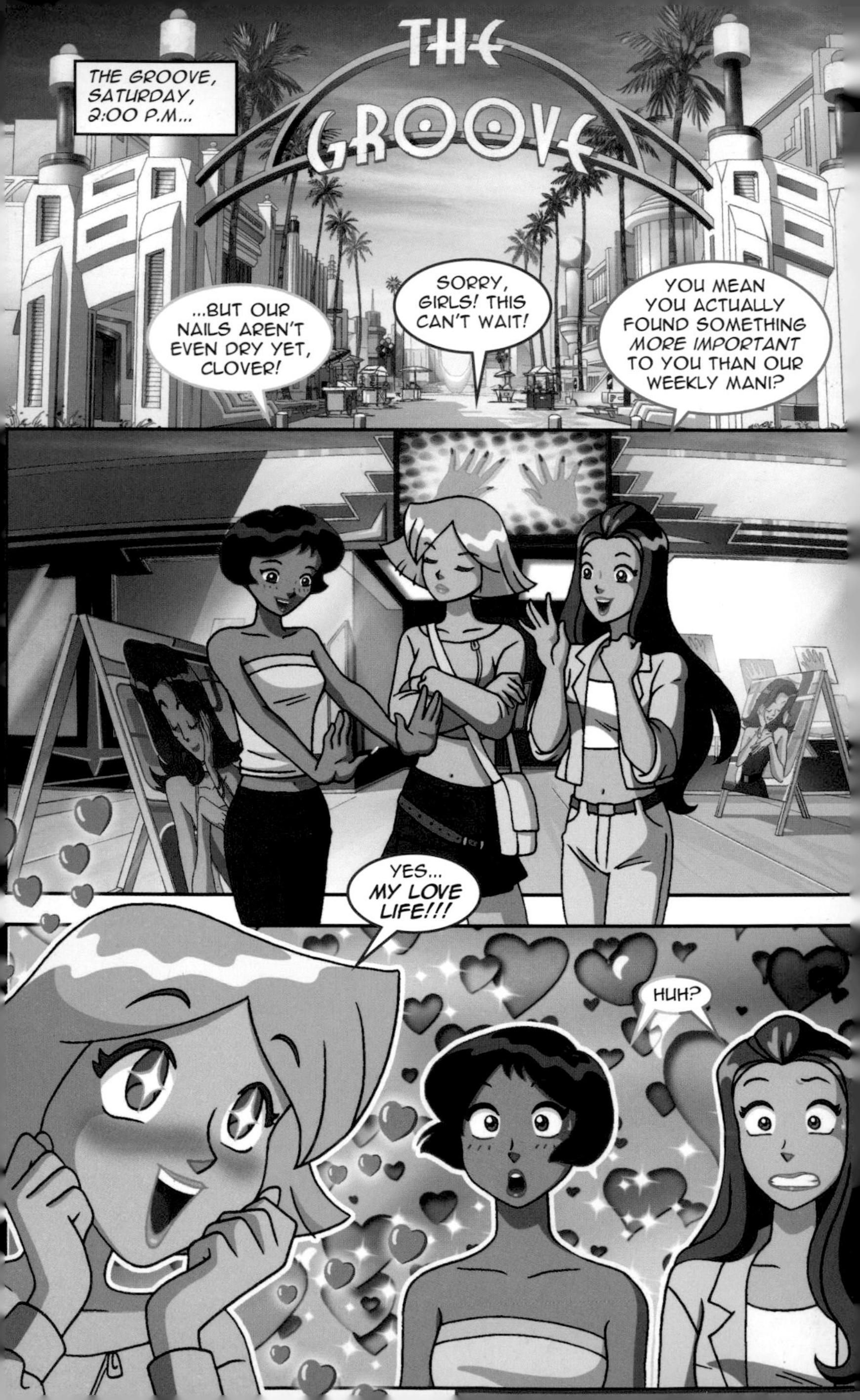
THE GROOVE
THE GROOVE, SATURDAY, 2:00 P.M...
...BUT OUR NAILS AREN'T EVEN DRY YET, CLOVER!
SORRY, GIRLS! THIS CAN'T WAIT!
YOU MEAN YOU ACTUALLY FOUND SOMETHING MORE IMPORTANT TO YOU THAN OUR WEEKLY MANI?
YES... MY LOVE LIFE!!!
HUH?

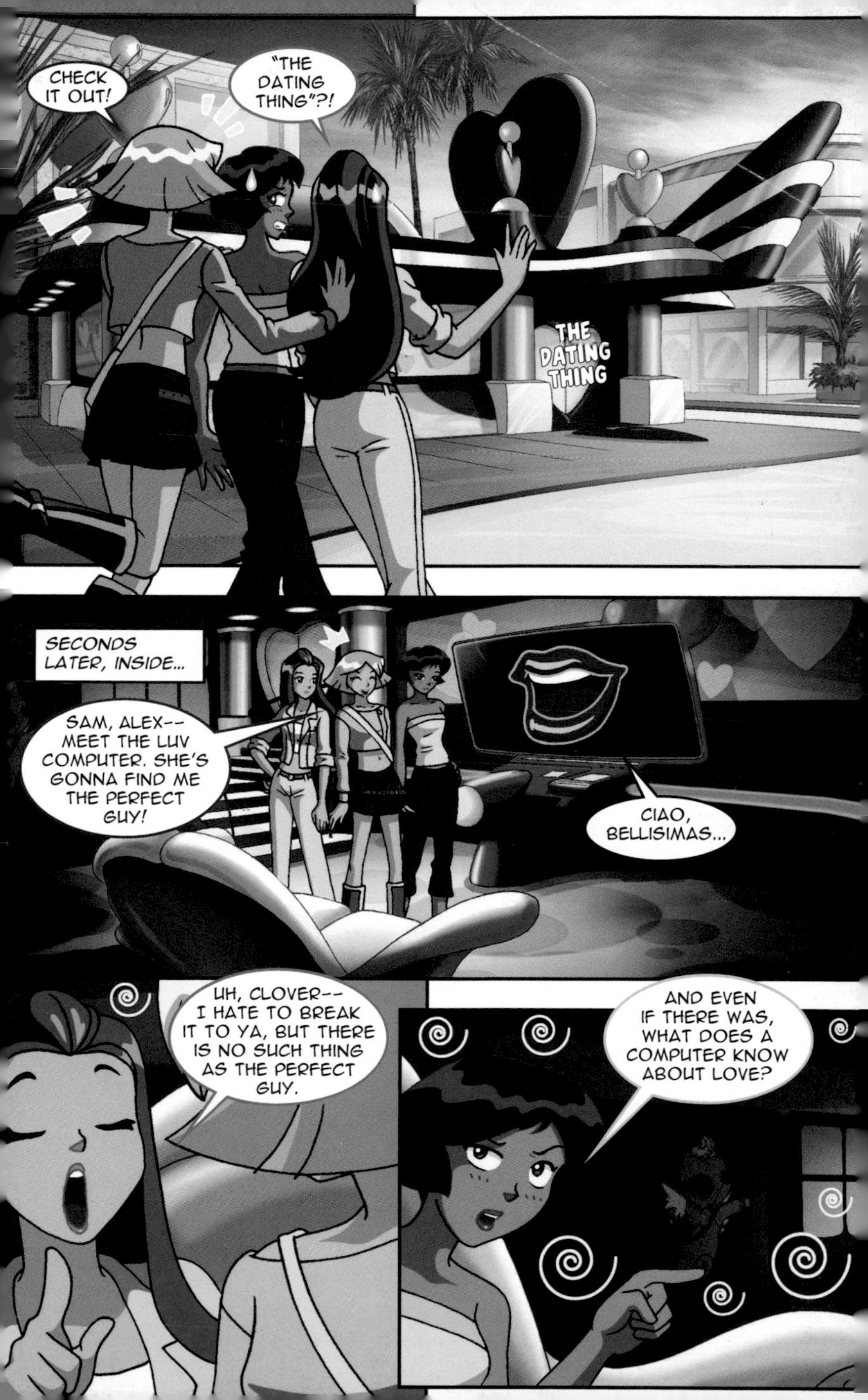
CHECK IT OUT!
"THE DATING THING"?!
THE DATING THING
SECONDS LATER, INSIDE...
SAM, ALEX-- MEET THE LUV COMPUTER. SHE'S GONNA FIND ME THE PERFECT GUY!
CIAO, BELLISIMAS...
UH, CLOVER-- I HATE TO BREAK IT TO YA, BUT THERE IS NO SUCH THING AS THE PERFECT GUY.
AND EVEN IF THERE WAS, WHAT DOES A COMPUTER KNOW ABOUT LOVE?

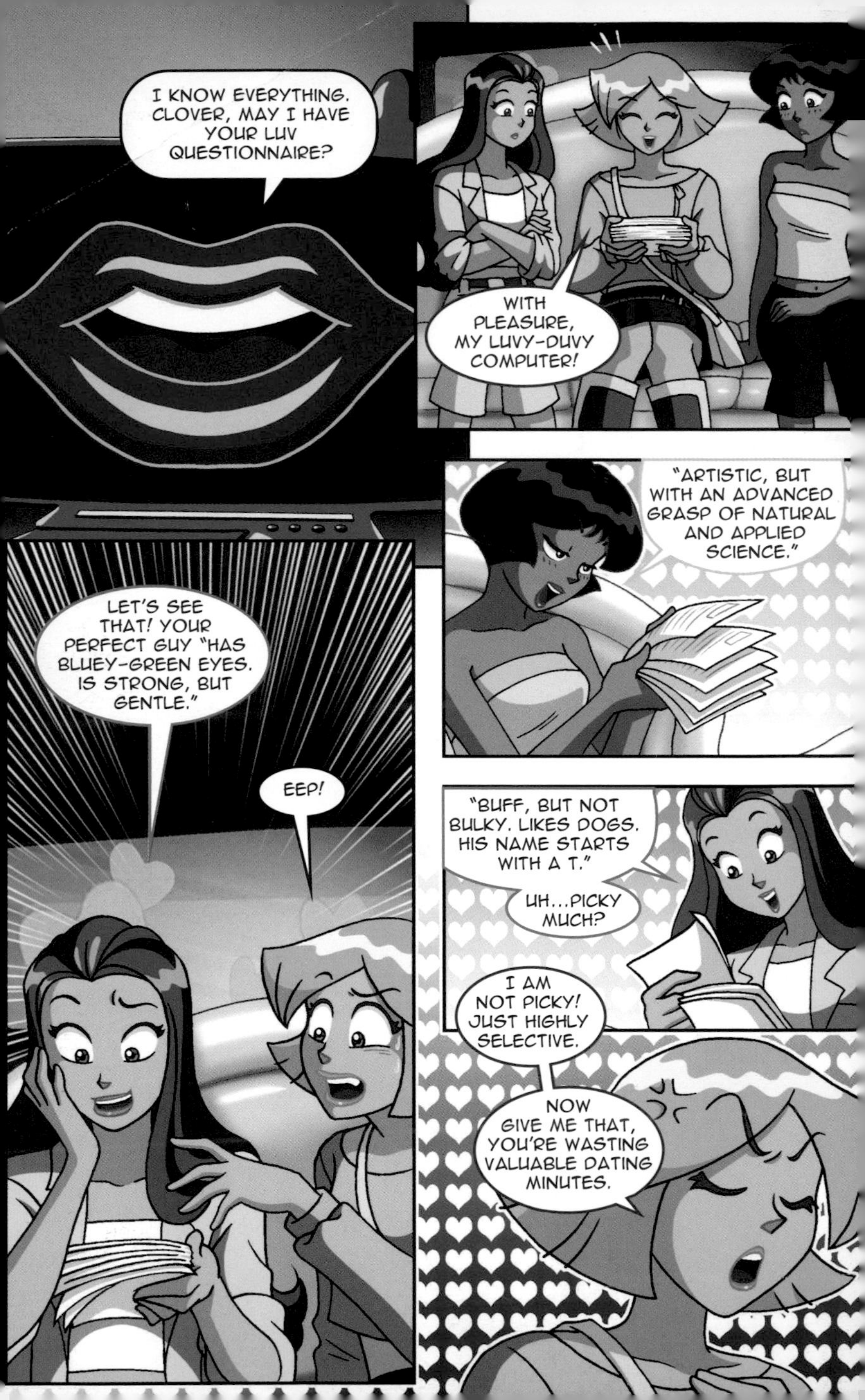
I KNOW EVERYTHING. CLOVER, MAY I HAVE YOUR LUV QUESTIONNAIRE?
WITH PLEASURE, MY LUVY-DUVY COMPUTER!
LET'S SEE THAT! YOUR PERFECT GUY "HAS BLUEY-GREEN EYES. IS STRONG, BUT GENTLE."
EEP!
"ARTISTIC, BUT WITH AN ADVANCED GRASP OF NATURAL AND APPLIED SCIENCE."
"BUFF, BUT NOT BULKY. LIKES DOGS. HIS NAME STARTS WITH A T."
UH...PICKY MUCH?
I AM NOT PICKY! JUST HIGHLY SELECTIVE.
NOW GIVE ME THAT, YOU'RE WASTING VALUABLE DATING MINUTES.

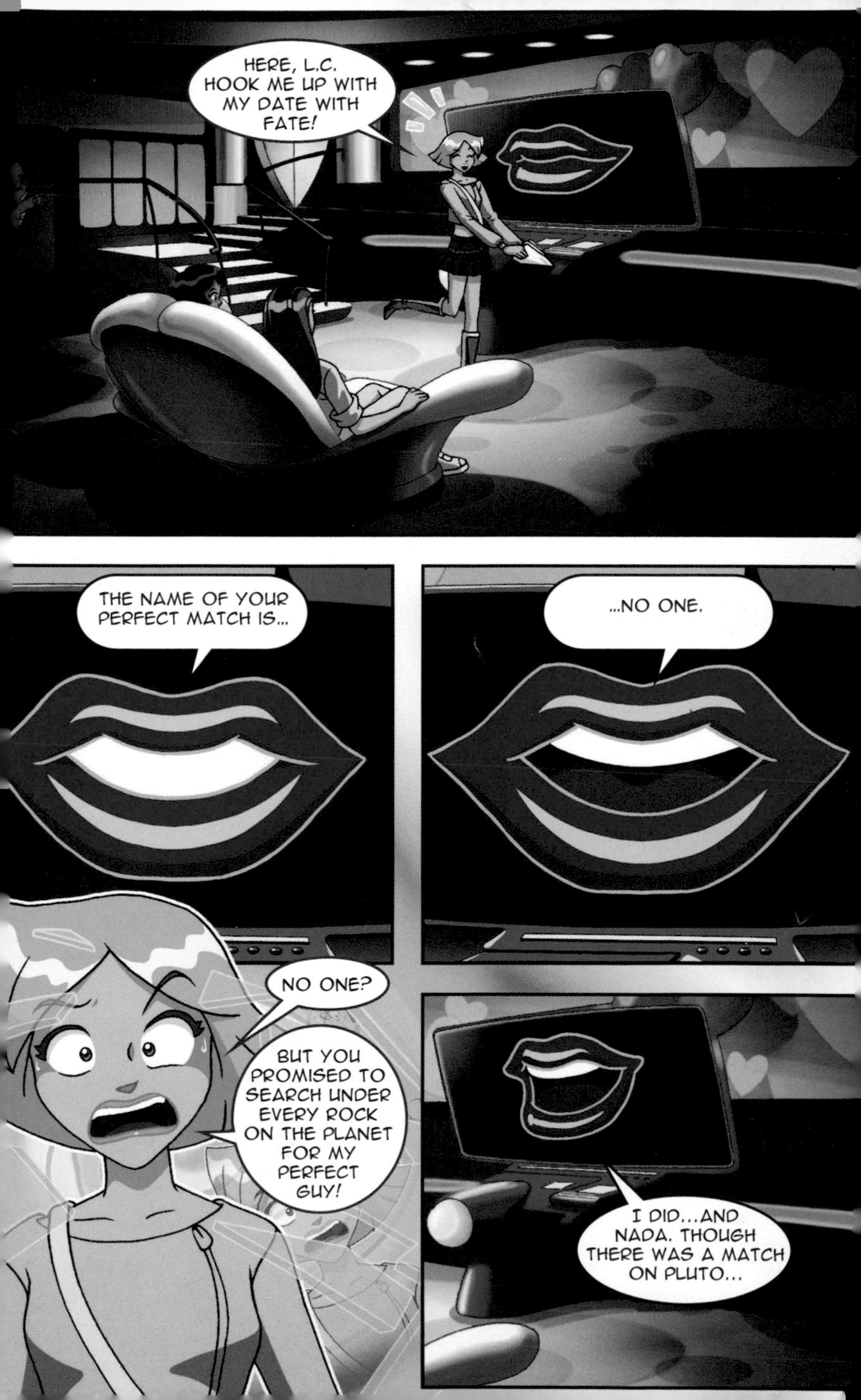
HERE, L.C. HOOK ME UP WITH MY DATE WITH FATE!
THE NAME OF YOUR PERFECT MATCH IS...
...NO ONE.
NO ONE?
BUT YOU PROMISED TO SEARCH UNDER EVERY ROCK ON THE PLANET FOR MY PERFECT GUY!
I DID...AND NADA. THOUGH THERE WAS A MATCH ON PLUTO...

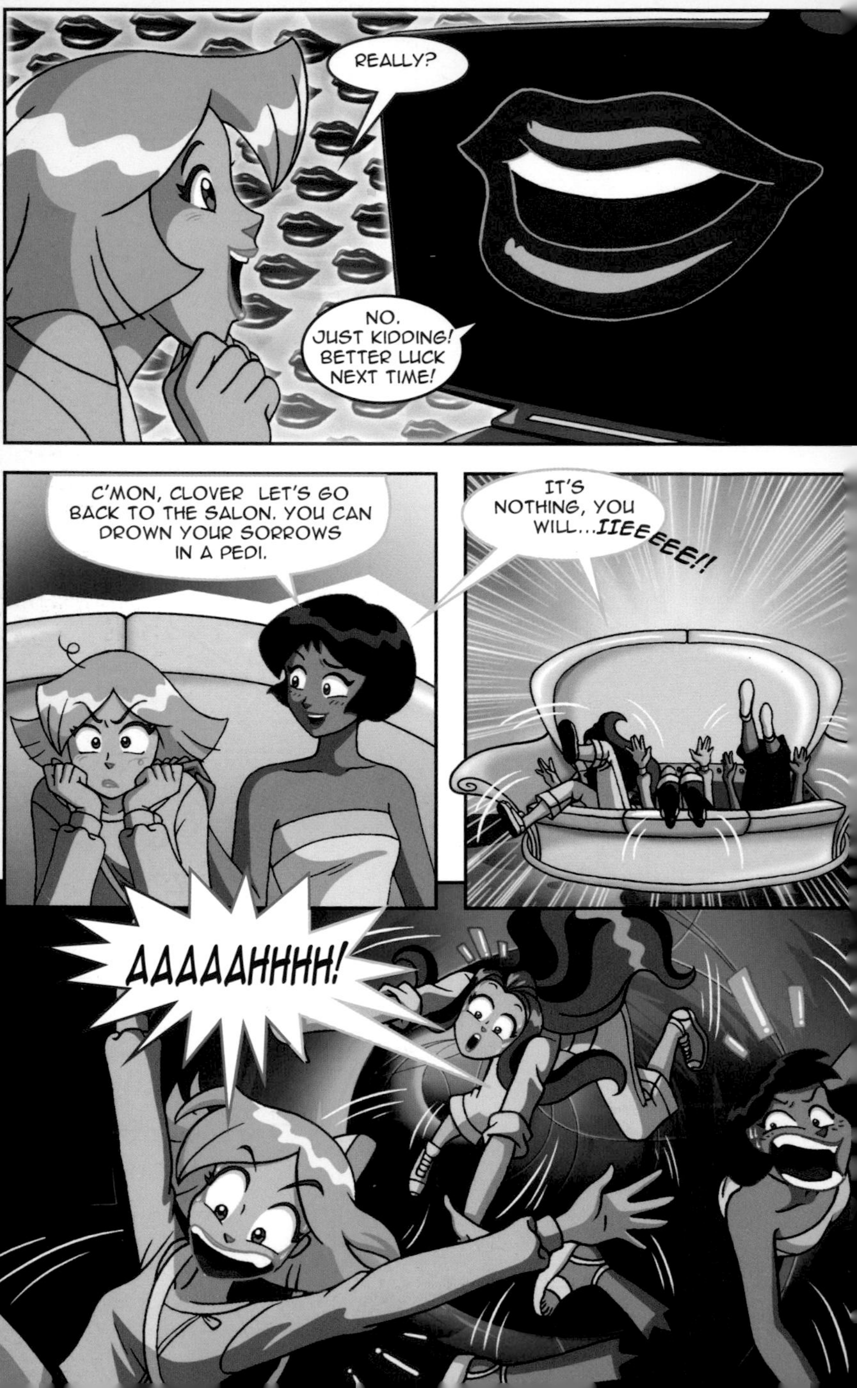
REALLY?
NO. JUST KIDDING! BETTER LUCK NEXT TIME!
C'MON, CLOVER LET'S GO BACK TO THE SALON. YOU CAN DROWN YOUR SORROWS IN A PEDI.
IT'S NOTHING, YOU WILL...IIEEEEEE!!
AAAAAHHHH!

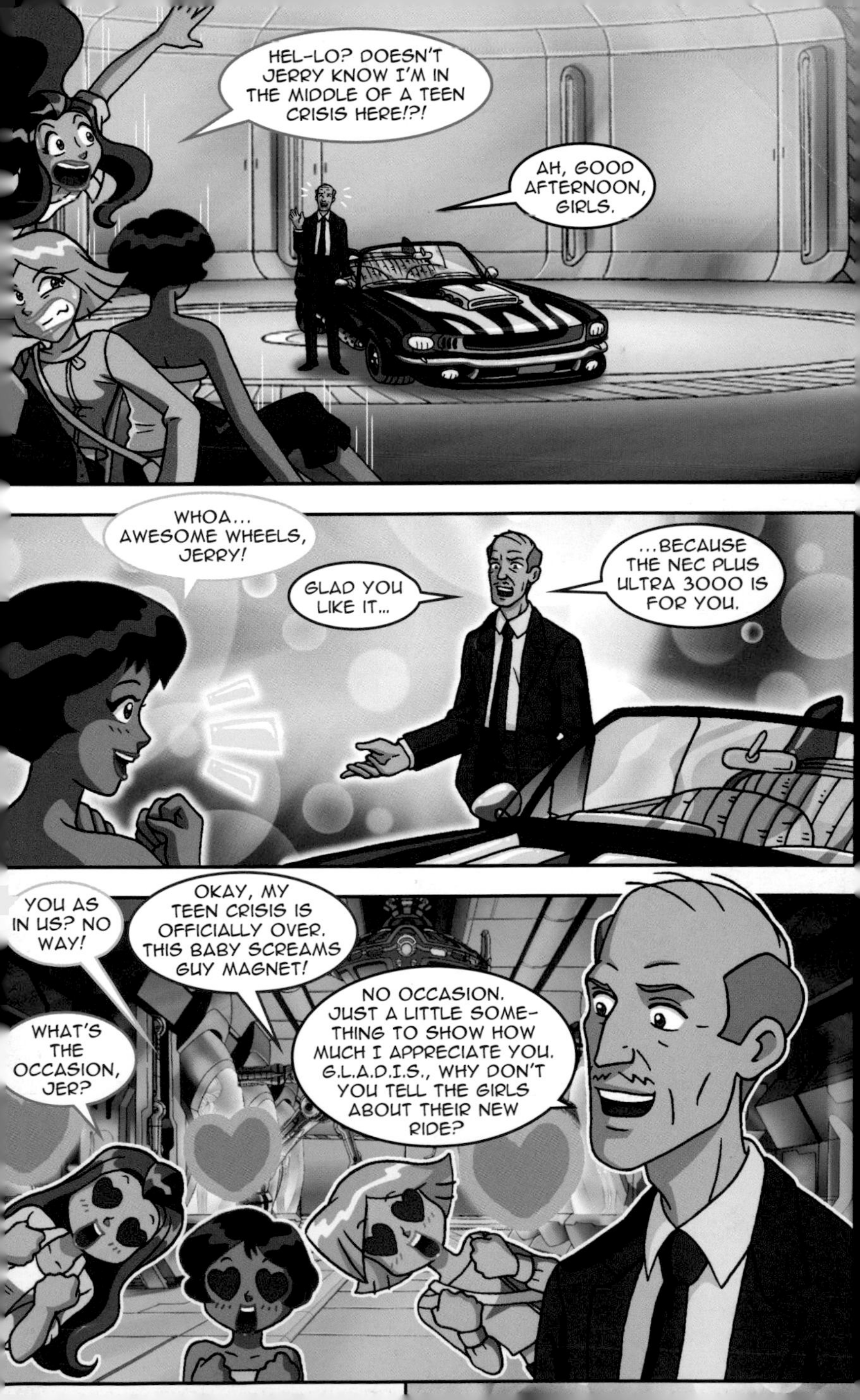
HEL-LO? DOESN'T JERRY KNOW I'M IN THE MIDDLE OF A TEEN CRISIS HERE!?!
AH, GOOD AFTERNOON, GIRLS.
WHOA... AWESOME WHEELS, JERRY!
GLAD YOU LIKE IT...
...BECAUSE THE NEC PLUS ULTRA 3000 IS FOR YOU.
YOU AS IN US? NO WAY!
OKAY, MY TEEN CRISIS IS OFFICIALLY OVER. THIS BABY SCREAMS GUY MAGNET!
WHAT'S THE OCCASION, JER?
NO OCCASION. JUST A LITTLE SOME-THING TO SHOW HOW MUCH I APPRECIATE YOU. G.L.A.D.I.S., WHY DON'T YOU TELL THE GIRLS ABOUT THEIR NEW RIDE?

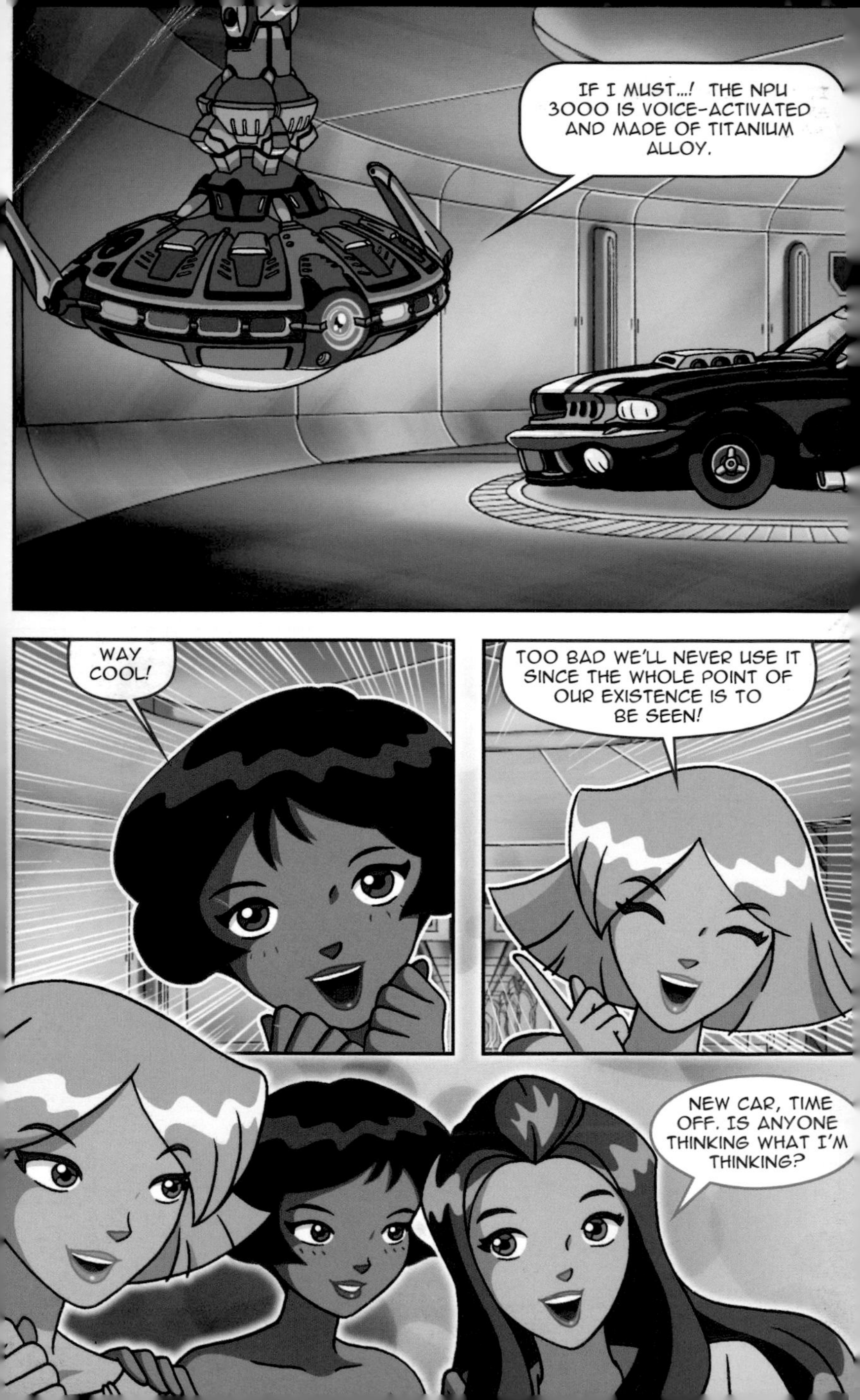
IF I MUST...! THE NPU 3000 IS VOICE-ACTIVATED AND MADE OF TITANIUM ALLOY.
WAY COOL!
TOO BAD WE'LL NEVER USE IT SINCE THE WHOLE POINT OF OUR EXISTENCE IS TO BE SEEN!
NEW CAR, TIME OFF. IS ANYONE THINKING WHAT I'M THINKING?

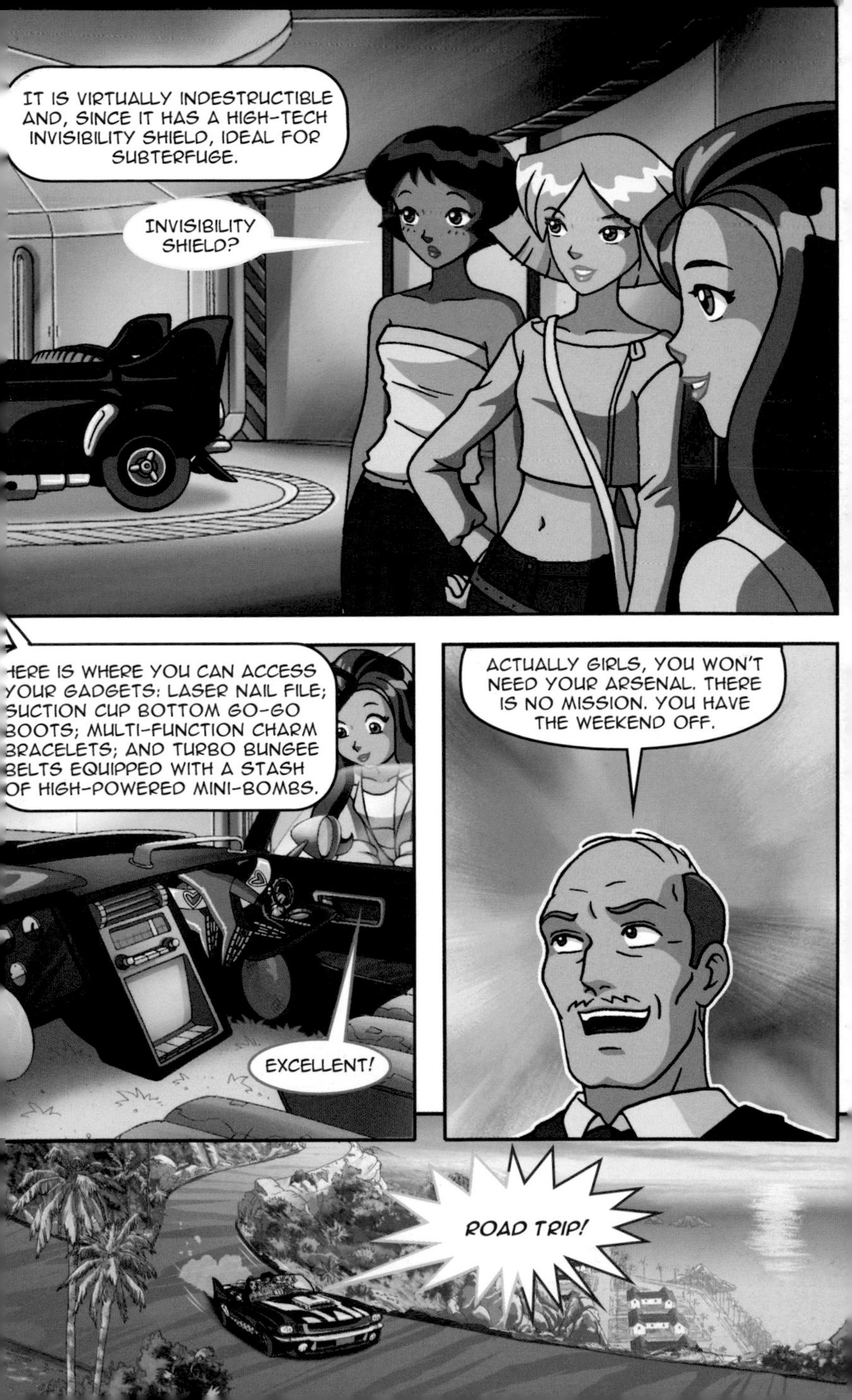
IT IS VIRTUALLY INDESTRUCTIBLE AND, SINCE IT HAS A HIGH-TECH INVISIBILITY SHIELD, IDEAL FOR SUBTERFUGE.
INVISIBILITY SHIELD?
HERE IS WHERE YOU CAN ACCESS YOUR GADGETS: LASER NAIL FILE; SUCTION CUP BOTTOM GO-GO BOOTS; MULTI-FUNCTION CHARM BRACELETS; AND TURBO BUNGEE BELTS EQUIPPED WITH A STASH OF HIGH-POWERED MINI-BOMBS.
EXCELLENT!
ACTUALLY GIRLS, YOU WON'T NEED YOUR ARSENAL. THERE IS NO MISSION. YOU HAVE THE WEEKEND OFF.
ROAD TRIP!

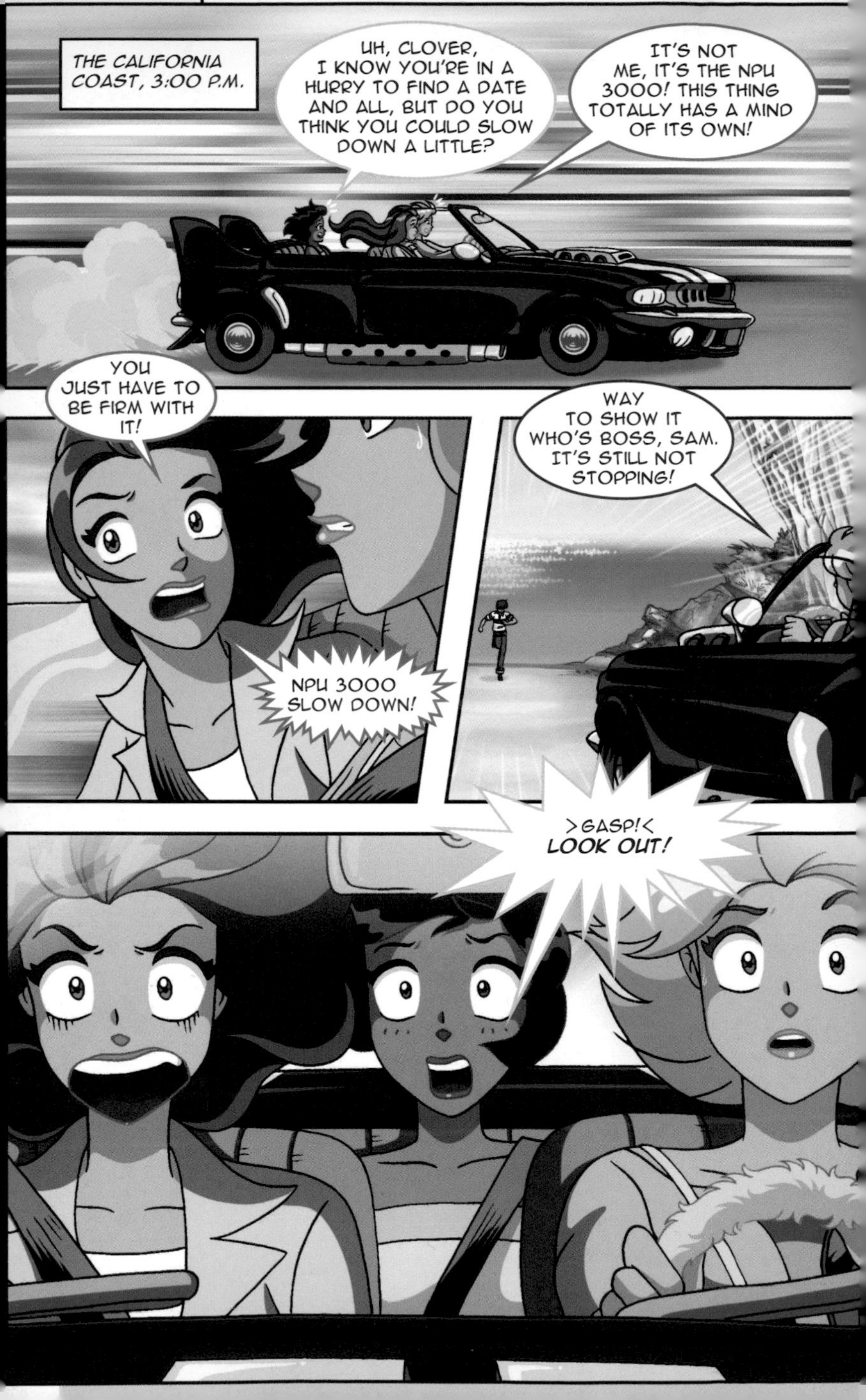
THE CALIFORNIA COAST, 3:00 P.M.
UH, CLOVER, I KNOW YOU'RE IN A HURRY TO FIND A DATE AND ALL, BUT DO YOU THINK YOU COULD SLOW DOWN A LITTLE?
IT'S NOT ME, IT'S THE NPU 3000! THIS THING TOTALLY HAS A MIND OF ITS OWN!
YOU JUST HAVE TO BE FIRM WITH IT!
NPU 3000 SLOW DOWN!
WAY TO SHOW IT WHO'S BOSS, SAM. IT'S STILL NOT STOPPING!
>GASP!<
LOOK OUT!

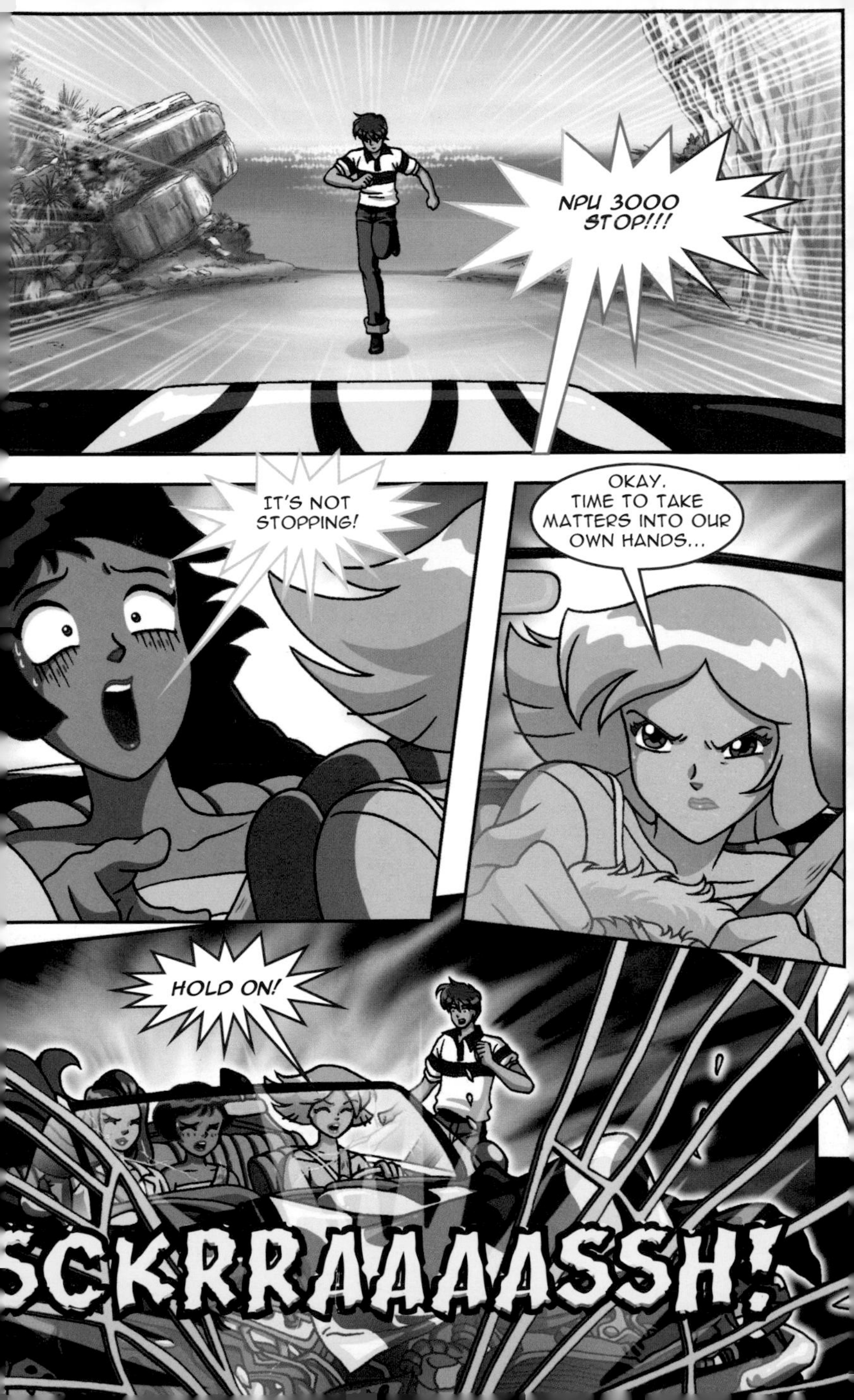
NPU 3000 STOP!!!
IT'S NOT STOPPING!
OKAY. TIME TO TAKE MATTERS INTO OUR OWN HANDS...
HOLD ON!
SCKRRAAAAASSH!

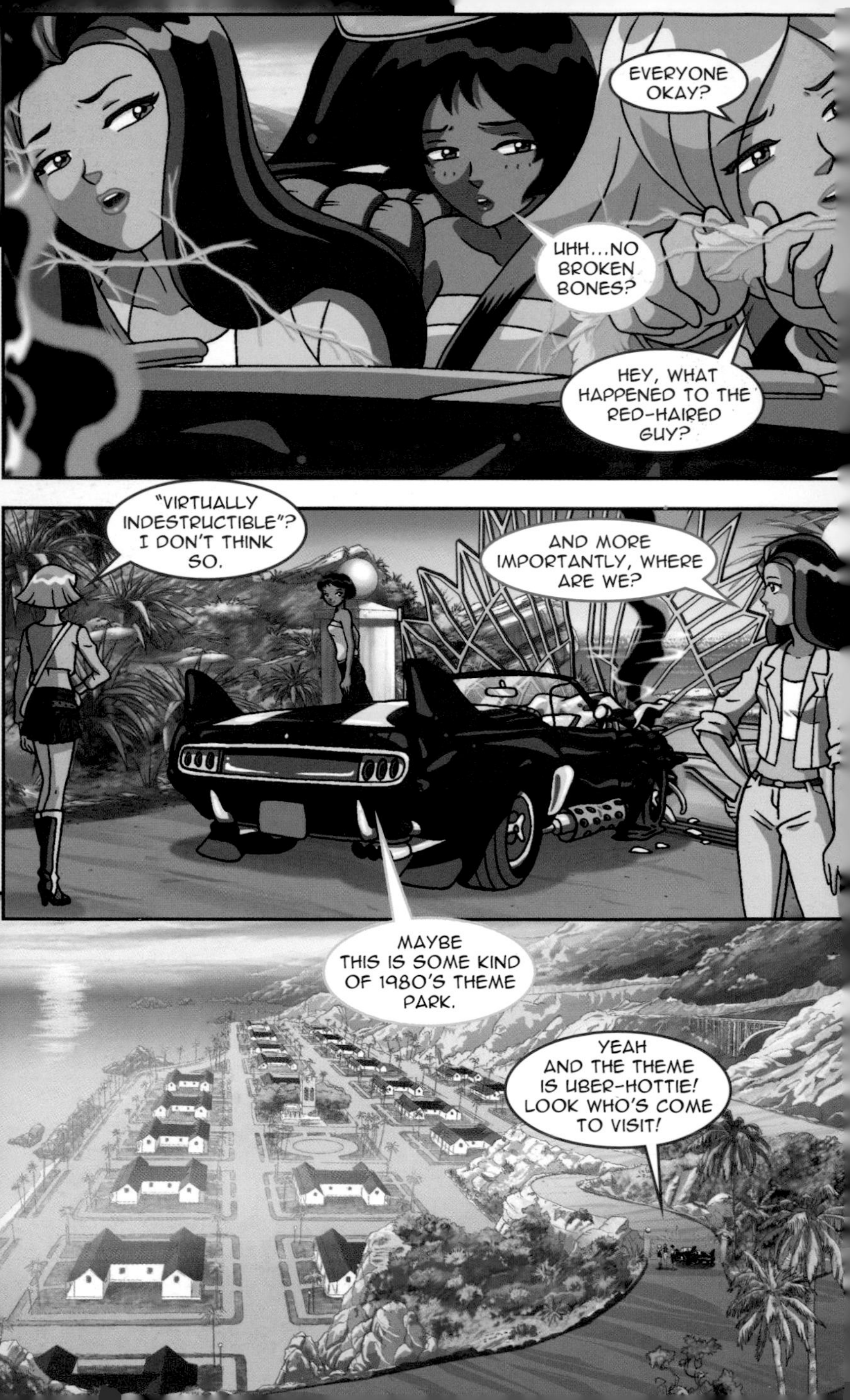
EVERYONE OKAY?
UHH...NO BROKEN BONES?
HEY, WHAT HAPPENED TO THE RED-HAIRED GUY?
"VIRTUALLY INDESTRUCTIBLE"? I DON'T THINK SO.
AND MORE IMPORTANTLY, WHERE ARE WE?
MAYBE THIS IS SOME KIND OF 1980'S THEME PARK.
YEAH AND THE THEME IS UBER-HOTTIE! LOOK WHO'S COME TO VISIT!

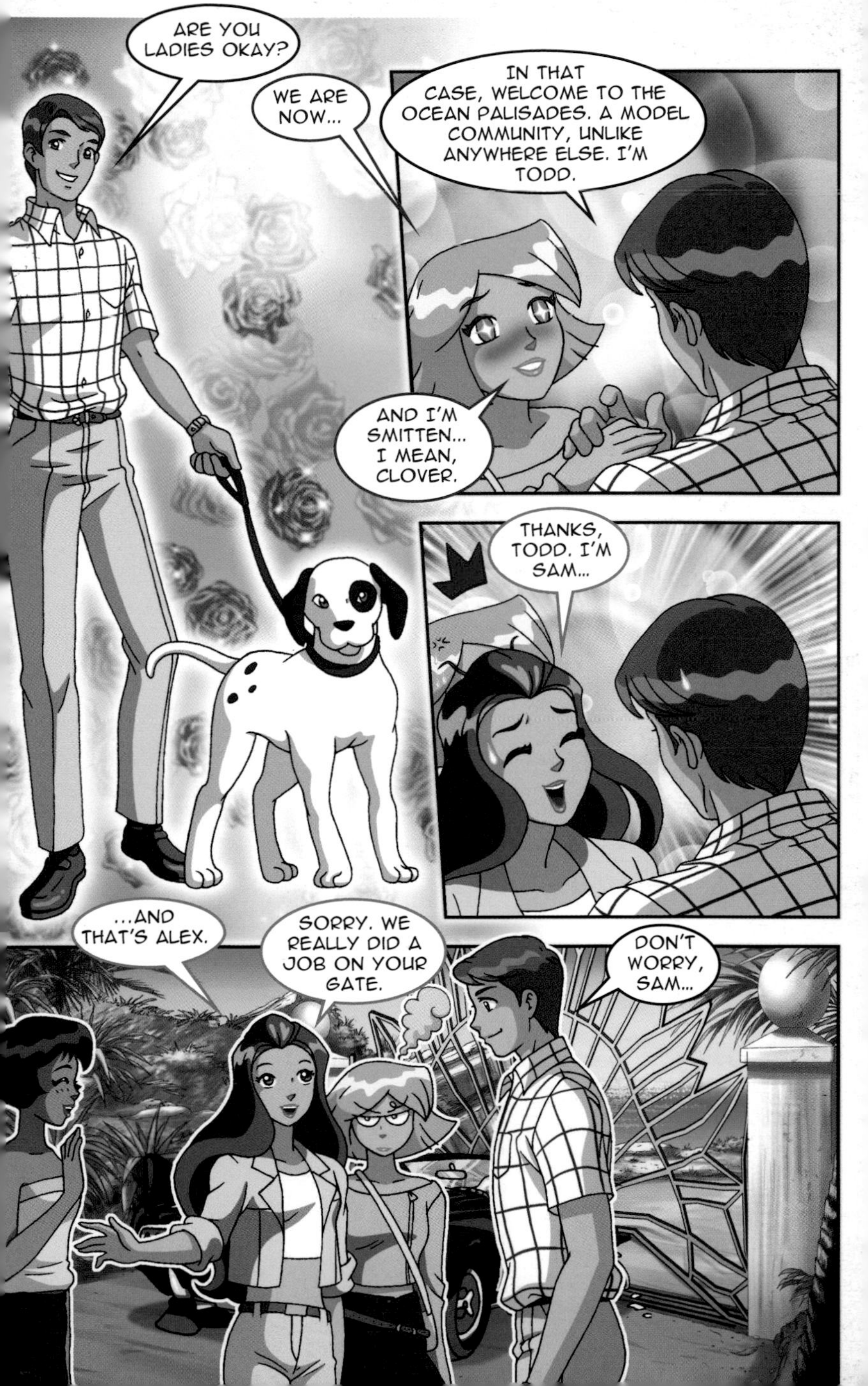
ARE YOU LADIES OKAY?
WE ARE NOW...
IN THAT CASE, WELCOME TO THE OCEAN PALISADES. A MODEL COMMUNITY, UNLIKE ANYWHERE ELSE. I'M TODD.
AND I'M SMITTEN... I MEAN, CLOVER.
THANKS, TODD. I'M SAM...
...AND THAT'S ALEX.
SORRY. WE REALLY DID A JOB ON YOUR GATE.
DON'T WORRY, SAM...

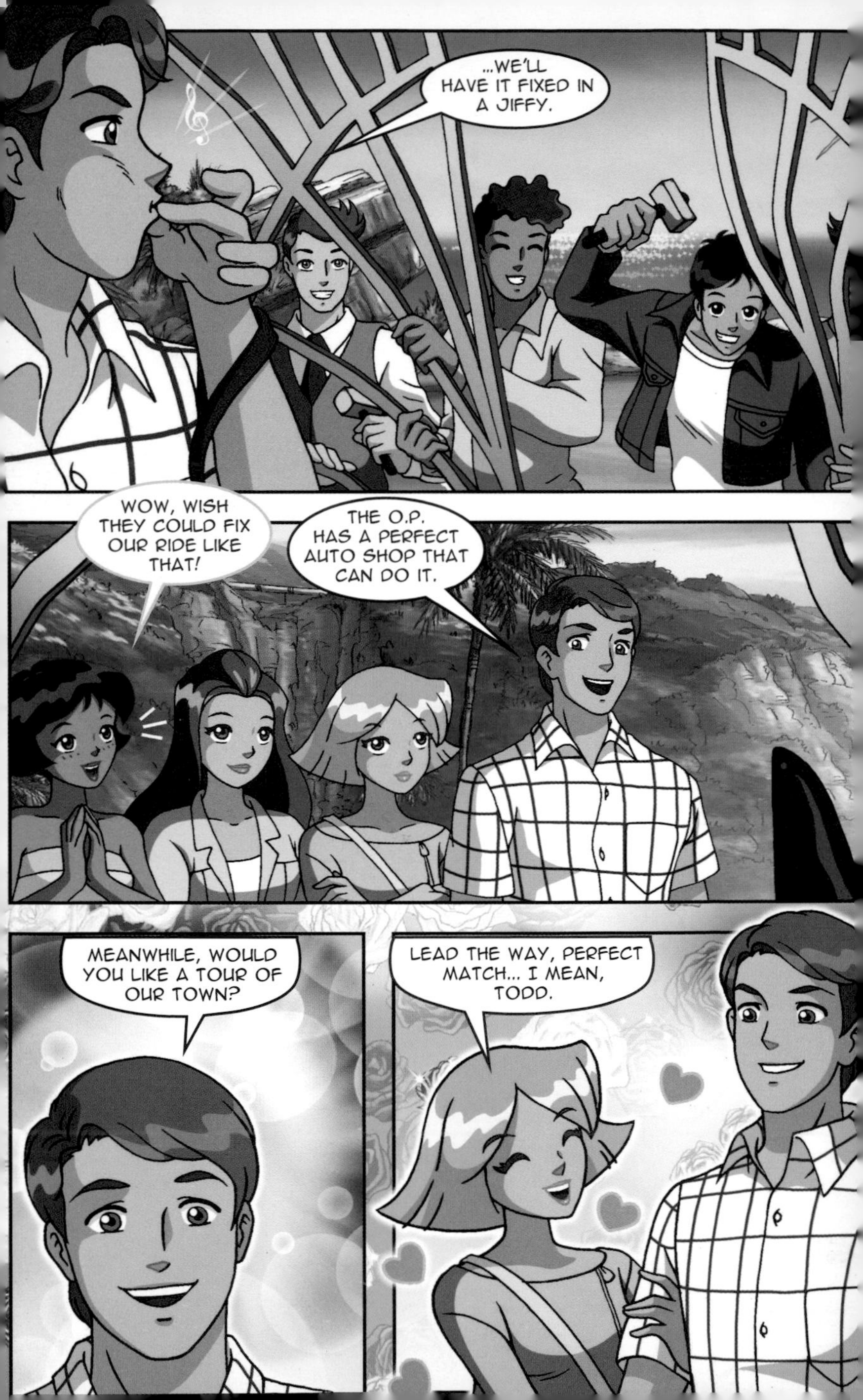
...WE'LL HAVE IT FIXED IN A JIFFY.
WOW, WISH THEY COULD FIX OUR RIDE LIKE THAT!
THE O.P. HAS A PERFECT AUTO SHOP THAT CAN DO IT.
MEANWHILE, WOULD YOU LIKE A TOUR OF OUR TOWN?
LEAD THE WAY, PERFECT MATCH... I MEAN, TODD.

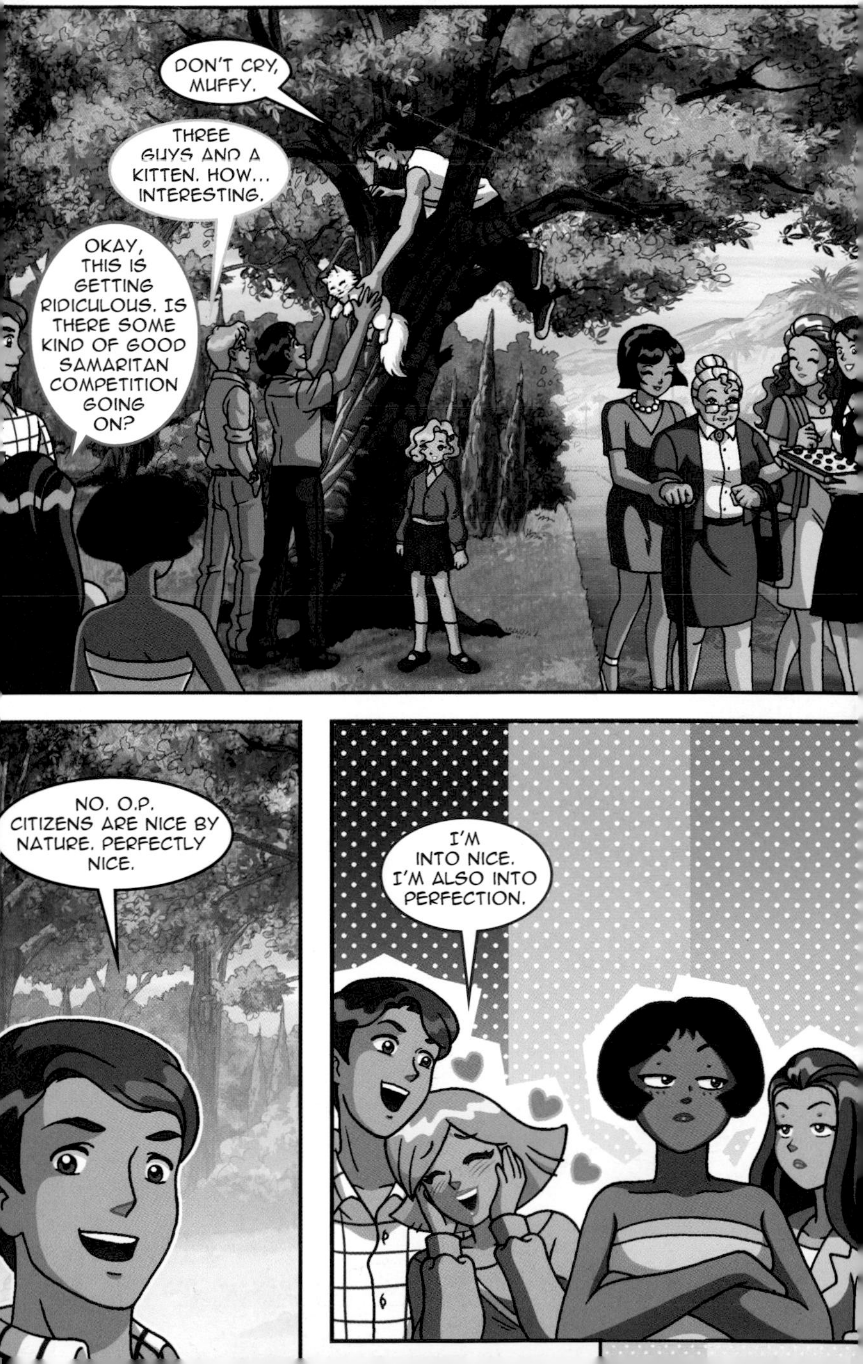
DON'T CRY, MUFFY.
THREE GUYS AND A KITTEN. HOW... INTERESTING.
OKAY, THIS IS GETTING RIDICULOUS. IS THERE SOME KIND OF GOOD SAMARITAN COMPETITION GOING ON?
NO. O.P. CITIZENS ARE NICE BY NATURE. PERFECTLY NICE.
I'M INTO NICE. I'M ALSO INTO PERFECTION.

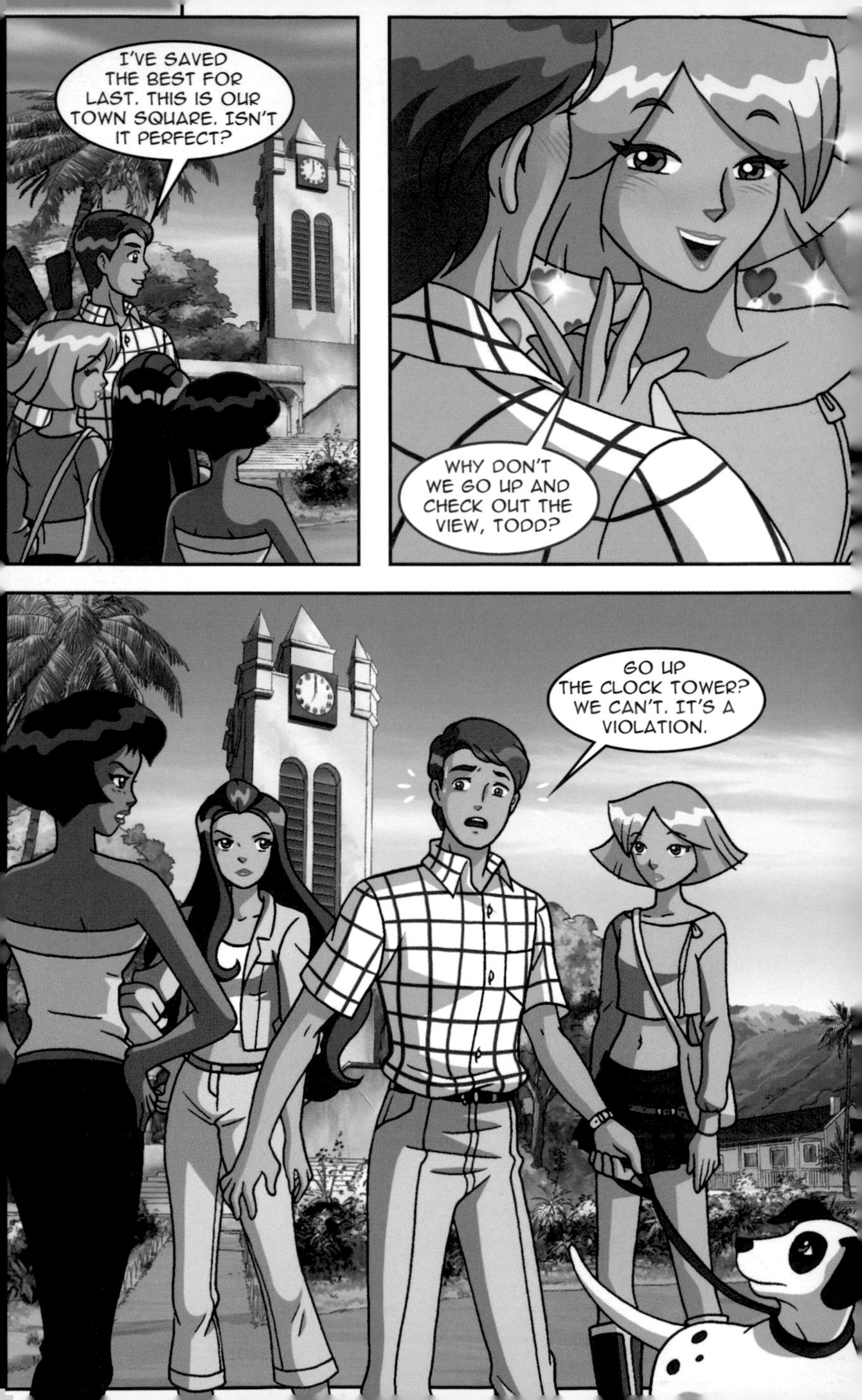
I'VE SAVED THE BEST FOR LAST. THIS IS OUR TOWN SQUARE. ISN'T IT PERFECT?
WHY DON'T WE GO UP AND CHECK OUT THE VIEW, TODD?
GO UP THE CLOCK TOWER? WE CAN'T. IT'S A VIOLATION.

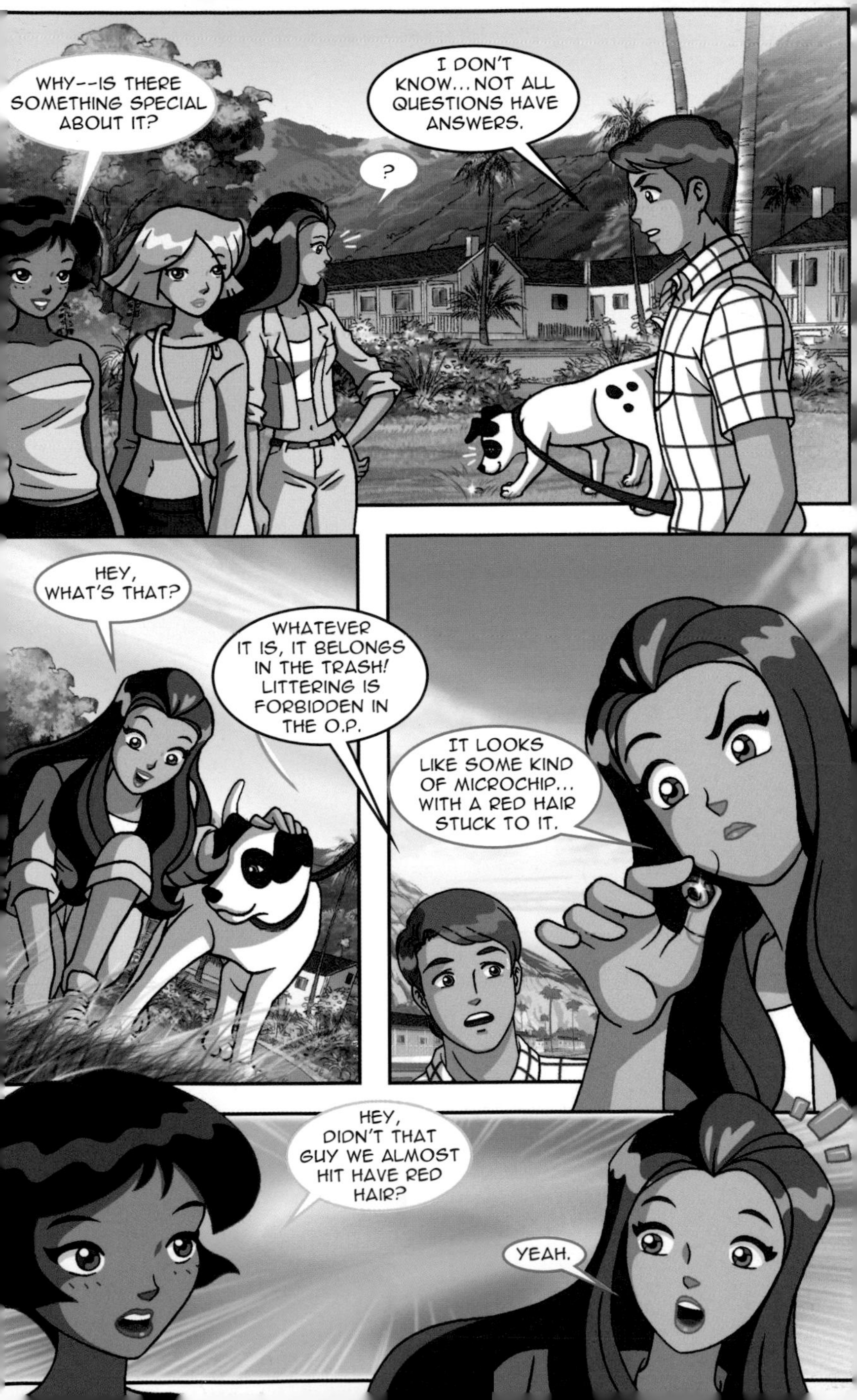
WHY--IS THERE SOMETHING SPECIAL ABOUT IT?
?
I DON'T KNOW... NOT ALL QUESTIONS HAVE ANSWERS.
HEY, WHAT'S THAT?
WHATEVER IT IS, IT BELONGS IN THE TRASH! LITTERING IS FORBIDDEN IN THE O.P.
IT LOOKS LIKE SOME KIND OF MICROCHIP... WITH A RED HAIR STUCK TO IT.
HEY, DIDN'T THAT GUY WE ALMOST HIT HAVE RED HAIR?
YEAH.

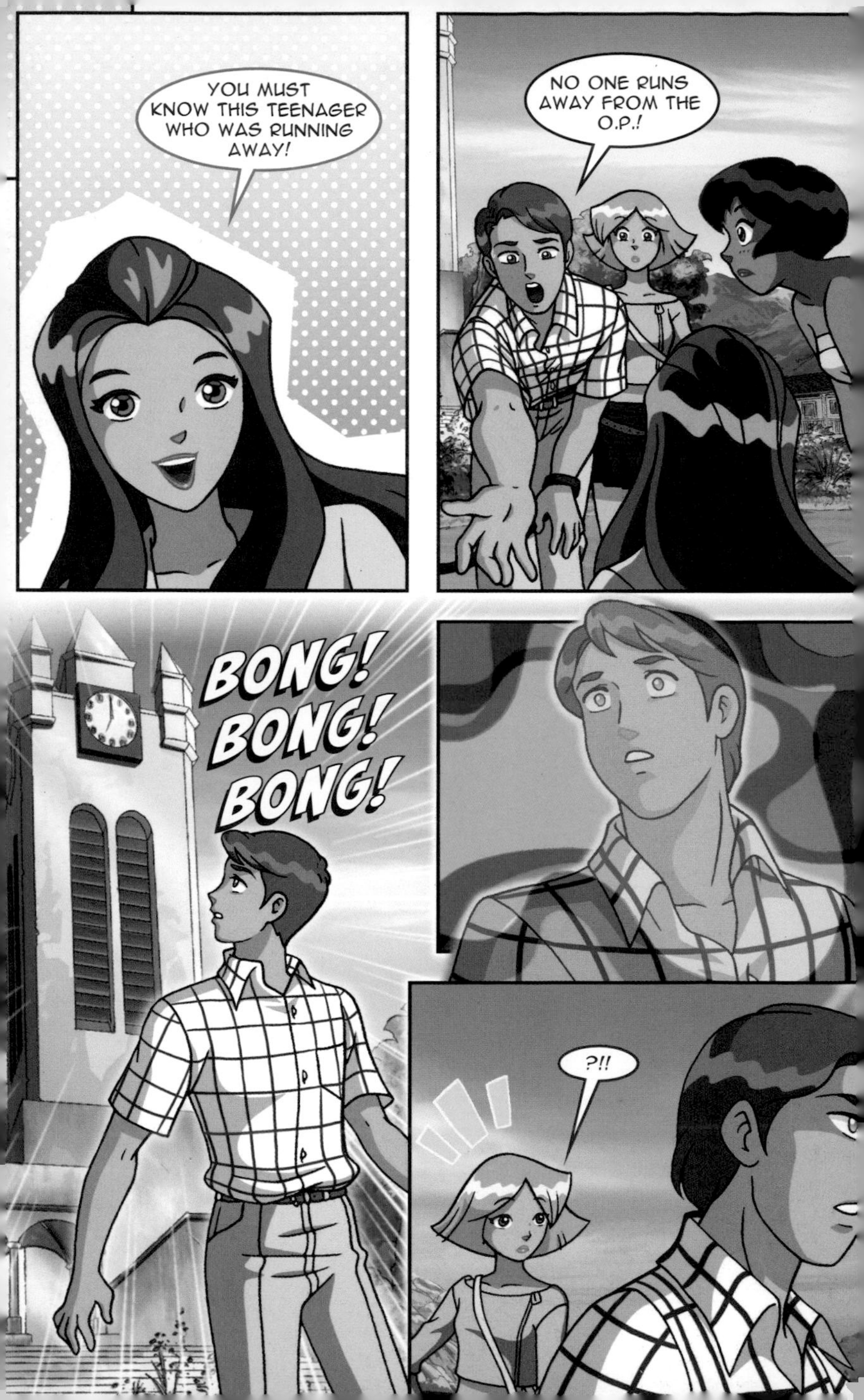
YOU MUST KNOW THIS TEENAGER WHO WAS RUNNING AWAY!
NO ONE RUNS AWAY FROM THE O.P.!
BONG! BONG! BONG!
?!!

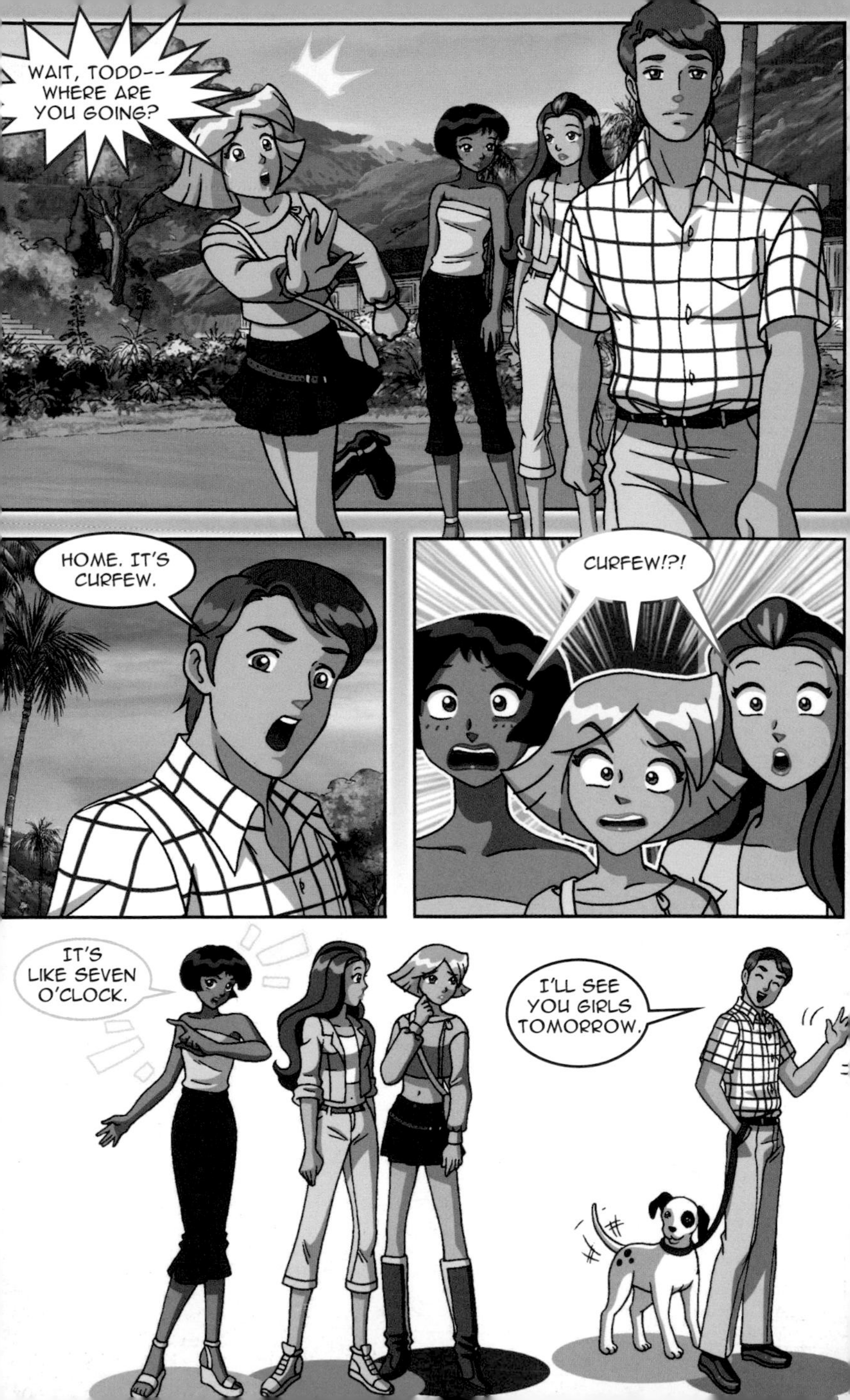
WAIT, TODD-- WHERE ARE YOU GOING?
HOME. IT'S CURFEW.
CURFEW!?!
IT'S LIKE SEVEN O'CLOCK.
I'LL SEE YOU GIRLS TOMORROW.

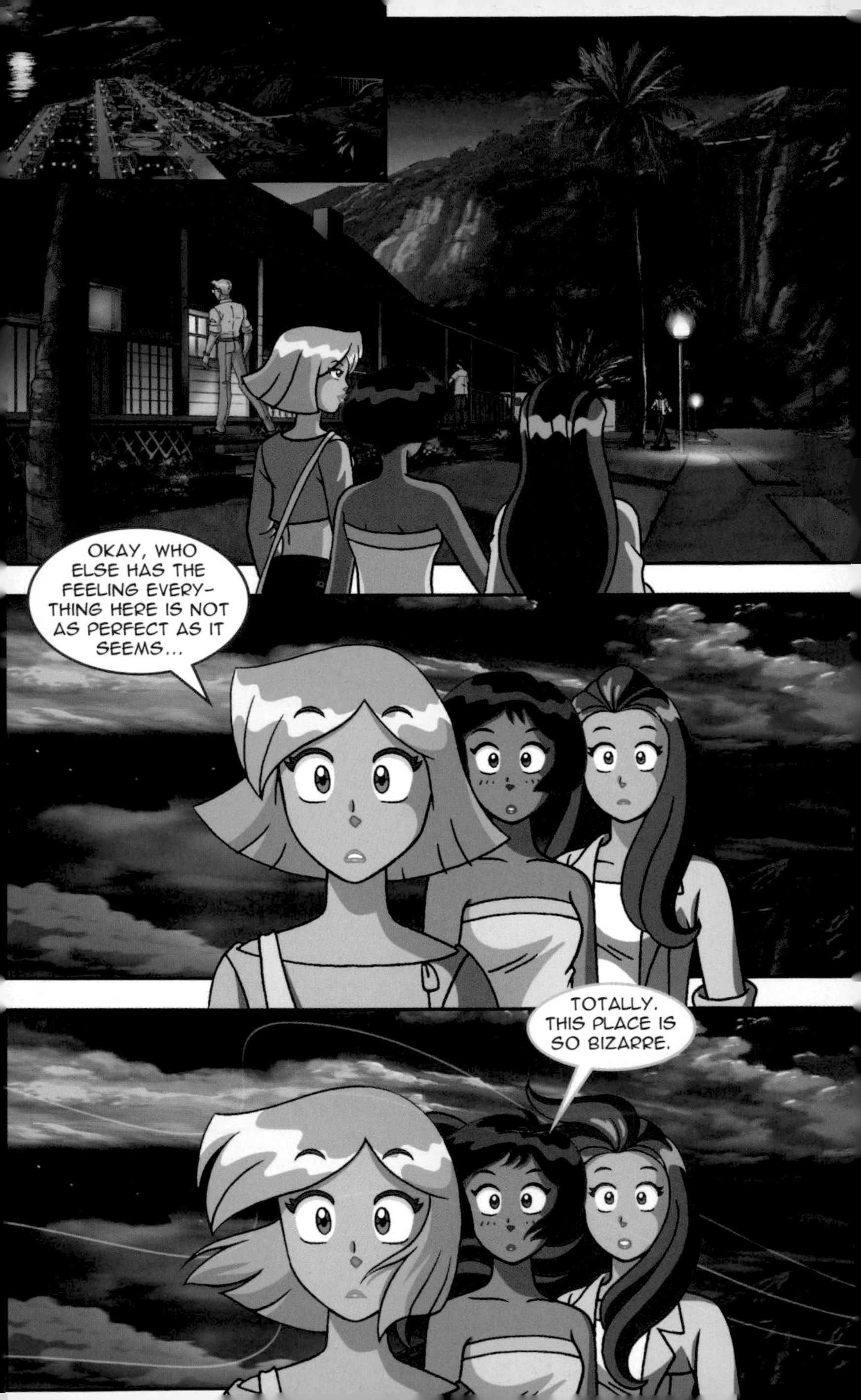
OKAY, WHO ELSE HAS THE FEELING EVERY-THING HERE IS NOT AS PERFECT AS IT SEEMS...
TOTALLY. THIS PLACE IS SO BIZARRE.

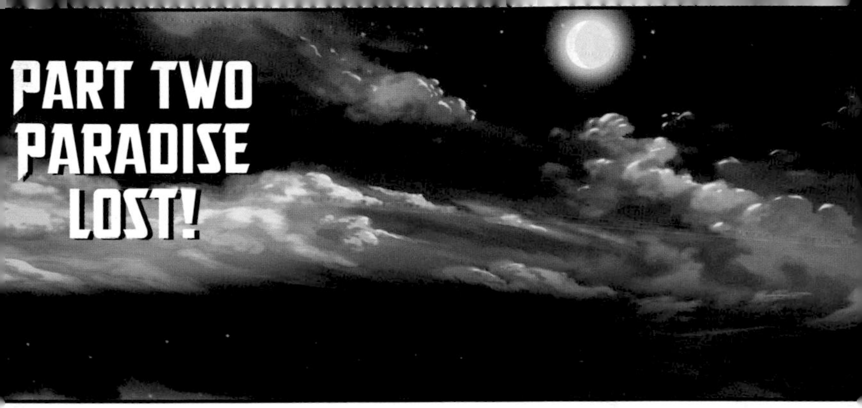
PART TWO
PARADISE
LOST!

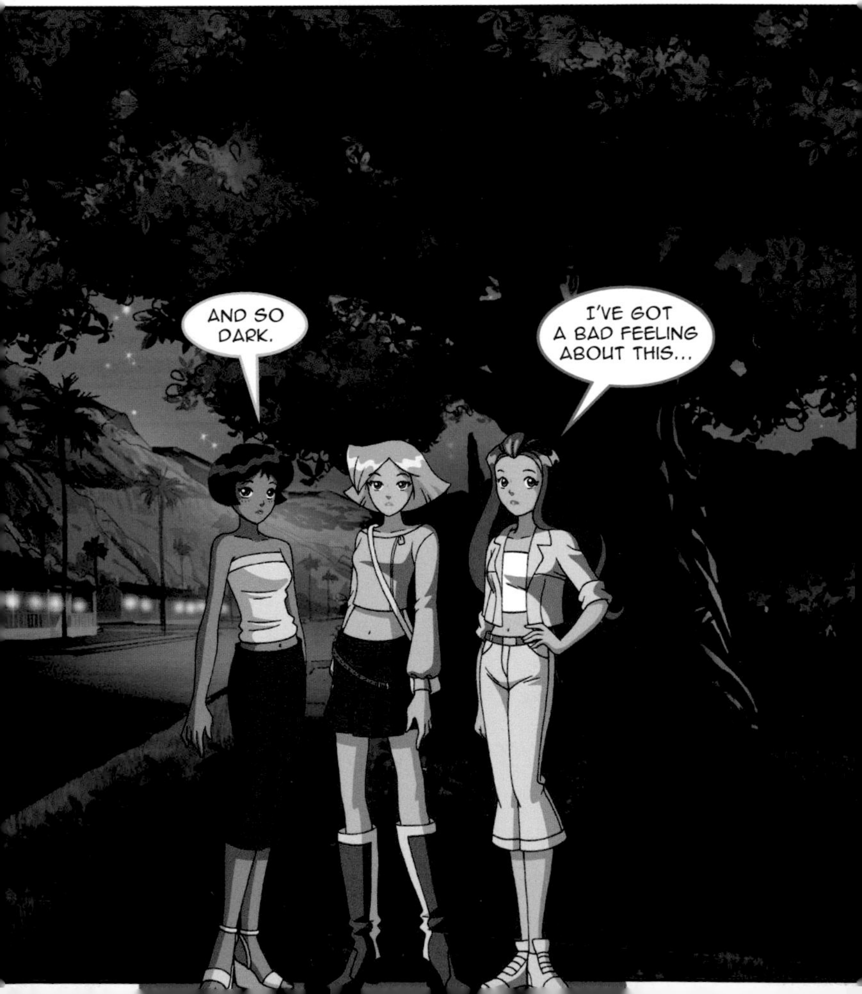
AND SO DARK.
I'VE GOT A BAD FEELING ABOUT THIS...

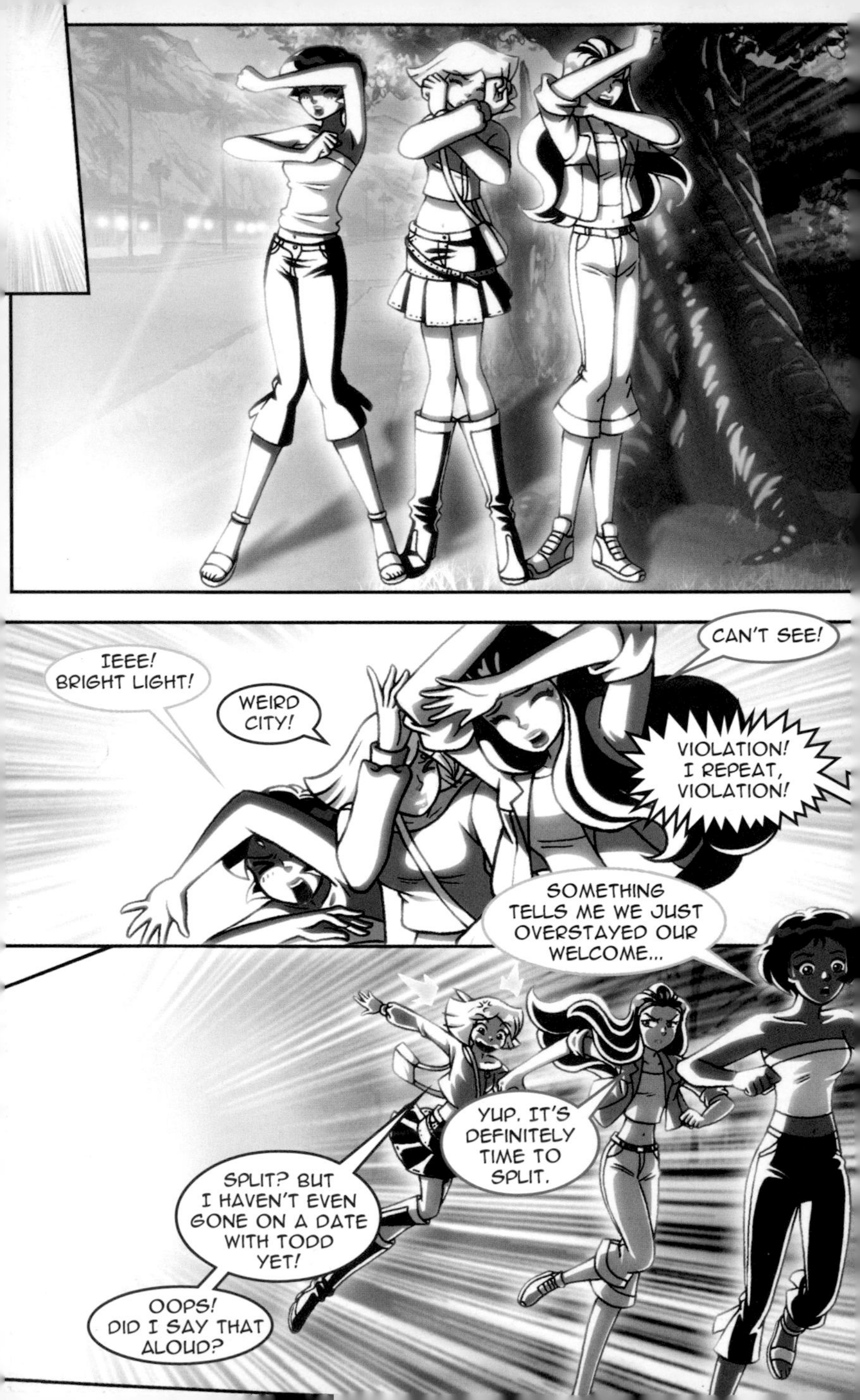
IEEE! BRIGHT LIGHT!
WEIRD CITY!
CAN'T SEE!
VIOLATION! I REPEAT, VIOLATION!
SOMETHING TELLS ME WE JUST OVERSTAYED OUR WELCOME...
YUP. IT'S DEFINITELY TIME TO SPLIT.
SPLIT? BUT I HAVEN'T EVEN GONE ON A DATE WITH TODD YET!
OOPS! DID I SAY THAT ALOUD?

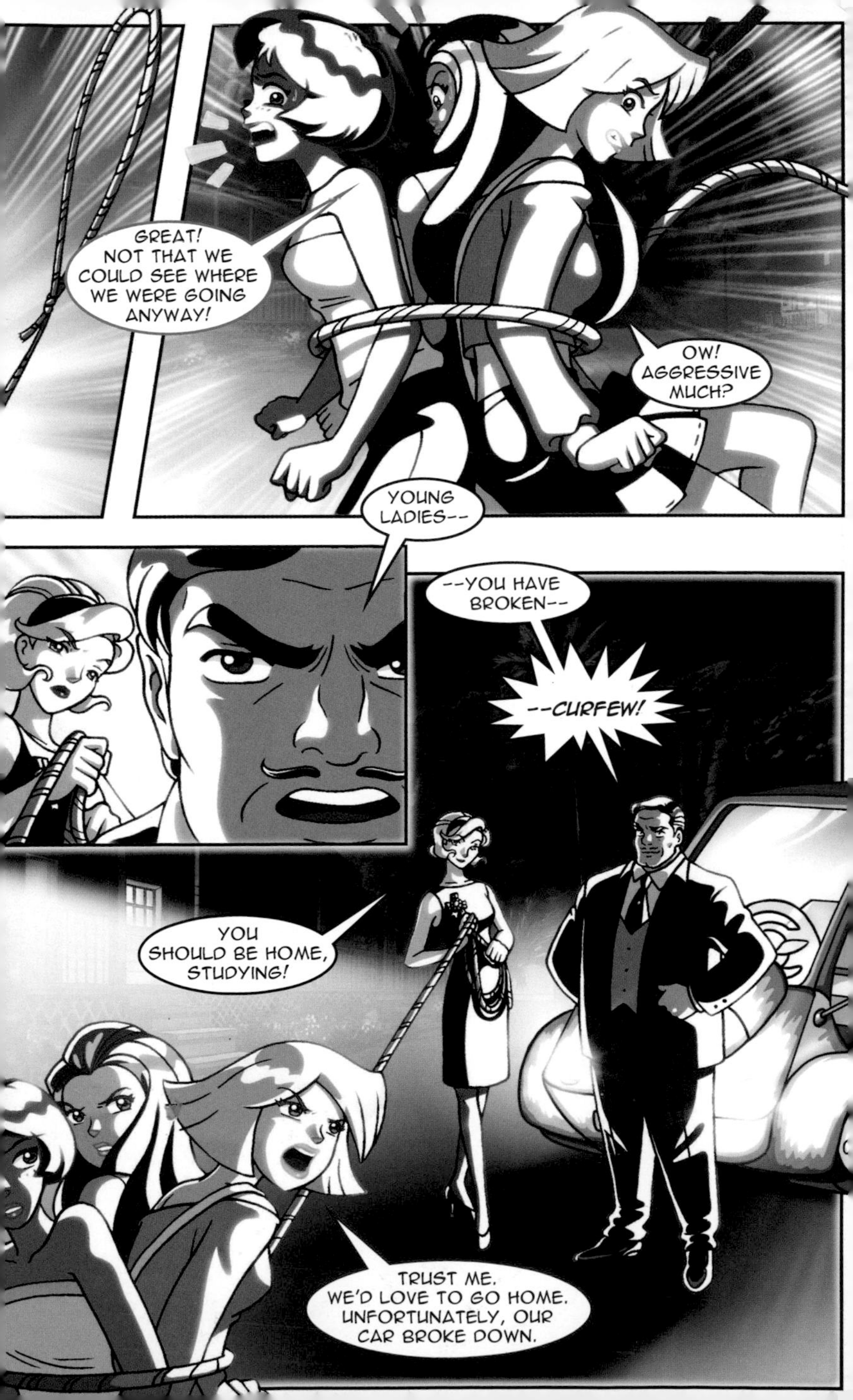
GREAT! NOT THAT WE COULD SEE WHERE WE WERE GOING ANYWAY!
OW! AGGRESSIVE MUCH?
YOUNG LADIES--
--YOU HAVE BROKEN--
--CURFEW!
YOU SHOULD BE HOME, STUDYING!
TRUST ME. WE'D LOVE TO GO HOME. UNFORTUNATELY, OUR CAR BROKE DOWN.

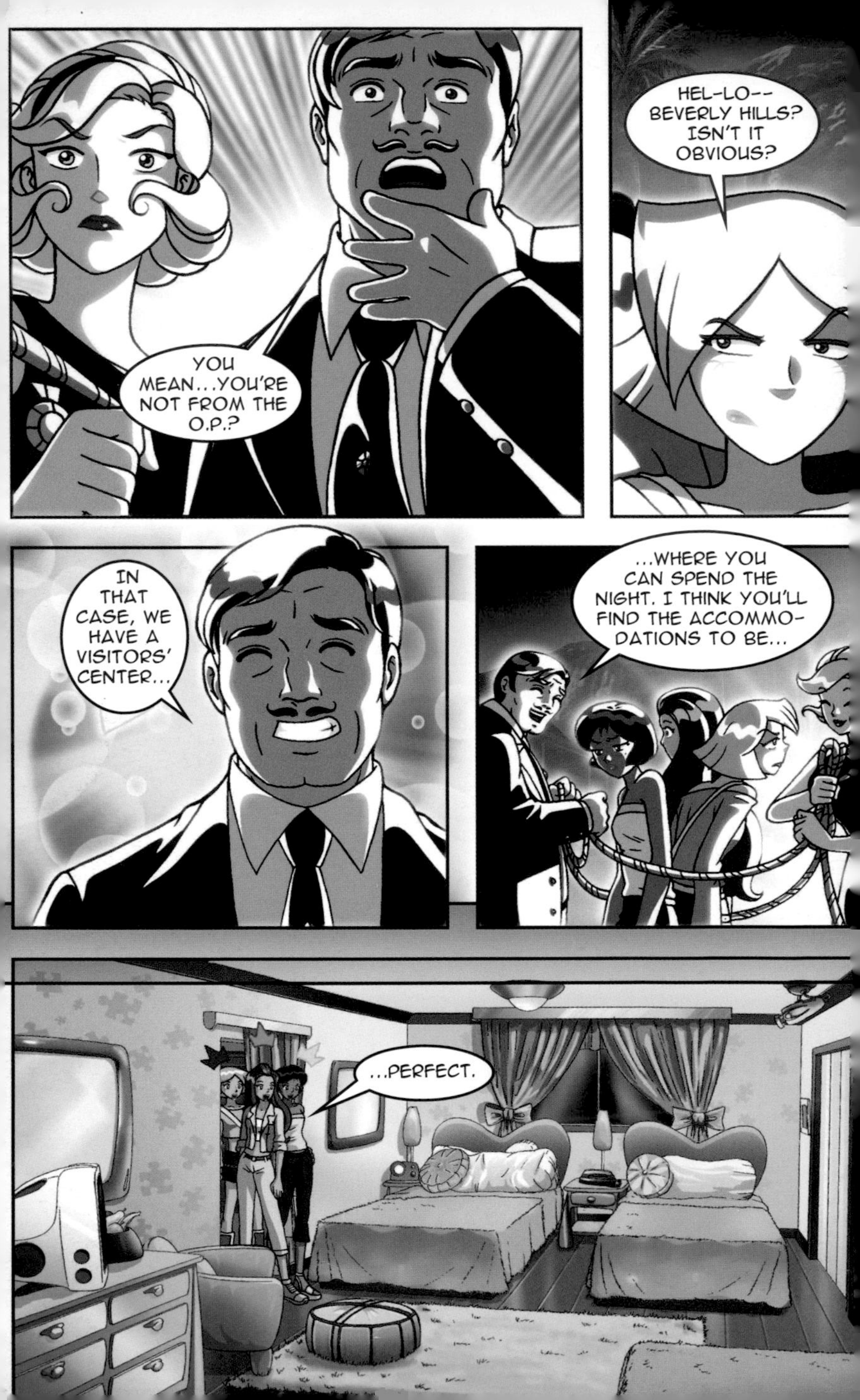
YOU MEAN...YOU'RE NOT FROM THE O.P.?
HEL-LO-- BEVERLY HILLS? ISN'T IT OBVIOUS?
IN THAT CASE, WE HAVE A VISITORS' CENTER...
...WHERE YOU CAN SPEND THE NIGHT. I THINK YOU'LL FIND THE ACCOMMO-DATIONS TO BE...
...PERFECT.

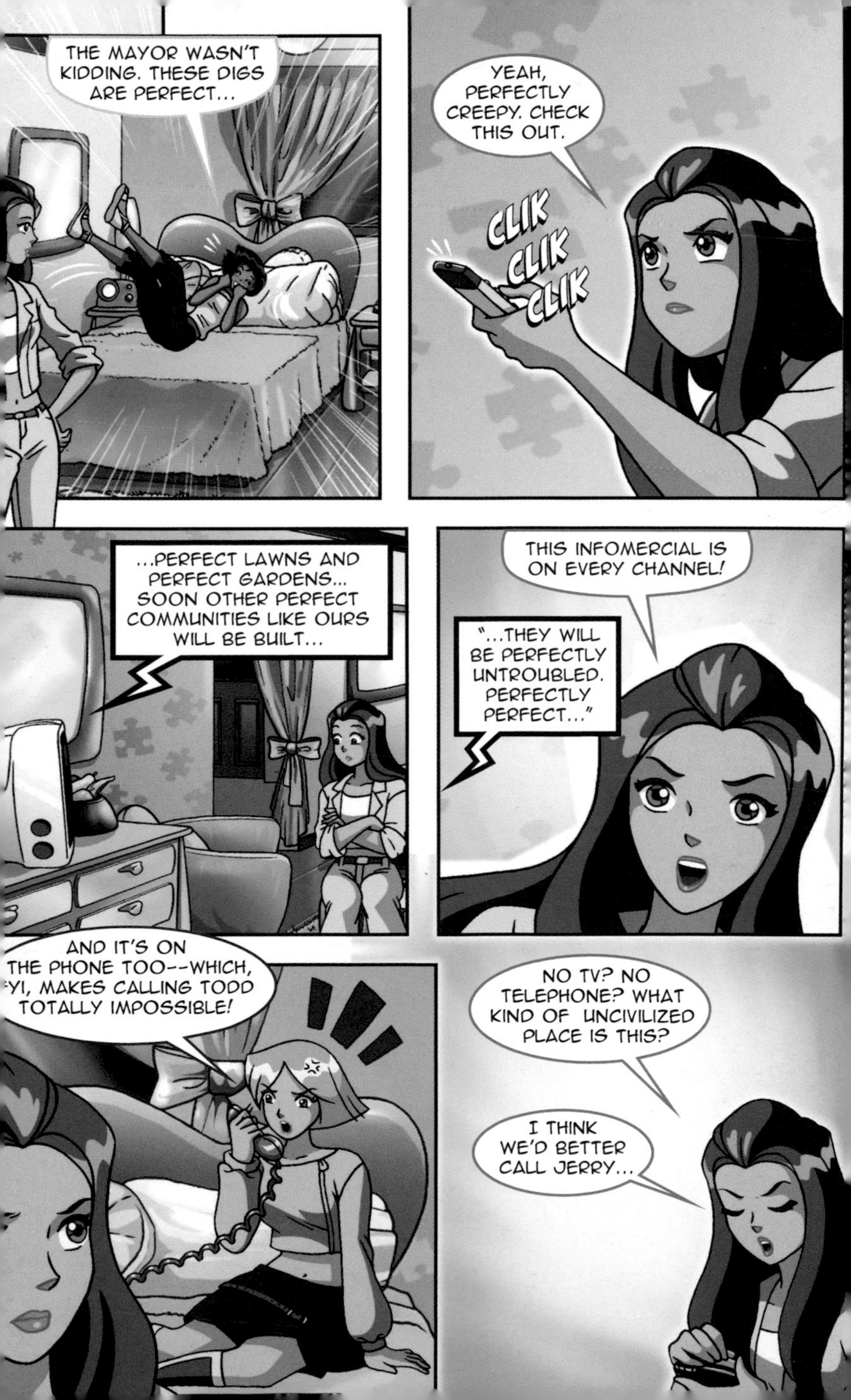
THE MAYOR WASN'T KIDDING. THESE DIGS ARE PERFECT...
YEAH, PERFECTLY CREEPY. CHECK THIS OUT.
CLIK CLIK CLIK
...PERFECT LAWNS AND PERFECT GARDENS... SOON OTHER PERFECT COMMUNITIES LIKE OURS WILL BE BUILT...
THIS INFOMERCIAL IS ON EVERY CHANNEL!
"...THEY WILL BE PERFECTLY UNTROUBLED. PERFECTLY PERFECT..."
AND IT'S ON THE PHONE TOO--WHICH, FYI, MAKES CALLING TODD TOTALLY IMPOSSIBLE!
NO TV? NO TELEPHONE? WHAT KIND OF UNCIVILIZED PLACE IS THIS?
I THINK WE'D BETTER CALL JERRY...

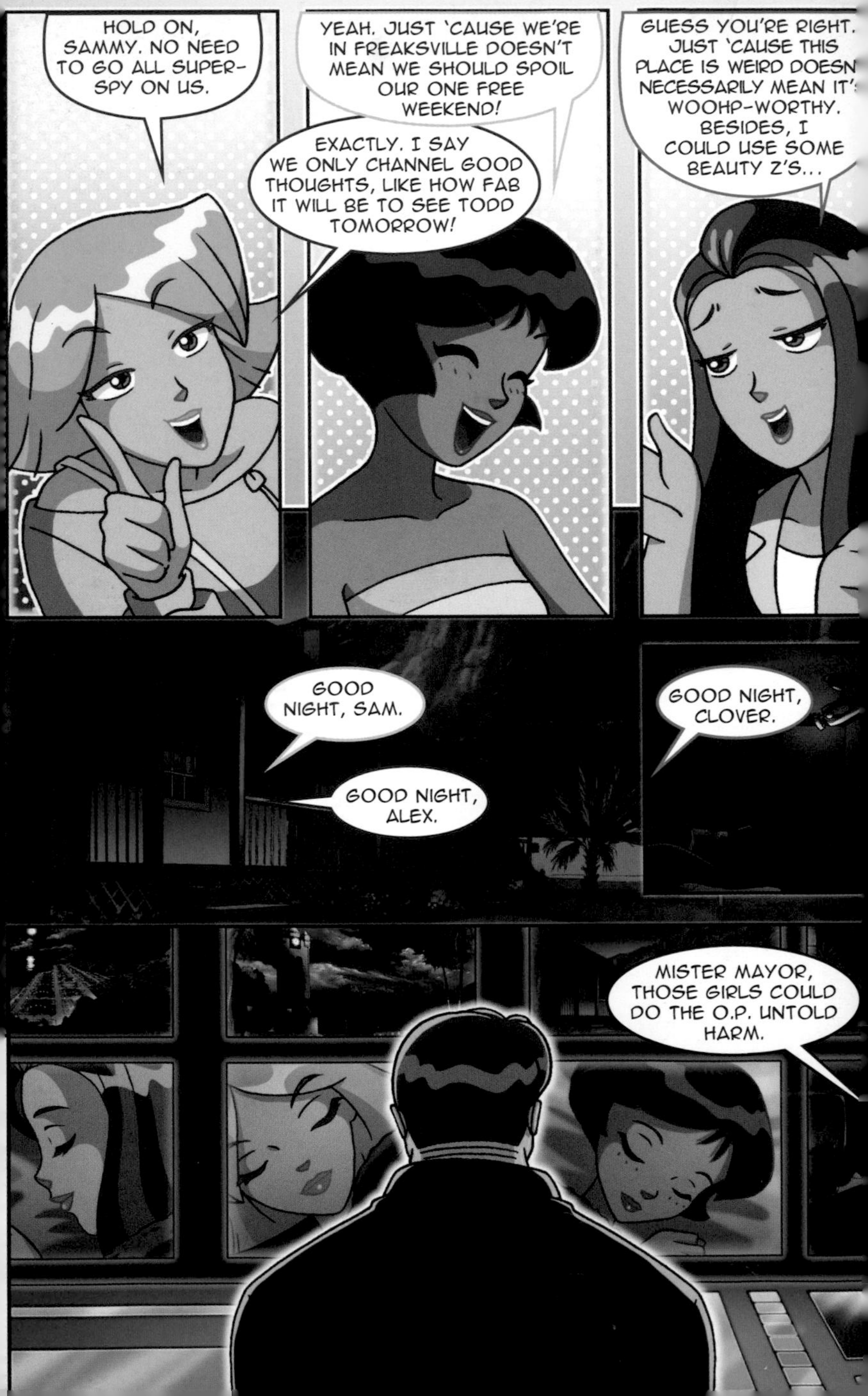
HOLD ON, SAMMY. NO NEED TO GO ALL SUPER-SPY ON US.
YEAH. JUST 'CAUSE WE'RE IN FREAKSVILLE DOESN'T MEAN WE SHOULD SPOIL OUR ONE FREE WEEKEND!
EXACTLY. I SAY WE ONLY CHANNEL GOOD THOUGHTS, LIKE HOW FAB IT WILL BE TO SEE TODD TOMORROW!
GUESS YOU'RE RIGHT. JUST 'CAUSE THIS PLACE IS WEIRD DOESN NECESSARILY MEAN IT' WOOHP-WORTHY. BESIDES, I COULD USE SOME BEAUTY Z'S...
GOOD NIGHT, SAM.
GOOD NIGHT, ALEX.
GOOD NIGHT, CLOVER.
MISTER MAYOR, THOSE GIRLS COULD DO THE O.P. UNTOLD HARM.

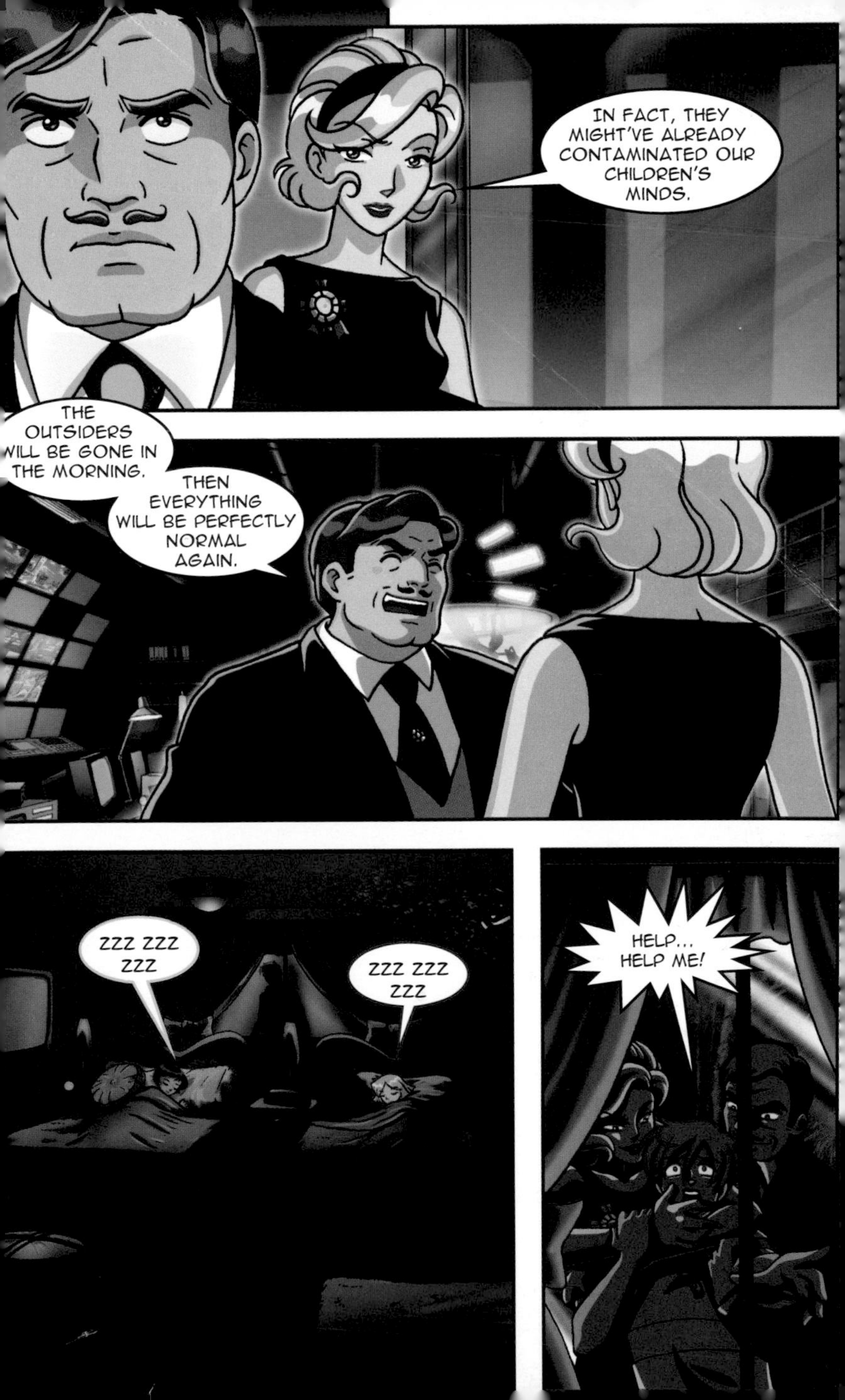
IN FACT, THEY MIGHT'VE ALREADY CONTAMINATED OUR CHILDREN'S MINDS.
THE OUTSIDERS WILL BE GONE IN THE MORNING.
THEN EVERYTHING WILL BE PERFECTLY NORMAL AGAIN.
ZZZ ZZZ ZZZ
ZZZ ZZZ ZZZ
HELP... HELP ME!

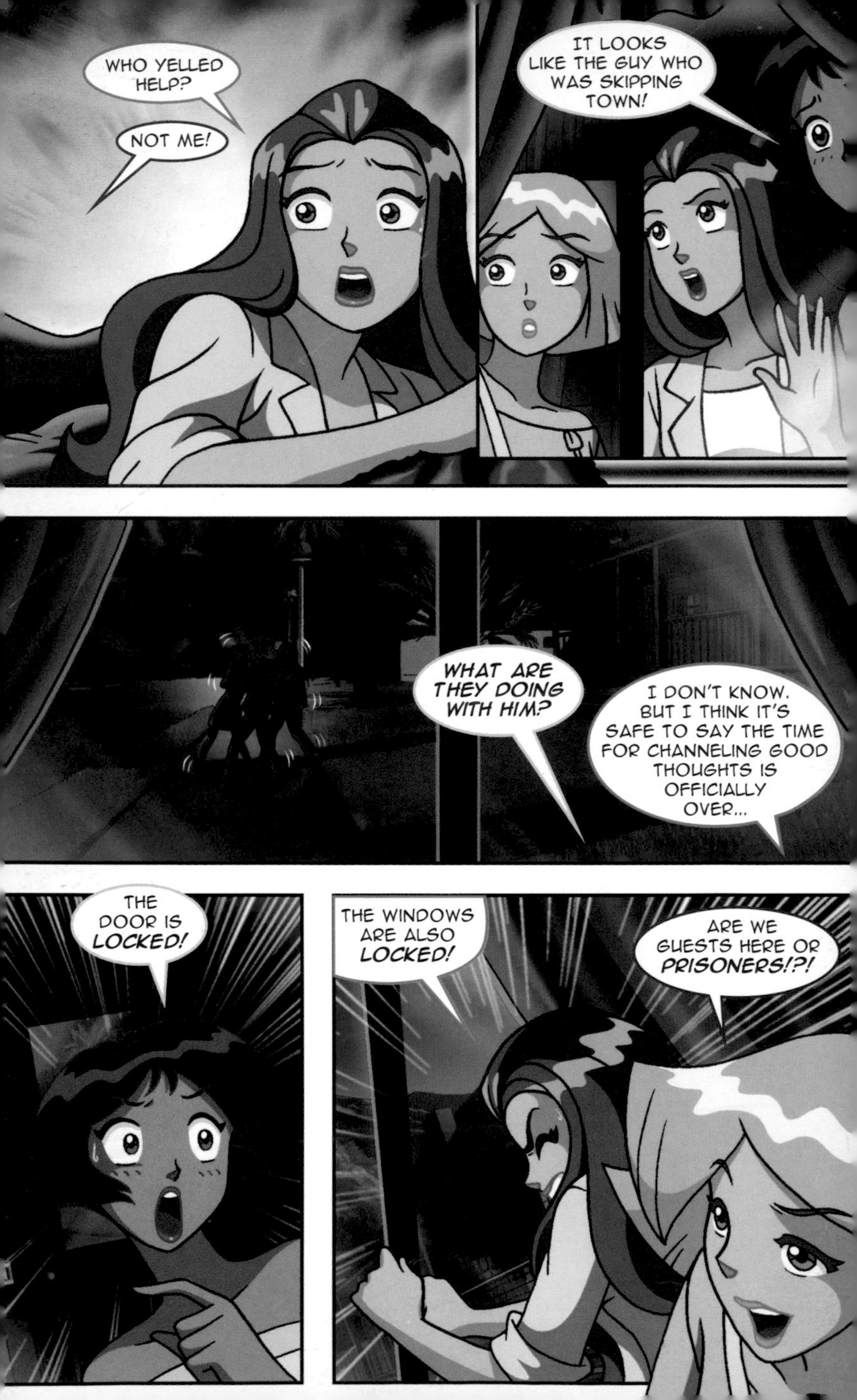
WHO YELLED HELP?
NOT ME!
IT LOOKS LIKE THE GUY WHO WAS SKIPPING TOWN!
WHAT ARE THEY DOING WITH HIM?
I DON'T KNOW. BUT I THINK IT'S SAFE TO SAY THE TIME FOR CHANNELING GOOD THOUGHTS IS OFFICIALLY OVER...
THE DOOR IS LOCKED!
THE WINDOWS ARE ALSO LOCKED!
ARE WE GUESTS HERE OR PRISONERS!?!

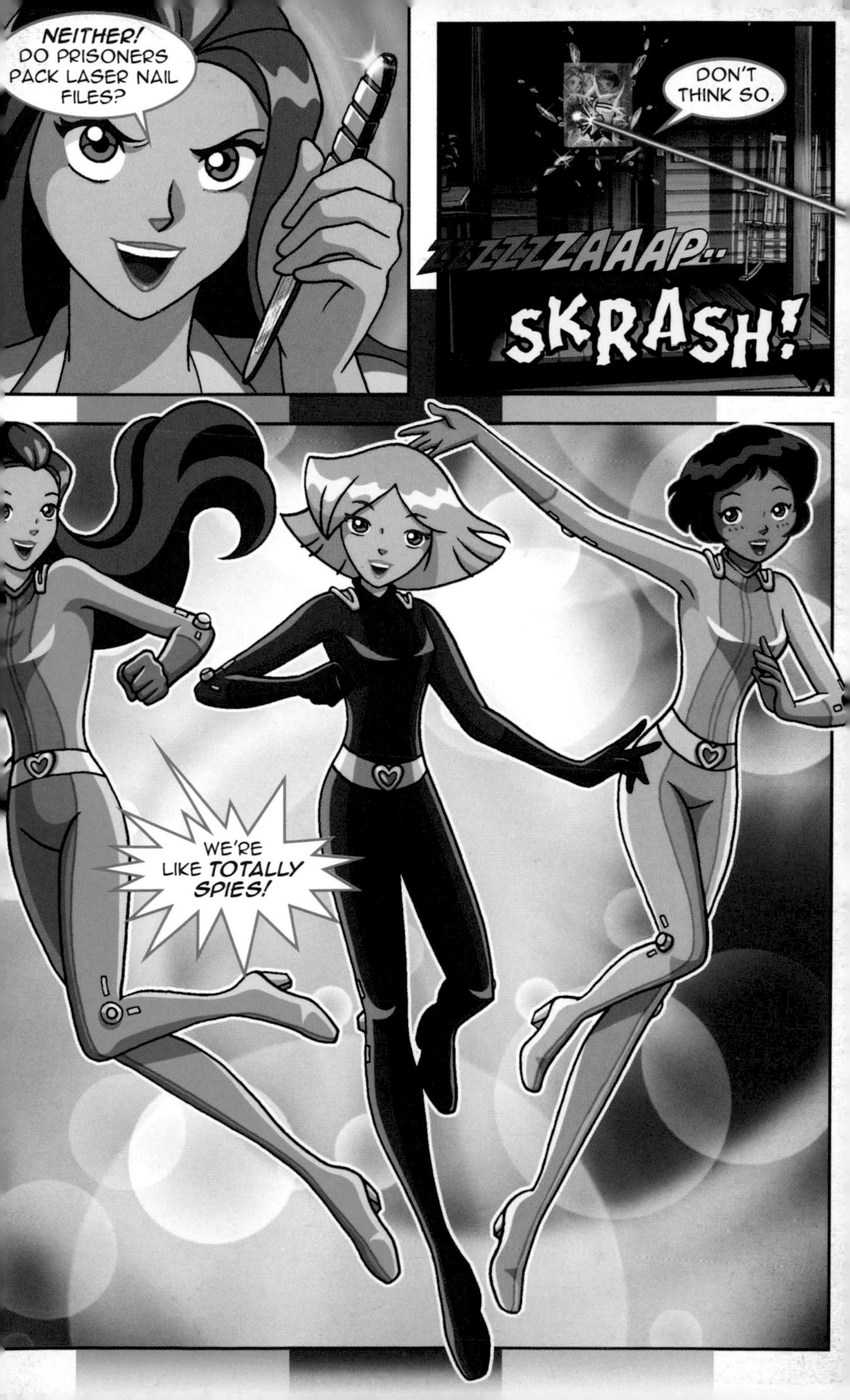
NEITHER! DO PRISONERS PACK LASER NAIL FILES?
DON'T THINK SO.
ZZZZZZZAAAP..
SKRASH!
WE'RE LIKE TOTALLY SPIES!

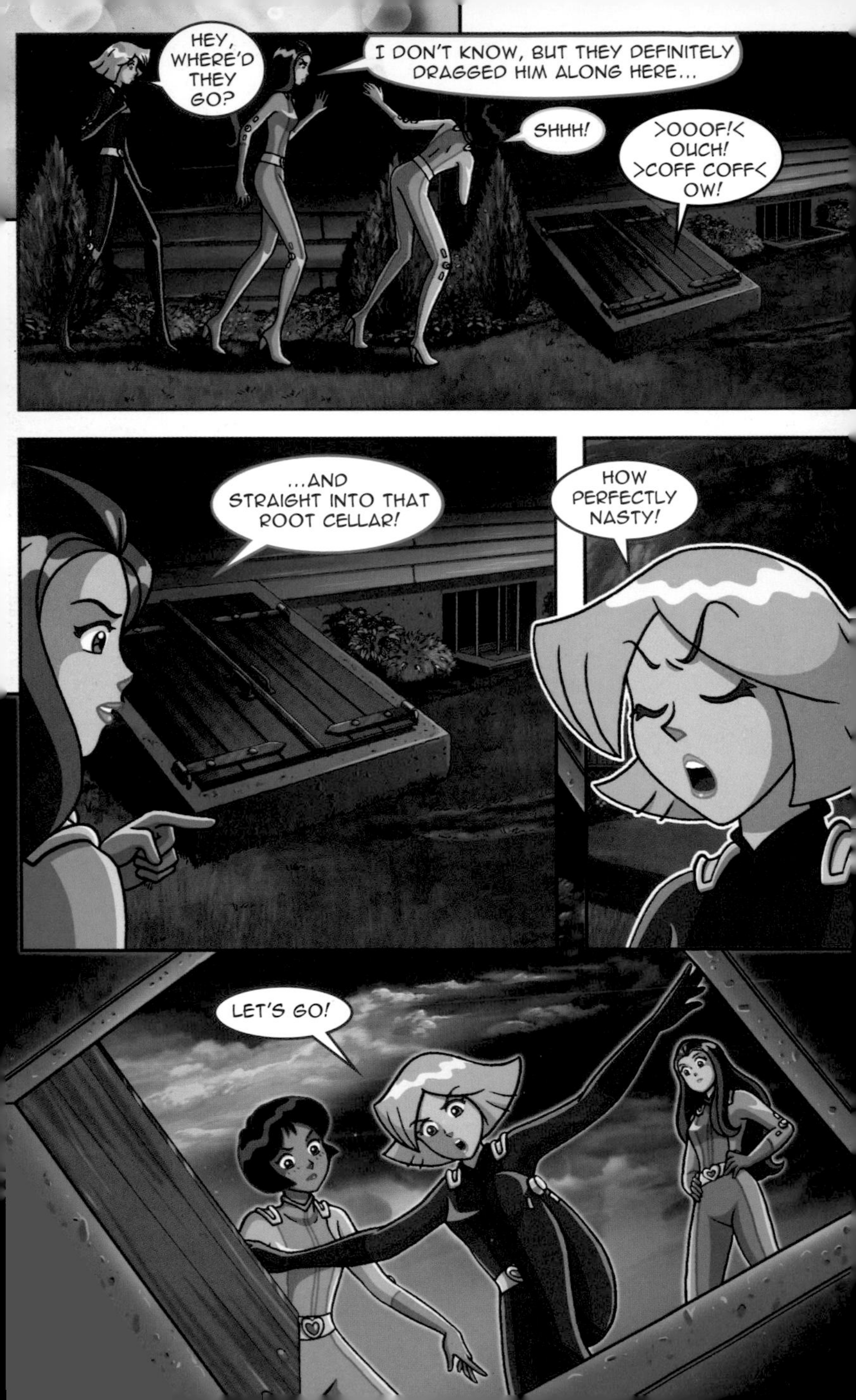
HEY, WHERE'D THEY GO?
I DON'T KNOW, BUT THEY DEFINITELY DRAGGED HIM ALONG HERE...
SHHH!
>OOOF!< OUCH! >COFF COFF< OW!
...AND STRAIGHT INTO THAT ROOT CELLAR!
HOW PERFECTLY NASTY!
LET'S GO!

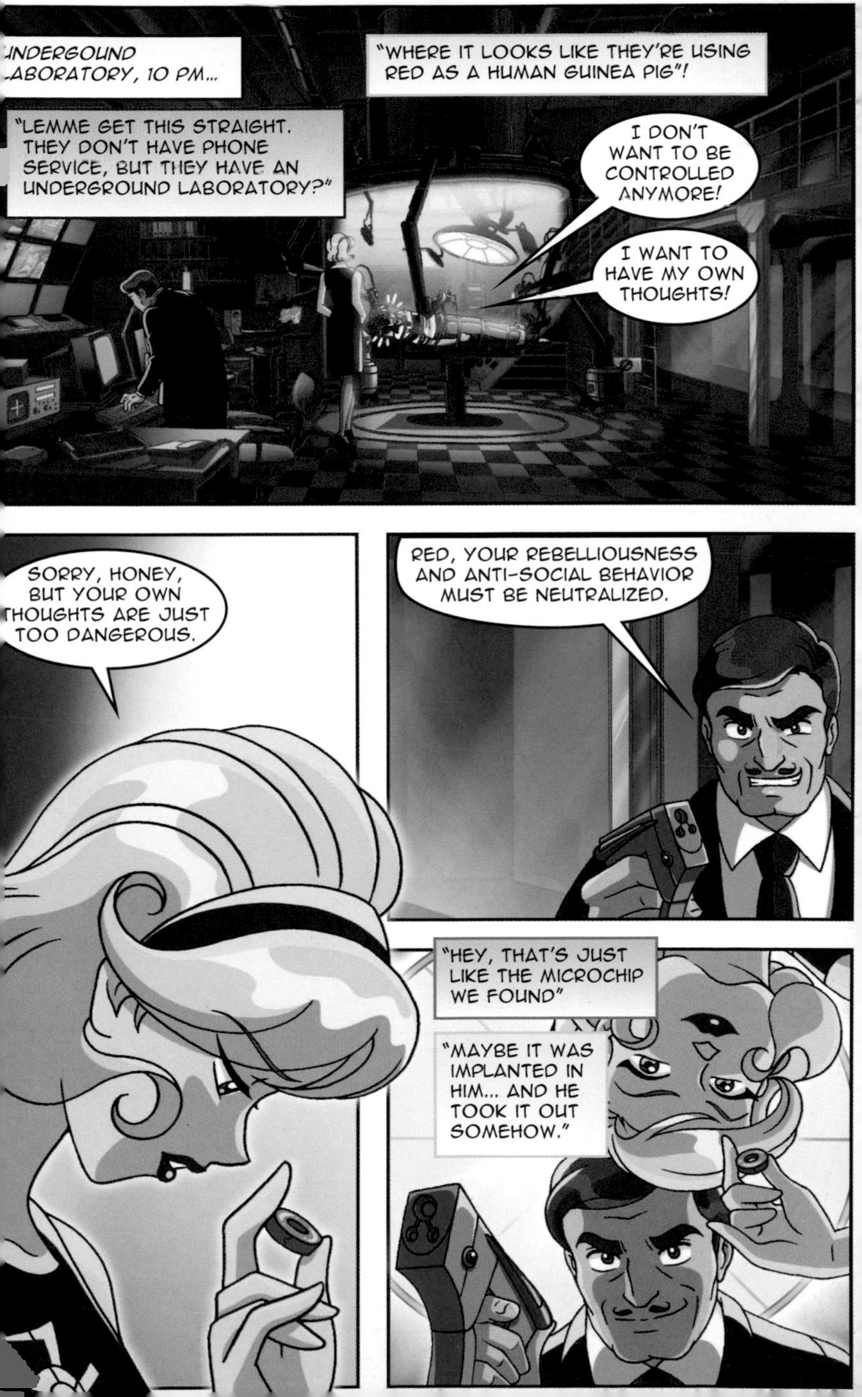
UNDERGOUND LABORATORY, 10 PM...
"LEMME GET THIS STRAIGHT. THEY DON'T HAVE PHONE SERVICE, BUT THEY HAVE AN UNDERGROUND LABORATORY?"
"WHERE IT LOOKS LIKE THEY'RE USING RED AS A HUMAN GUINEA PIG"!
I DON'T WANT TO BE CONTROLLED ANYMORE!
I WANT TO HAVE MY OWN THOUGHTS!
SORRY, HONEY, BUT YOUR OWN THOUGHTS ARE JUST TOO DANGEROUS.
RED, YOUR REBELLIOUSNESS AND ANTI-SOCIAL BEHAVIOR MUST BE NEUTRALIZED.
"HEY, THAT'S JUST LIKE THE MICROCHIP WE FOUND"
"MAYBE IT WAS IMPLANTED IN HIM... AND HE TOOK IT OUT SOMEHOW."

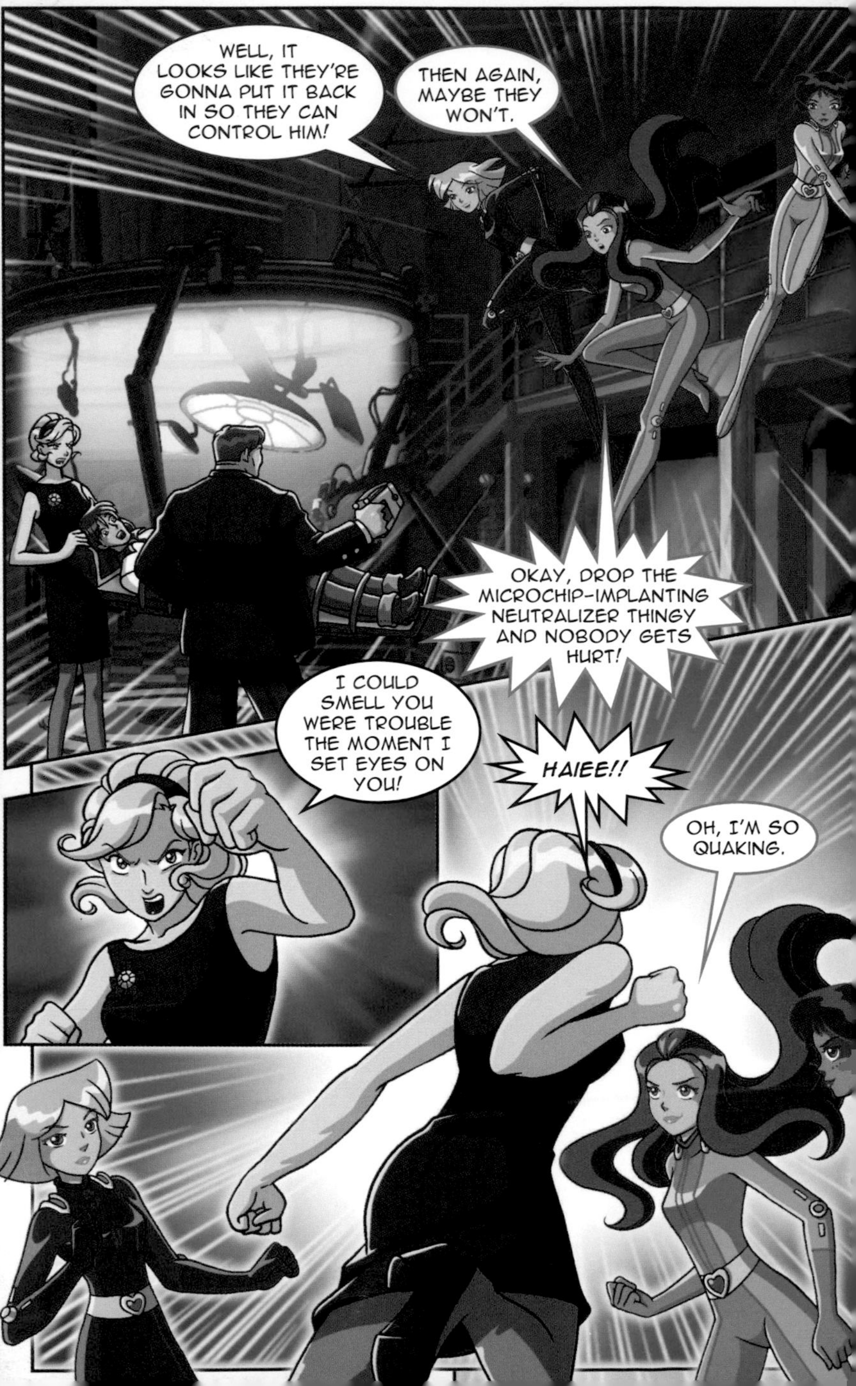
WELL, IT LOOKS LIKE THEY'RE GONNA PUT IT BACK IN SO THEY CAN CONTROL HIM!
THEN AGAIN, MAYBE THEY WON'T.
OKAY, DROP THE MICROCHIP-IMPLANTING NEUTRALIZER THINGY AND NOBODY GETS HURT!
I COULD SMELL YOU WERE TROUBLE THE MOMENT I SET EYES ON YOU!
HAIEE!!
OH, I'M SO QUAKING.

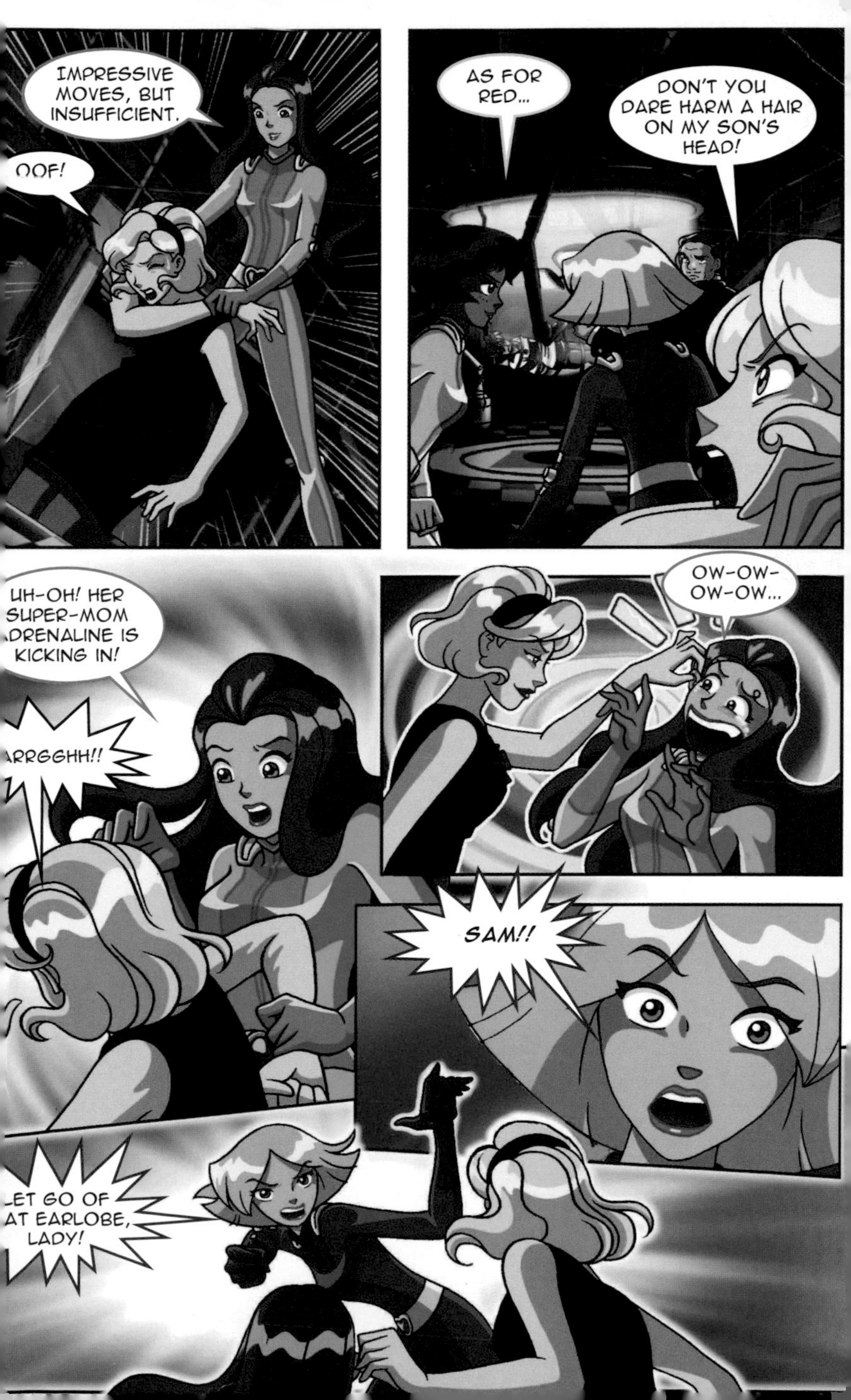
IMPRESSIVE MOVES, BUT INSUFFICIENT.
OOF!
AS FOR RED...
DON'T YOU DARE HARM A HAIR ON MY SON'S HEAD!
UH-OH! HER SUPER-MOM ADRENALINE IS KICKING IN!
ARRGGHH!!
OW-OW-OW-OW...
SAM!!
LET GO OF THAT EARLOBE, LADY!

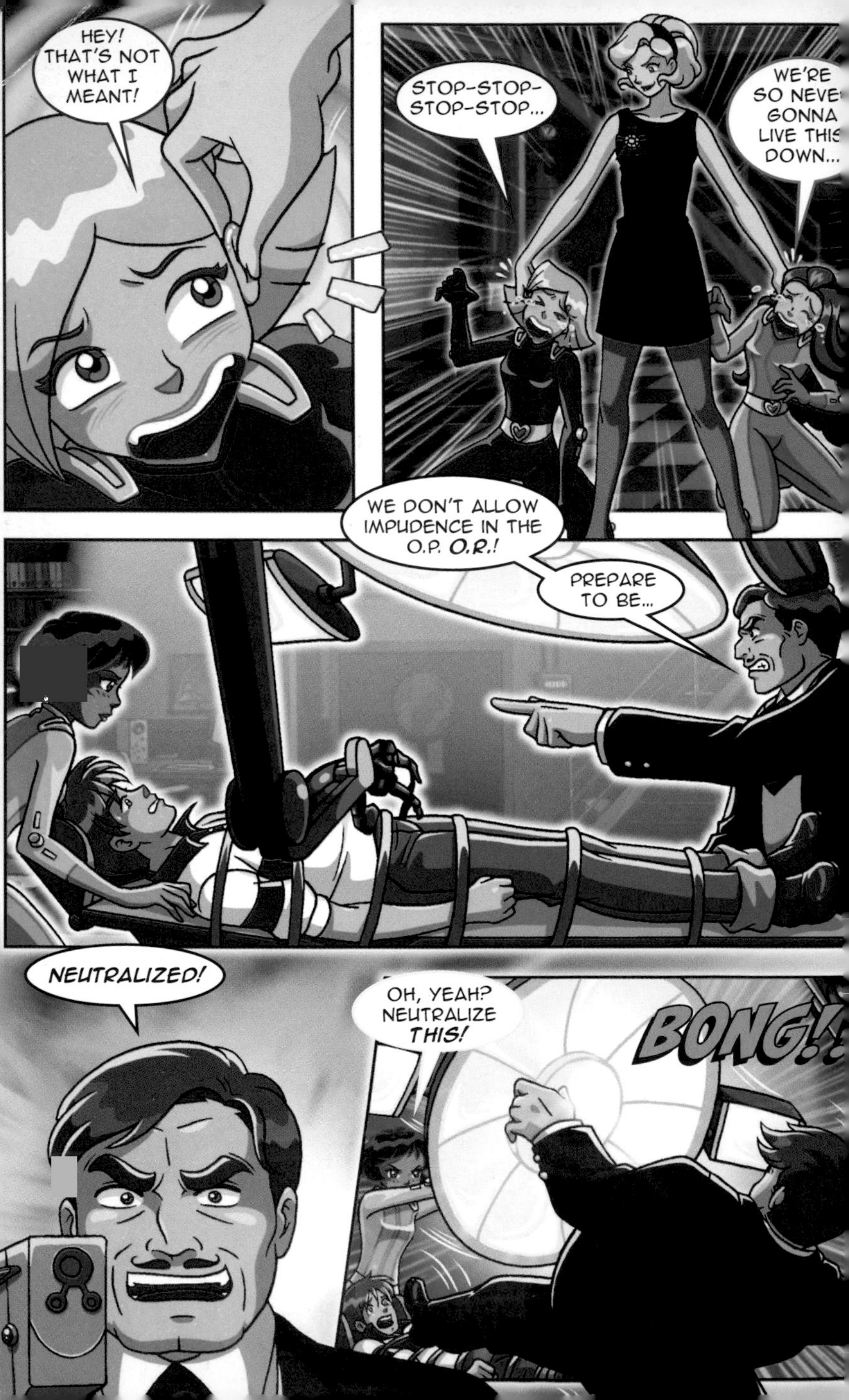
HEY! THAT'S NOT WHAT I MEANT!
STOP-STOP-STOP-STOP...
WE'RE SO NEVE GONNA LIVE THIS DOWN...
WE DON'T ALLOW IMPUDENCE IN THE O.P. *O.R.*!
PREPARE TO BE...
NEUTRALIZED!
OH, YEAH? NEUTRALIZE *THIS!*
BONG!!

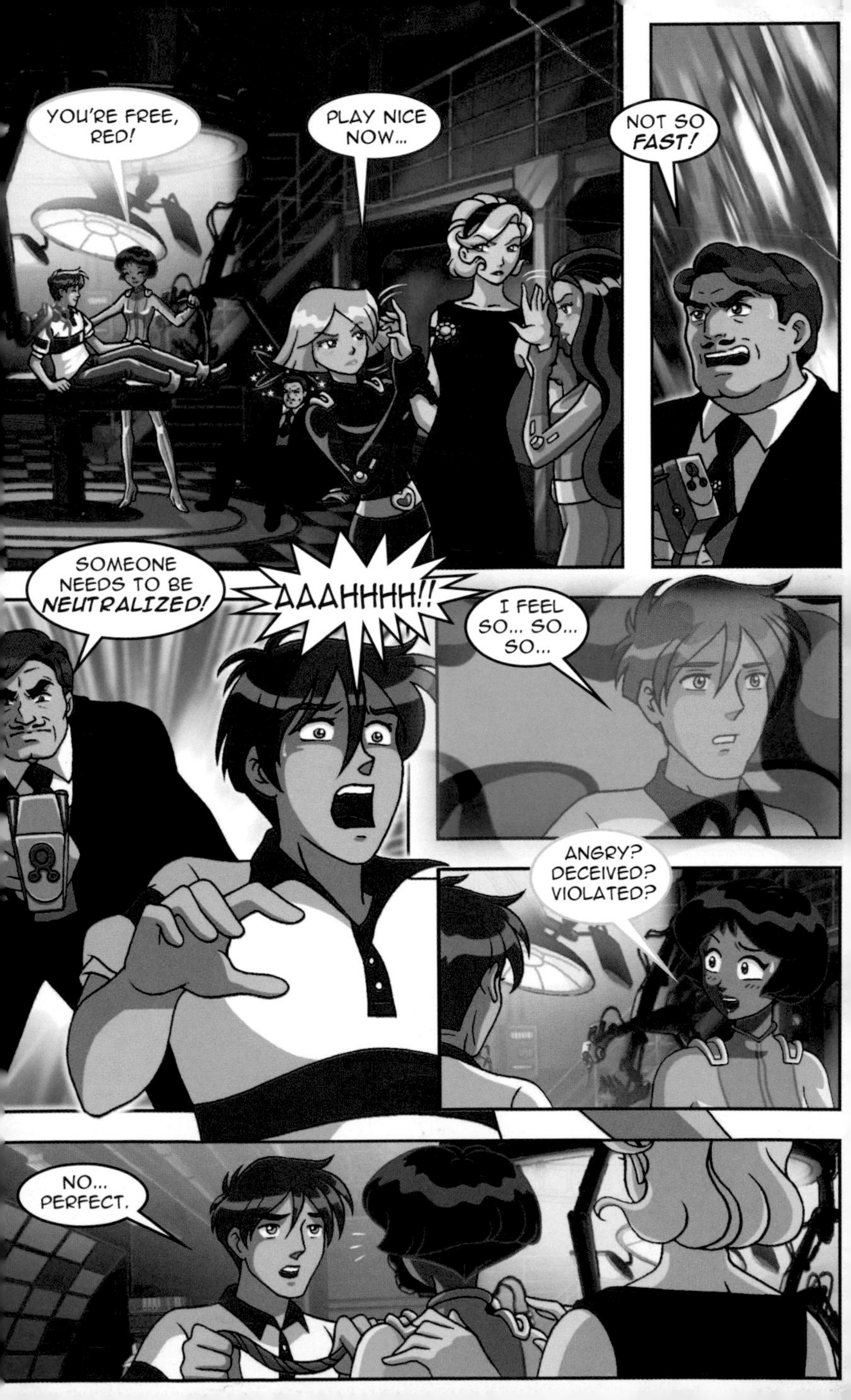
YOU'RE FREE, RED!
PLAY NICE NOW...
NOT SO FAST!
SOMEONE NEEDS TO BE NEUTRALIZED!
AAAHHHH!!
I FEEL SO... SO... SO...
ANGRY? DECEIVED? VIOLATED?
NO... PERFECT.

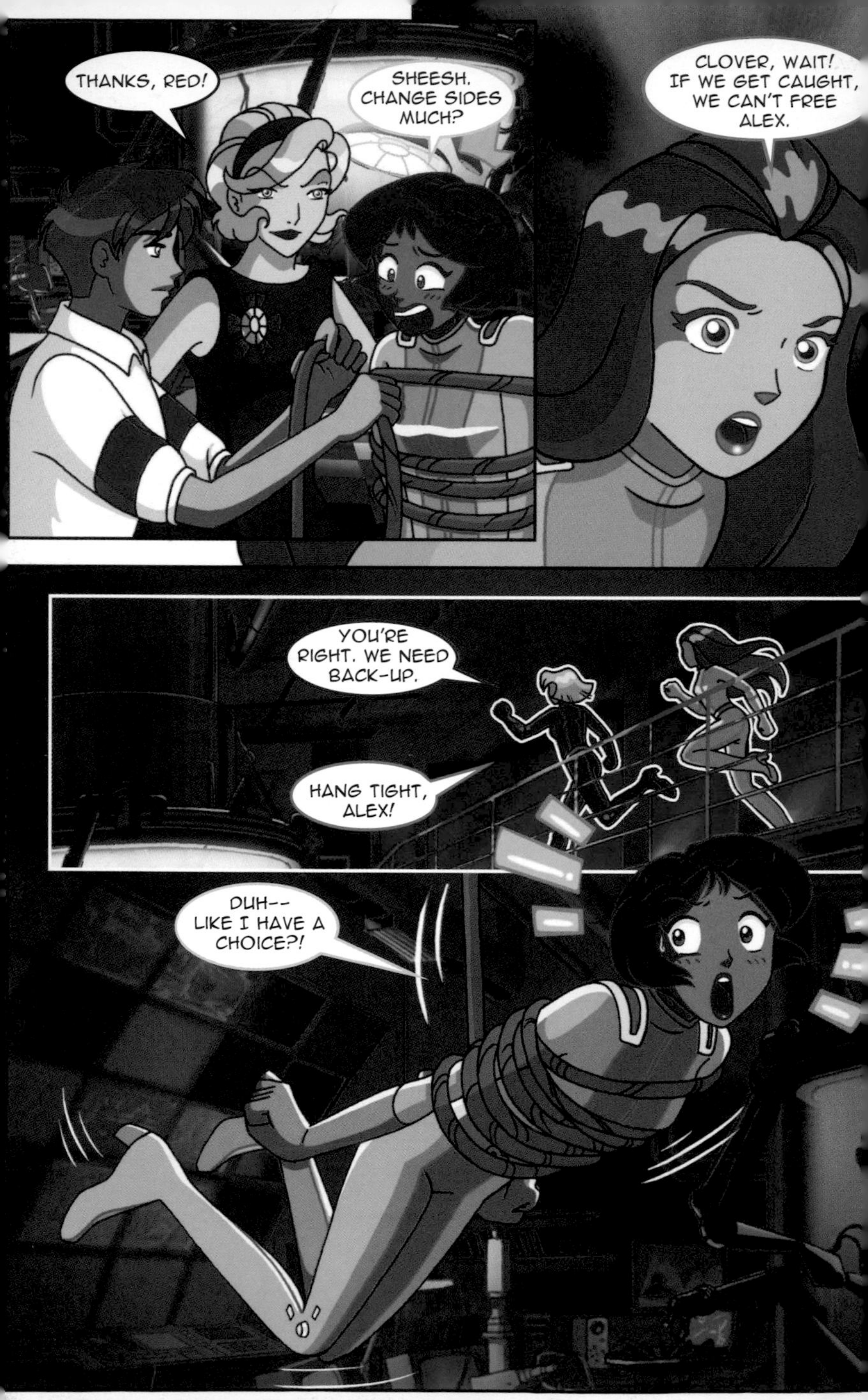
THANKS, RED!
SHEESH. CHANGE SIDES MUCH?
CLOVER, WAIT! IF WE GET CAUGHT, WE CAN'T FREE ALEX.
YOU'RE RIGHT. WE NEED BACK-UP.
HANG TIGHT, ALEX!
DUH-- LIKE I HAVE A CHOICE?!

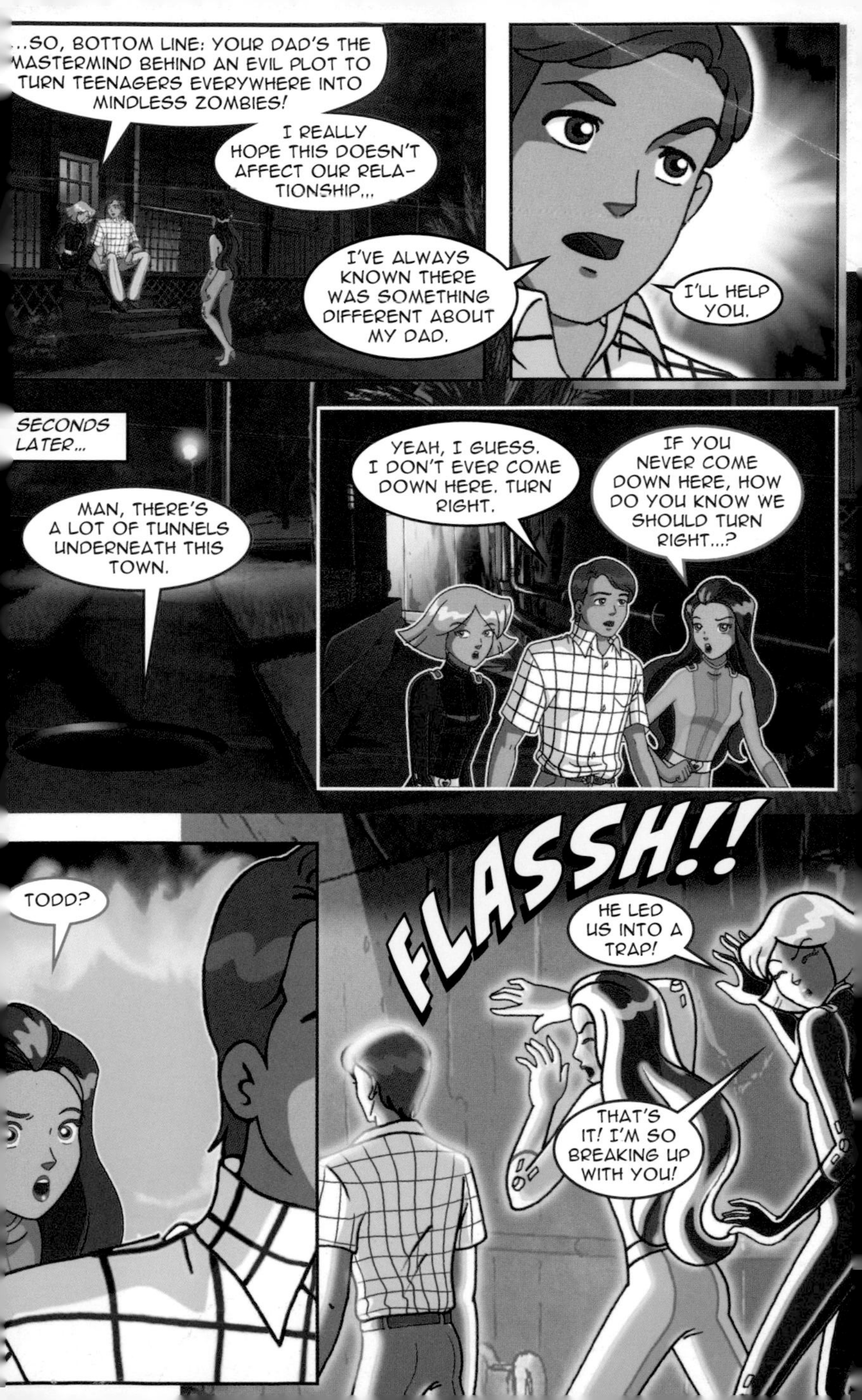
...SO, BOTTOM LINE: YOUR DAD'S THE MASTERMIND BEHIND AN EVIL PLOT TO TURN TEENAGERS EVERYWHERE INTO MINDLESS ZOMBIES!
I REALLY HOPE THIS DOESN'T AFFECT OUR RELA-TIONSHIP...
I'VE ALWAYS KNOWN THERE WAS SOMETHING DIFFERENT ABOUT MY DAD.
I'LL HELP YOU.
SECONDS LATER...
MAN, THERE'S A LOT OF TUNNELS UNDERNEATH THIS TOWN.
YEAH, I GUESS. I DON'T EVER COME DOWN HERE. TURN RIGHT.
IF YOU NEVER COME DOWN HERE, HOW DO YOU KNOW WE SHOULD TURN RIGHT...?
TODD?
FLASSH!!
HE LED US INTO A TRAP!
THAT'S IT! I'M SO BREAKING UP WITH YOU!

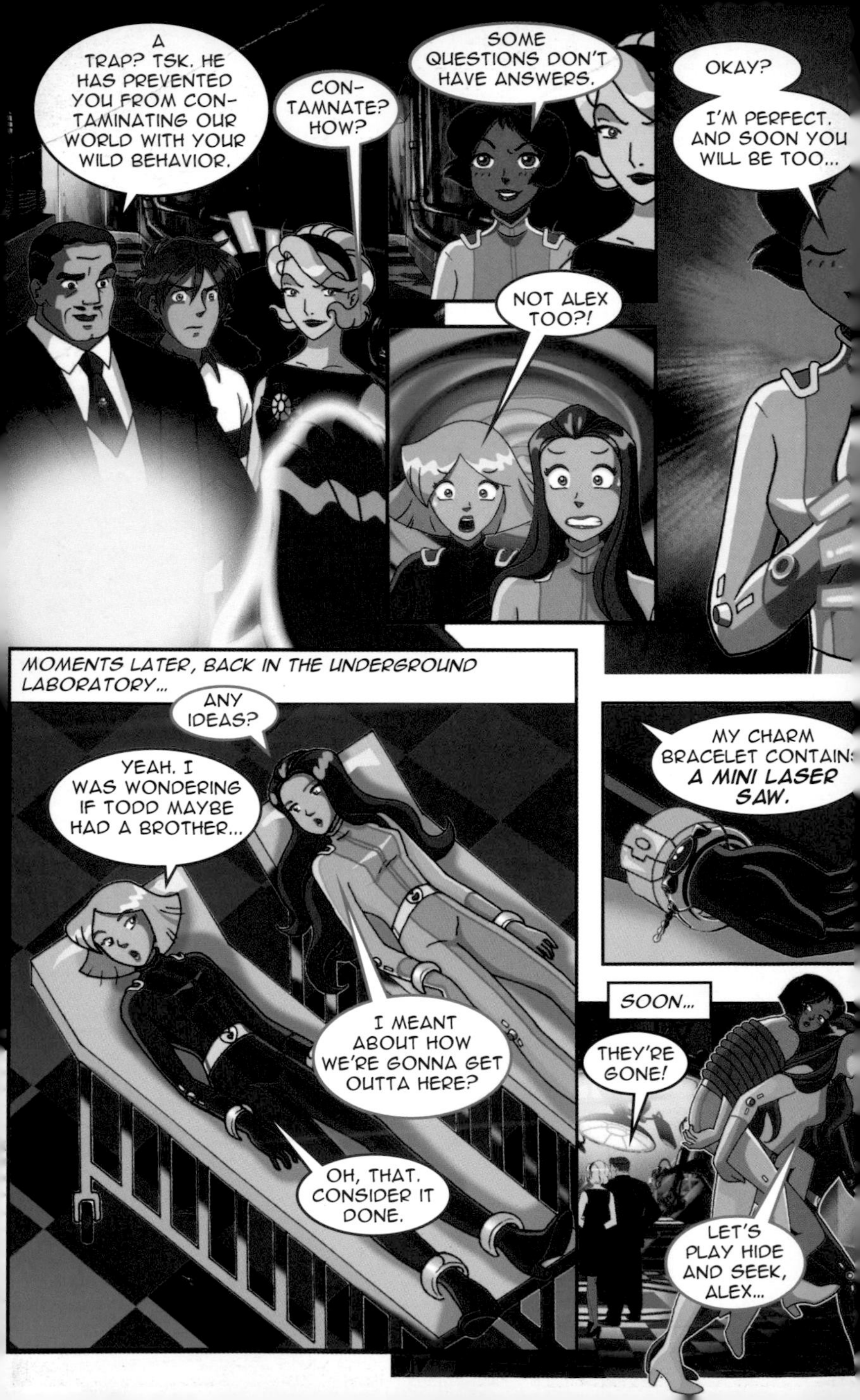
A TRAP? TSK. HE HAS PREVENTED YOU FROM CON-TAMINATING OUR WORLD WITH YOUR WILD BEHAVIOR.
CON-TAMNATE? HOW?
SOME QUESTIONS DON'T HAVE ANSWERS.
NOT ALEX TOO?!
OKAY?
I'M PERFECT. AND SOON YOU WILL BE TOO...
MOMENTS LATER, BACK IN THE UNDERGROUND LABORATORY...
ANY IDEAS?
YEAH. I WAS WONDERING IF TODD MAYBE HAD A BROTHER...
I MEANT ABOUT HOW WE'RE GONNA GET OUTTA HERE?
OH, THAT. CONSIDER IT DONE.
MY CHARM BRACELET CONTAIN: A MINI LASER SAW.
SOON...
THEY'RE GONE!
LET'S PLAY HIDE AND SEEK, ALEX...

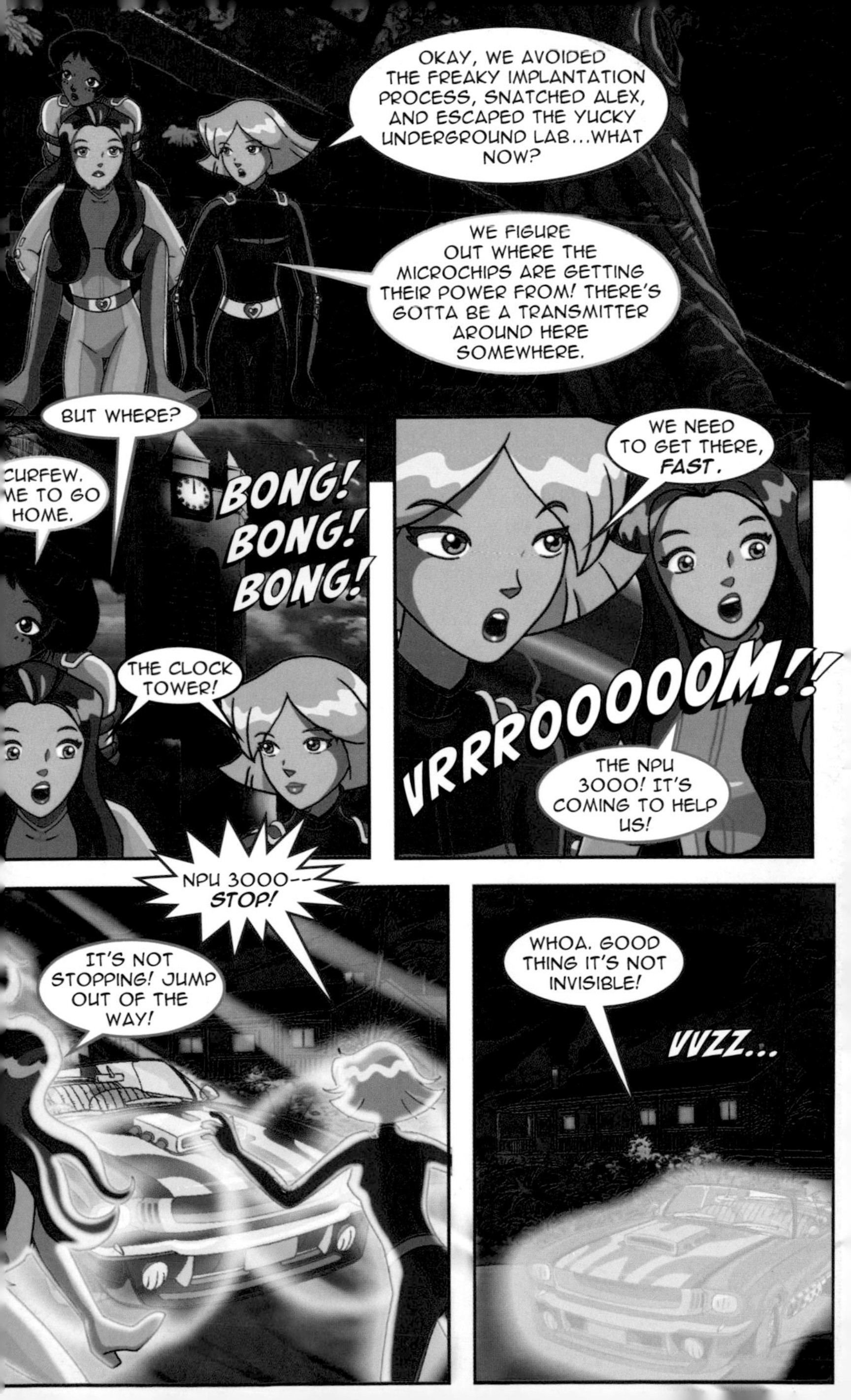
OKAY, WE AVOIDED THE FREAKY IMPLANTATION PROCESS, SNATCHED ALEX, AND ESCAPED THE YUCKY UNDERGROUND LAB...WHAT NOW?
WE FIGURE OUT WHERE THE MICROCHIPS ARE GETTING THEIR POWER FROM! THERE'S GOTTA BE A TRANSMITTER AROUND HERE SOMEWHERE.
BUT WHERE?
CURFEW. ME TO GO HOME.
BONG! BONG! BONG!
THE CLOCK TOWER!
WE NEED TO GET THERE, ***FAST***.
VRRROOOOOOM!!
THE NPU 3000! IT'S COMING TO HELP US!
NPU 3000-- ***STOP!***
IT'S NOT STOPPING! JUMP OUT OF THE WAY!
WHOA. GOOD THING IT'S NOT INVISIBLE!
VVZZ...

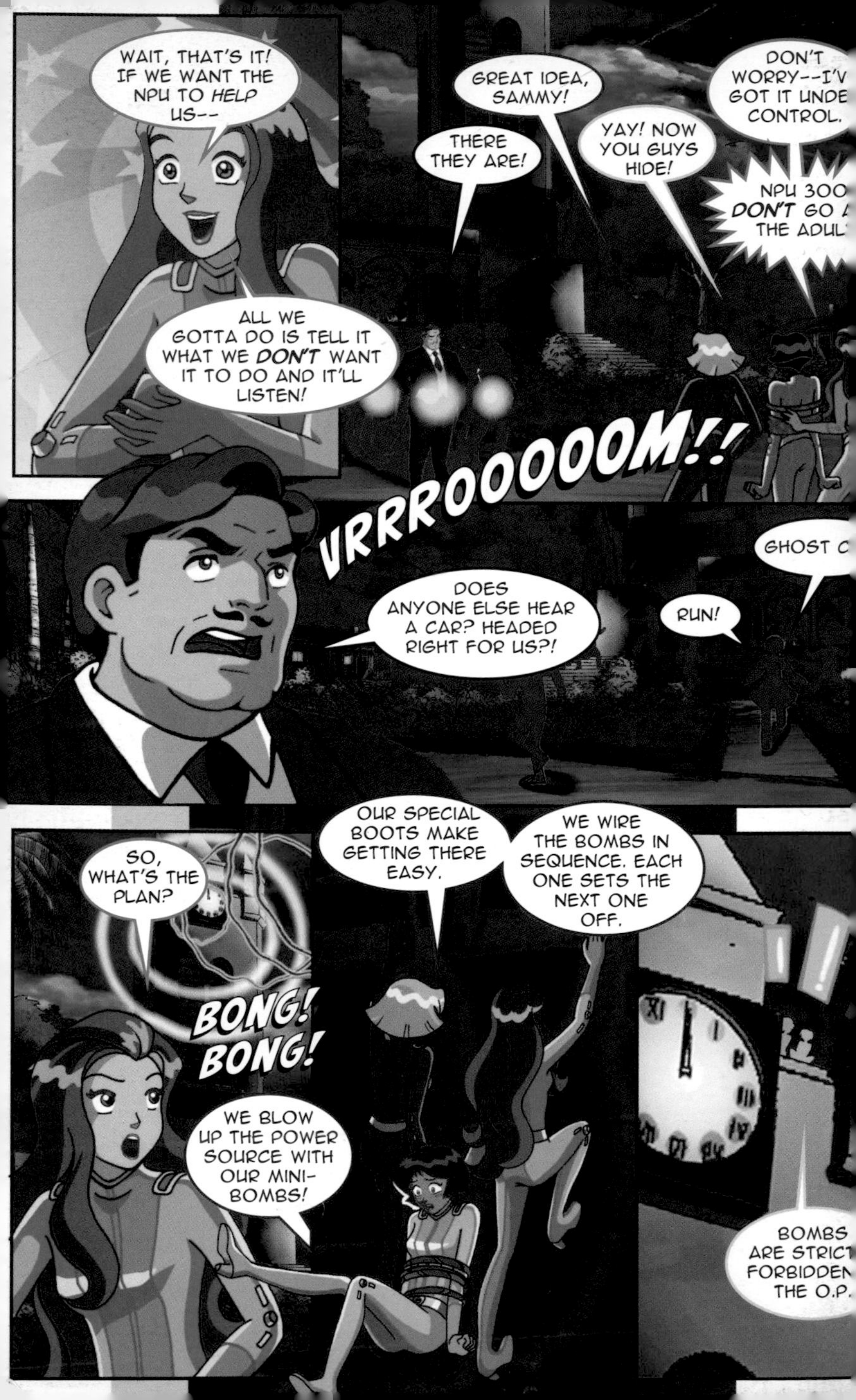
WAIT, THAT'S IT! IF WE WANT THE NPU TO *HELP* US--
ALL WE GOTTA DO IS TELL IT WHAT WE ***DON'T*** WANT IT TO DO AND IT'LL LISTEN!
GREAT IDEA, SAMMY!
THERE THEY ARE!
YAY! NOW YOU GUYS HIDE!
DON'T WORRY--I'V GOT IT UNDE CONTROL.
NPU 300 ***DON'T*** GO A THE ADUL
VRRROOOOOM!!
DOES ANYONE ELSE HEAR A CAR? HEADED RIGHT FOR US?!
RUN!
GHOST C
SO, WHAT'S THE PLAN?
BONG! BONG!
WE BLOW UP THE POWER SOURCE WITH OUR MINI-BOMBS!
OUR SPECIAL BOOTS MAKE GETTING THERE EASY.
WE WIRE THE BOMBS IN SEQUENCE. EACH ONE SETS THE NEXT ONE OFF.
BOMBS ARE STRICT FORBIDDEN THE O.P.

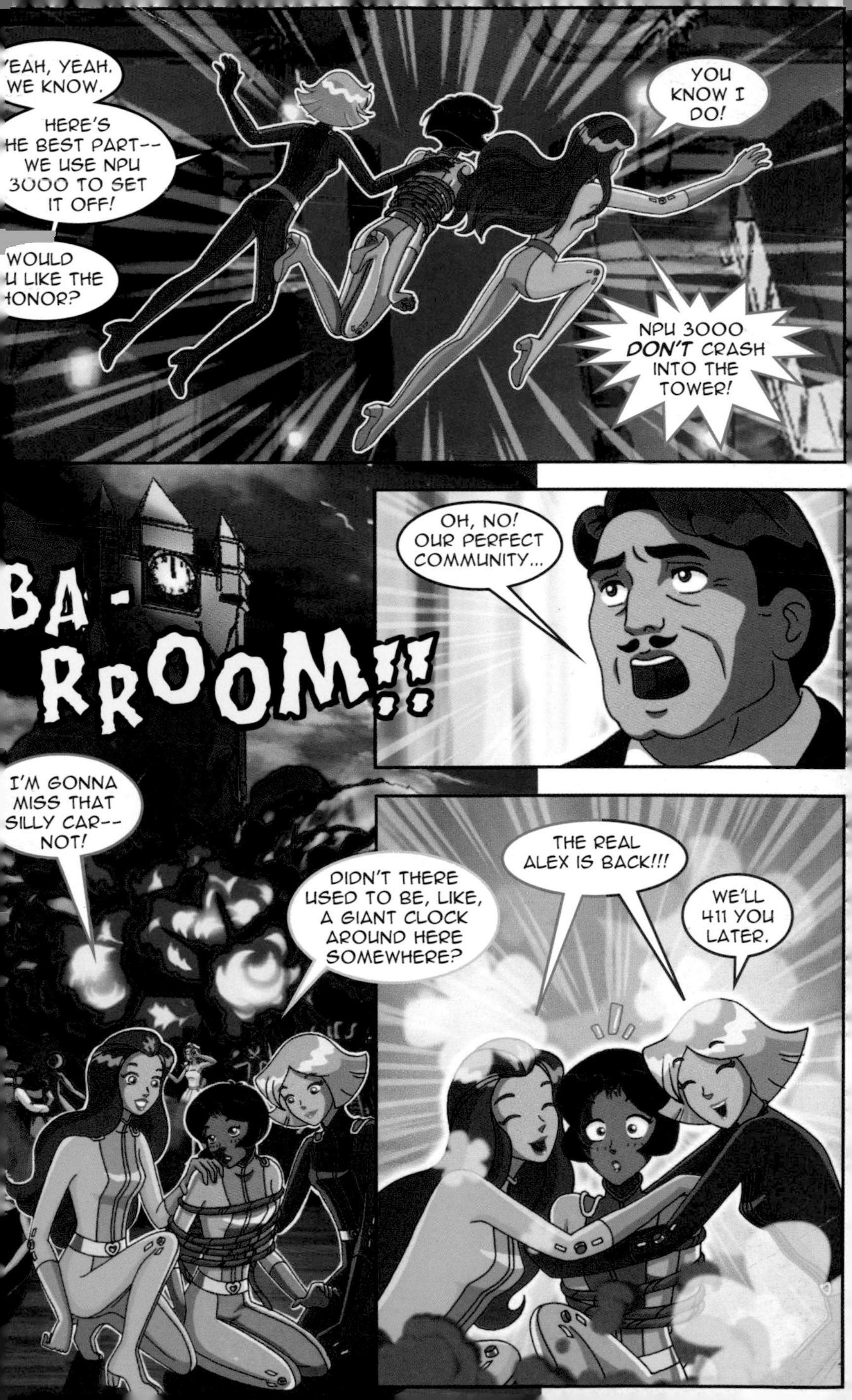

'EAH, YEAH. WE KNOW.
HERE'S HE BEST PART-- WE USE NPU 3000 TO SET IT OFF!
WOULD U LIKE THE HONOR?
YOU KNOW I DO!
NPU 3000 DON'T CRASH INTO THE TOWER!
BA-RROOM!!
OH, NO! OUR PERFECT COMMUNITY...
I'M GONNA MISS THAT SILLY CAR-- NOT!
DIDN'T THERE USED TO BE, LIKE, A GIANT CLOCK AROUND HERE SOMEWHERE?
THE REAL ALEX IS BACK!!!
WE'LL 411 YOU LATER.

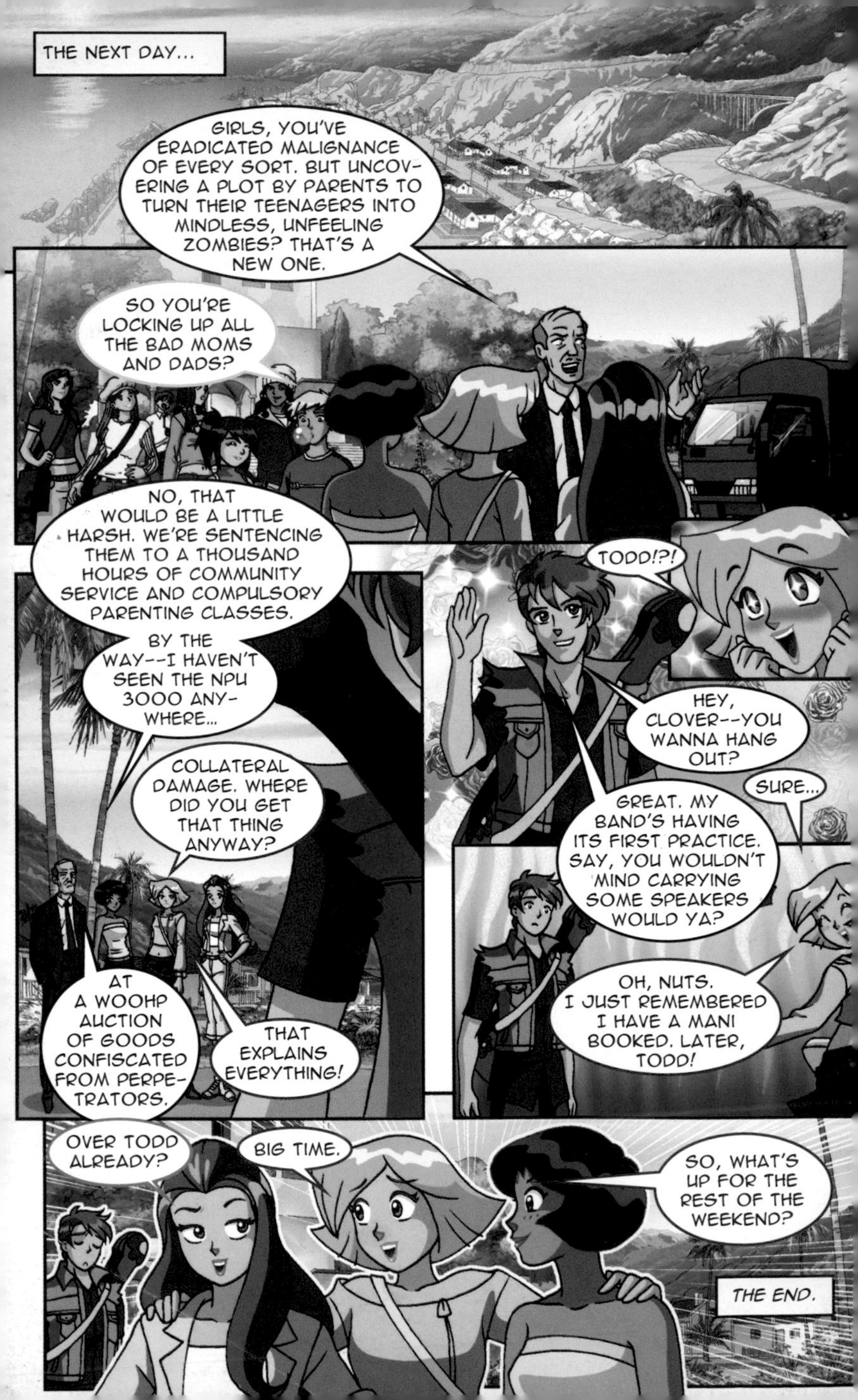
THE NEXT DAY...
GIRLS, YOU'VE ERADICATED MALIGNANCE OF EVERY SORT. BUT UNCOVERING A PLOT BY PARENTS TO TURN THEIR TEENAGERS INTO MINDLESS, UNFEELING ZOMBIES? THAT'S A NEW ONE.
SO YOU'RE LOCKING UP ALL THE BAD MOMS AND DADS?
NO, THAT WOULD BE A LITTLE HARSH. WE'RE SENTENCING THEM TO A THOUSAND HOURS OF COMMUNITY SERVICE AND COMPULSORY PARENTING CLASSES.
BY THE WAY--I HAVEN'T SEEN THE NPU 3000 ANYWHERE...
COLLATERAL DAMAGE. WHERE DID YOU GET THAT THING ANYWAY?
AT A WOOHP AUCTION OF GOODS CONFISCATED FROM PERPETRATORS.
THAT EXPLAINS EVERYTHING!
TODD!?!
HEY, CLOVER--YOU WANNA HANG OUT?
SURE...
GREAT. MY BAND'S HAVING ITS FIRST PRACTICE. SAY, YOU WOULDN'T MIND CARRYING SOME SPEAKERS WOULD YA?
OH, NUTS. I JUST REMEMBERED I HAVE A MANI BOOKED. LATER, TODD!
OVER TODD ALREADY?
BIG TIME.
SO, WHAT'S UP FOR THE REST OF THE WEEKEND?
THE END.

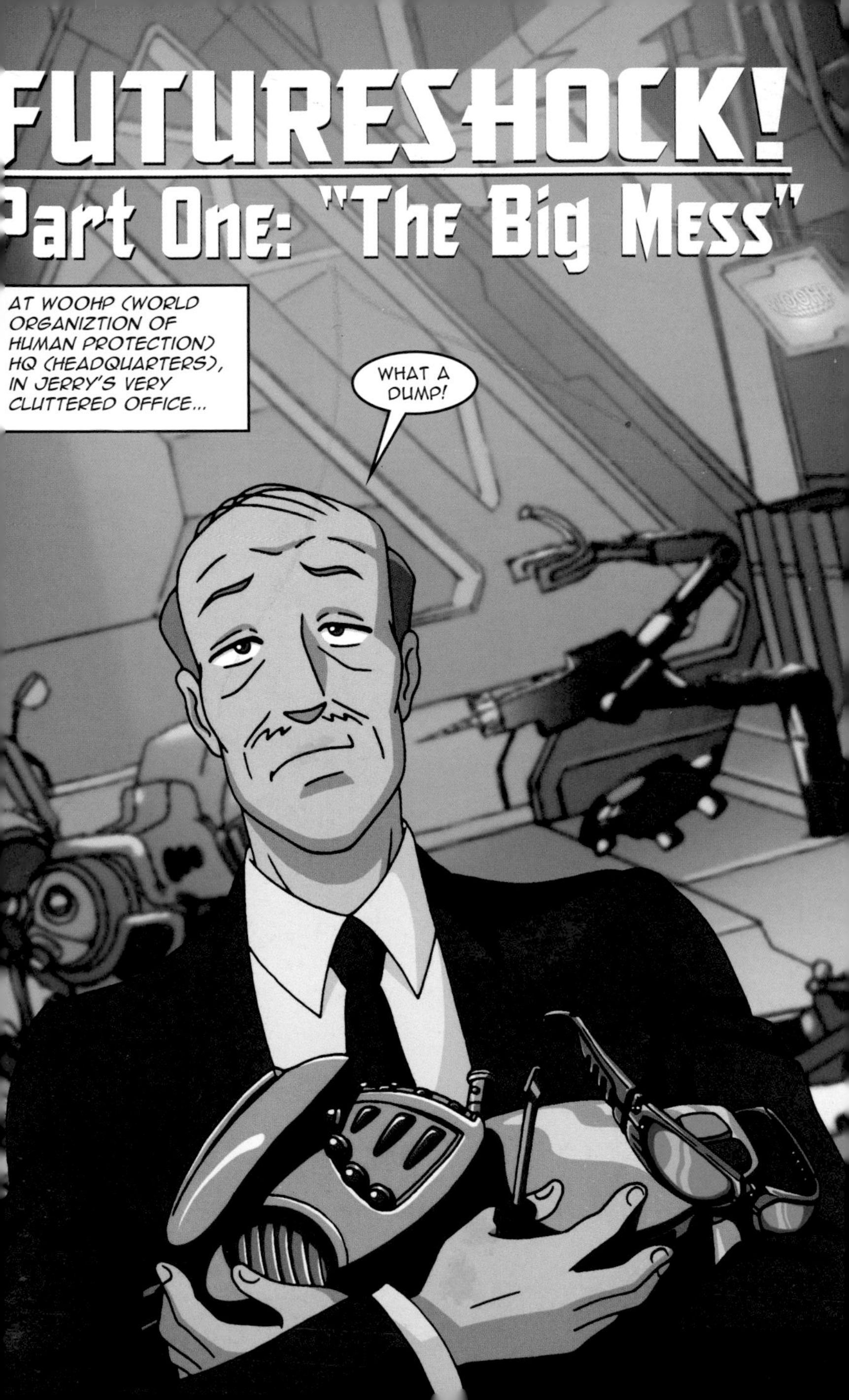
FUTURESHOCK!
Part One: "The Big Mess"
AT WOOHP (WORLD ORGANIZTION OF HUMAN PROTECTION) HQ (HEADQUARTERS), IN JERRY'S VERY CLUTTERED OFFICE...
WHAT A DUMP!

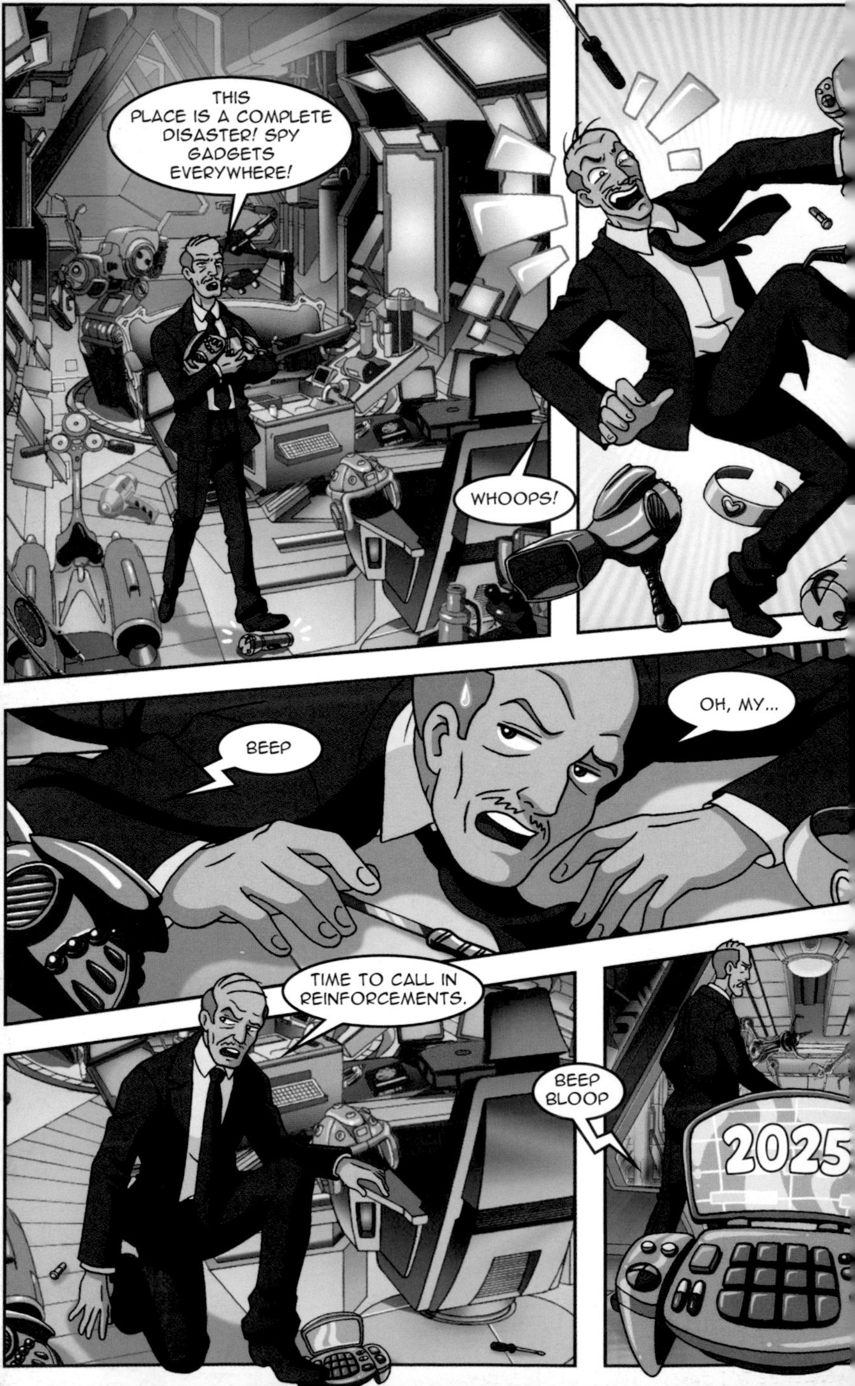
THIS PLACE IS A COMPLETE DISASTER! SPY GADGETS EVERYWHERE!
WHOOPS!
BEEP
OH, MY...
TIME TO CALL IN REINFORCEMENTS.
BEEP BLOOP
2025

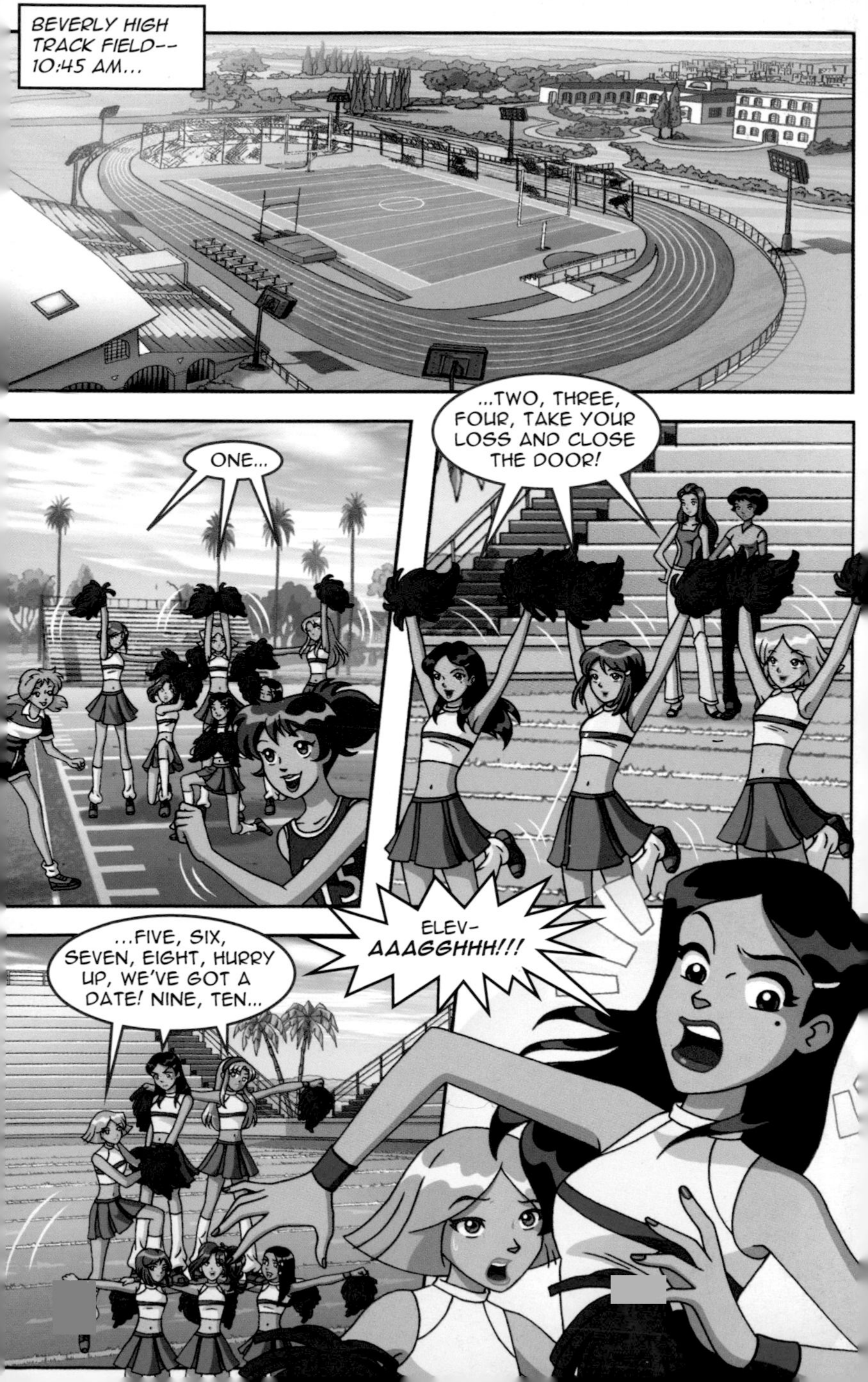
BEVERLY HIGH TRACK FIELD--10:45 AM...
ONE...
...TWO, THREE, FOUR, TAKE YOUR LOSS AND CLOSE THE DOOR!
...FIVE, SIX, SEVEN, EIGHT, HURRY UP, WE'VE GOT A DATE! NINE, TEN...
ELEV-AAAGGHHH!!!

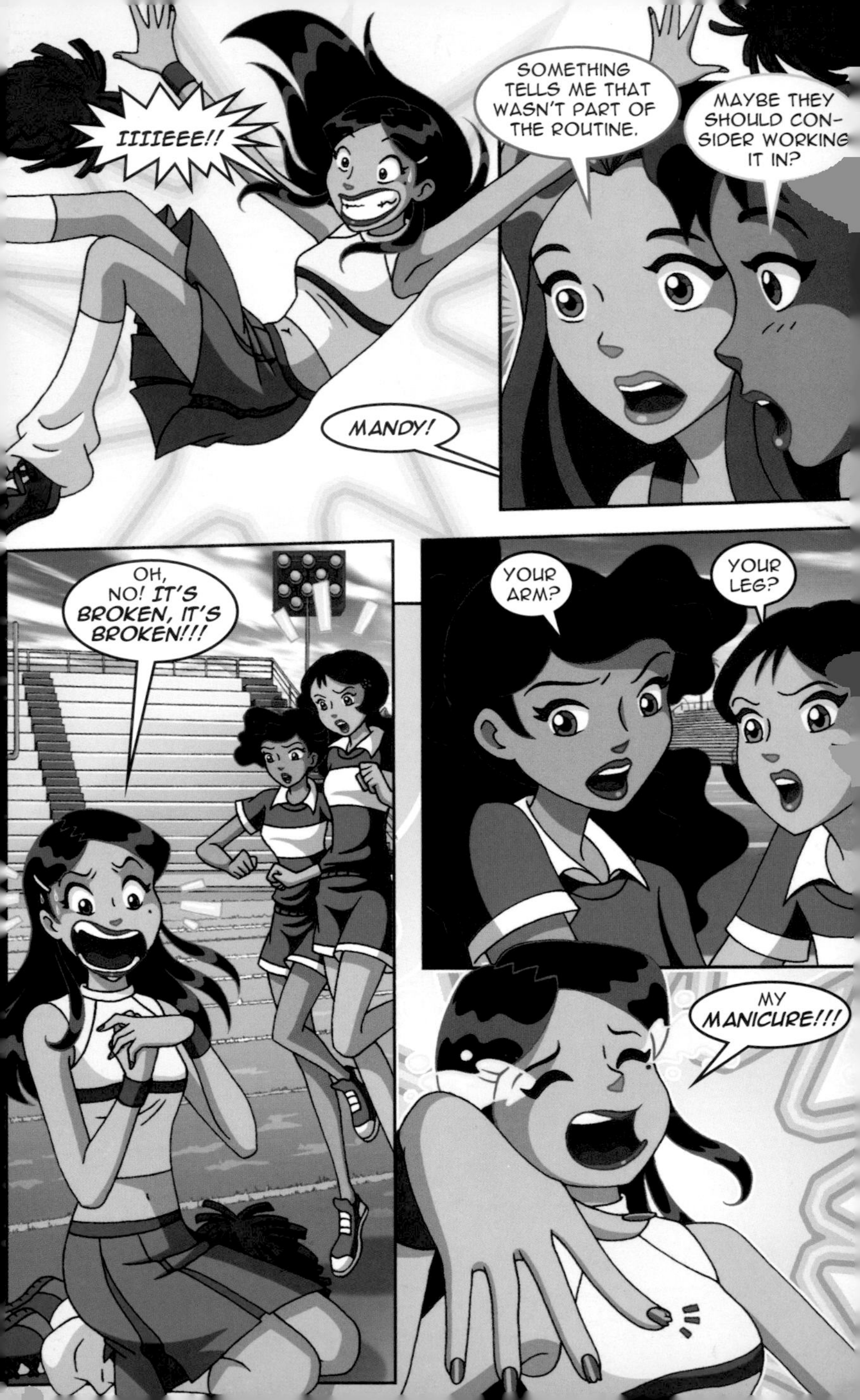
IIIIEEE!!
MANDY!
SOMETHING TELLS ME THAT WASN'T PART OF THE ROUTINE.
MAYBE THEY SHOULD CON-SIDER WORKING IT IN?
OH, NO! IT'S BROKEN, IT'S BROKEN!!!
YOUR ARM?
YOUR LEG?
MY MANICURE!!!

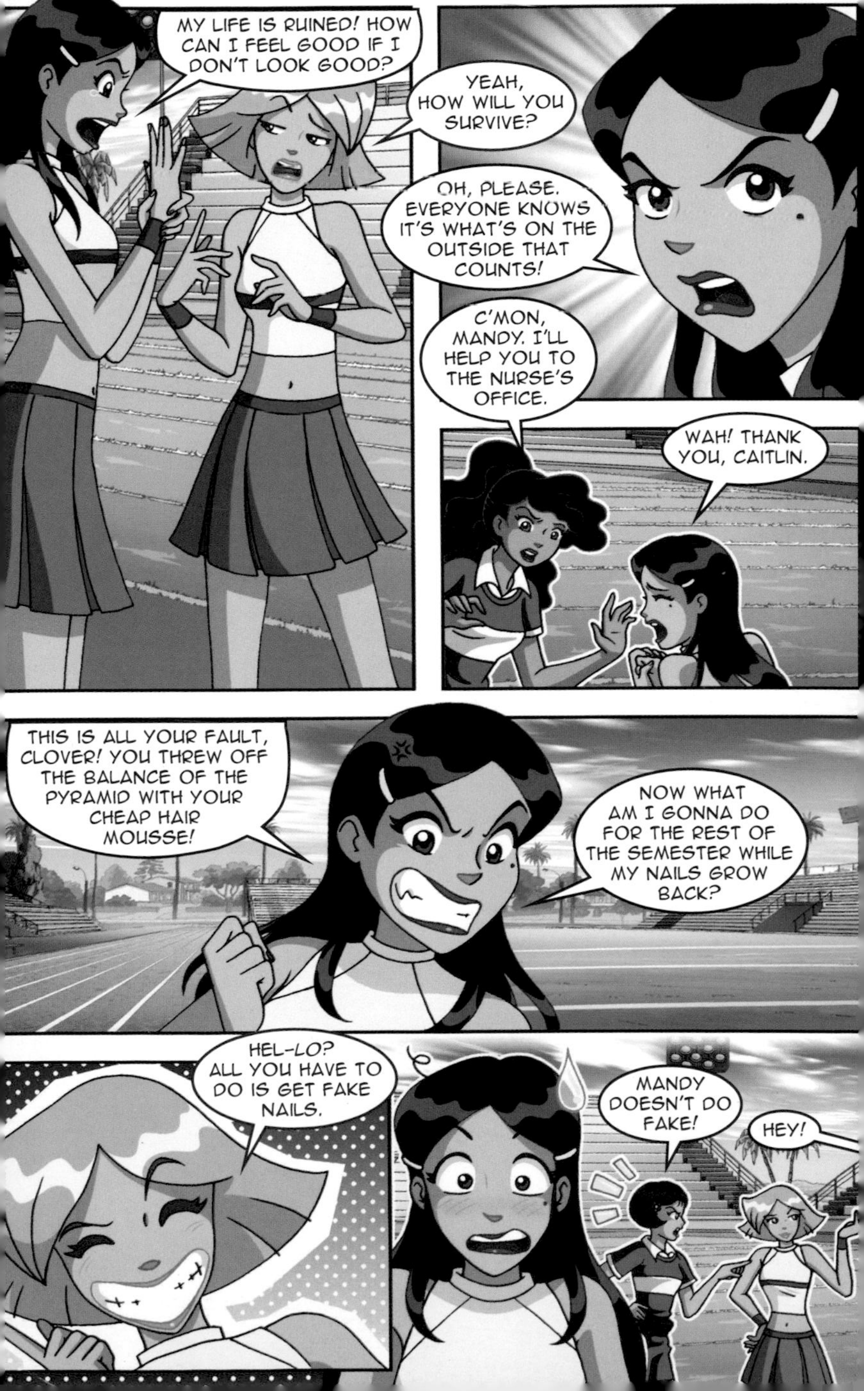
MY LIFE IS RUINED! HOW CAN I FEEL GOOD IF I DON'T LOOK GOOD?
YEAH, HOW WILL YOU SURVIVE?
OH, PLEASE. EVERYONE KNOWS IT'S WHAT'S ON THE OUTSIDE THAT COUNTS!
C'MON, MANDY. I'LL HELP YOU TO THE NURSE'S OFFICE.
WAH! THANK YOU, CAITLIN.
THIS IS ALL YOUR FAULT, CLOVER! YOU THREW OFF THE BALANCE OF THE PYRAMID WITH YOUR CHEAP HAIR MOUSSE!
NOW WHAT AM I GONNA DO FOR THE REST OF THE SEMESTER WHILE MY NAILS GROW BACK?
HEL-*LO*? ALL YOU HAVE TO DO IS GET FAKE NAILS.
MANDY DOESN'T DO FAKE!
HEY!

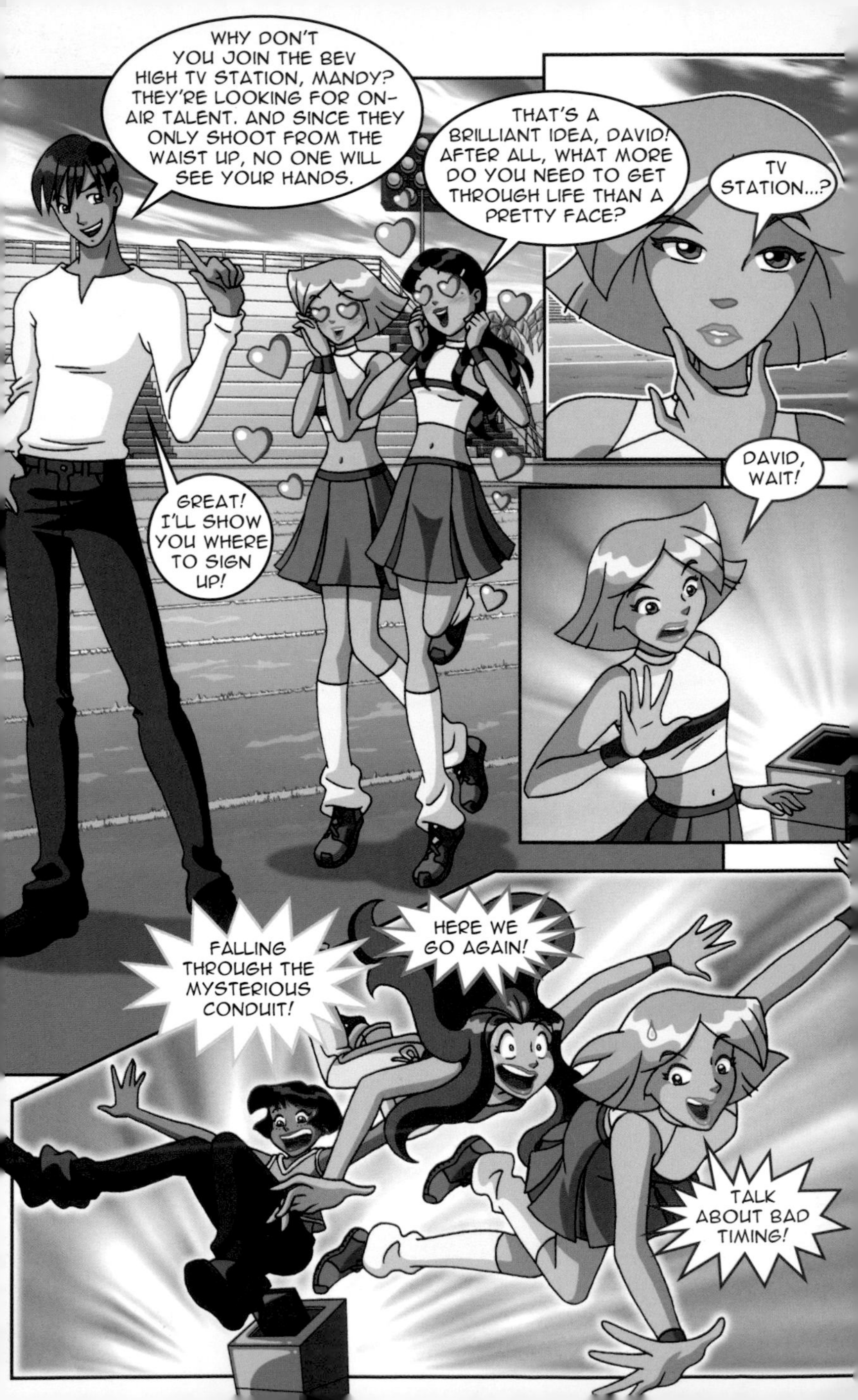
WHY DON'T YOU JOIN THE BEV HIGH TV STATION, MANDY? THEY'RE LOOKING FOR ON-AIR TALENT. AND SINCE THEY ONLY SHOOT FROM THE WAIST UP, NO ONE WILL SEE YOUR HANDS.
THAT'S A BRILLIANT IDEA, DAVID! AFTER ALL, WHAT MORE DO YOU NEED TO GET THROUGH LIFE THAN A PRETTY FACE?
GREAT! I'LL SHOW YOU WHERE TO SIGN UP!
TV STATION...?
DAVID, WAIT!
FALLING THROUGH THE MYSTERIOUS CONDUIT!
HERE WE GO AGAIN!
TALK ABOUT BAD TIMING!

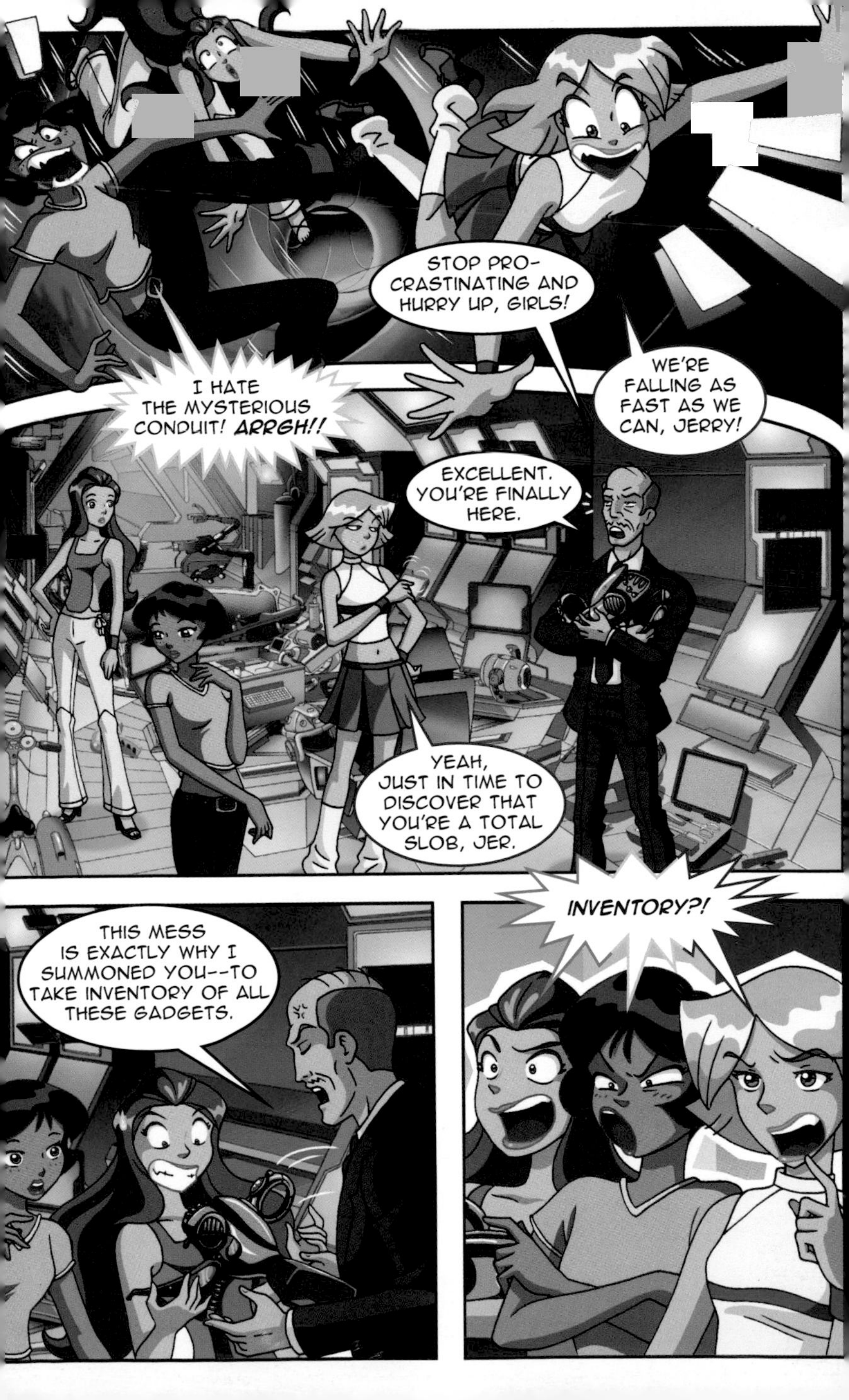
I HATE THE MYSTERIOUS CONDUIT! ***ARRGH!!***
STOP PRO-CRASTINATING AND HURRY UP, GIRLS!
WE'RE FALLING AS FAST AS WE CAN, JERRY!
EXCELLENT. YOU'RE FINALLY HERE.
YEAH, JUST IN TIME TO DISCOVER THAT YOU'RE A TOTAL SLOB, JER.
THIS MESS IS EXACTLY WHY I SUMMONED YOU--TO TAKE INVENTORY OF ALL THESE GADGETS.
INVENTORY?!

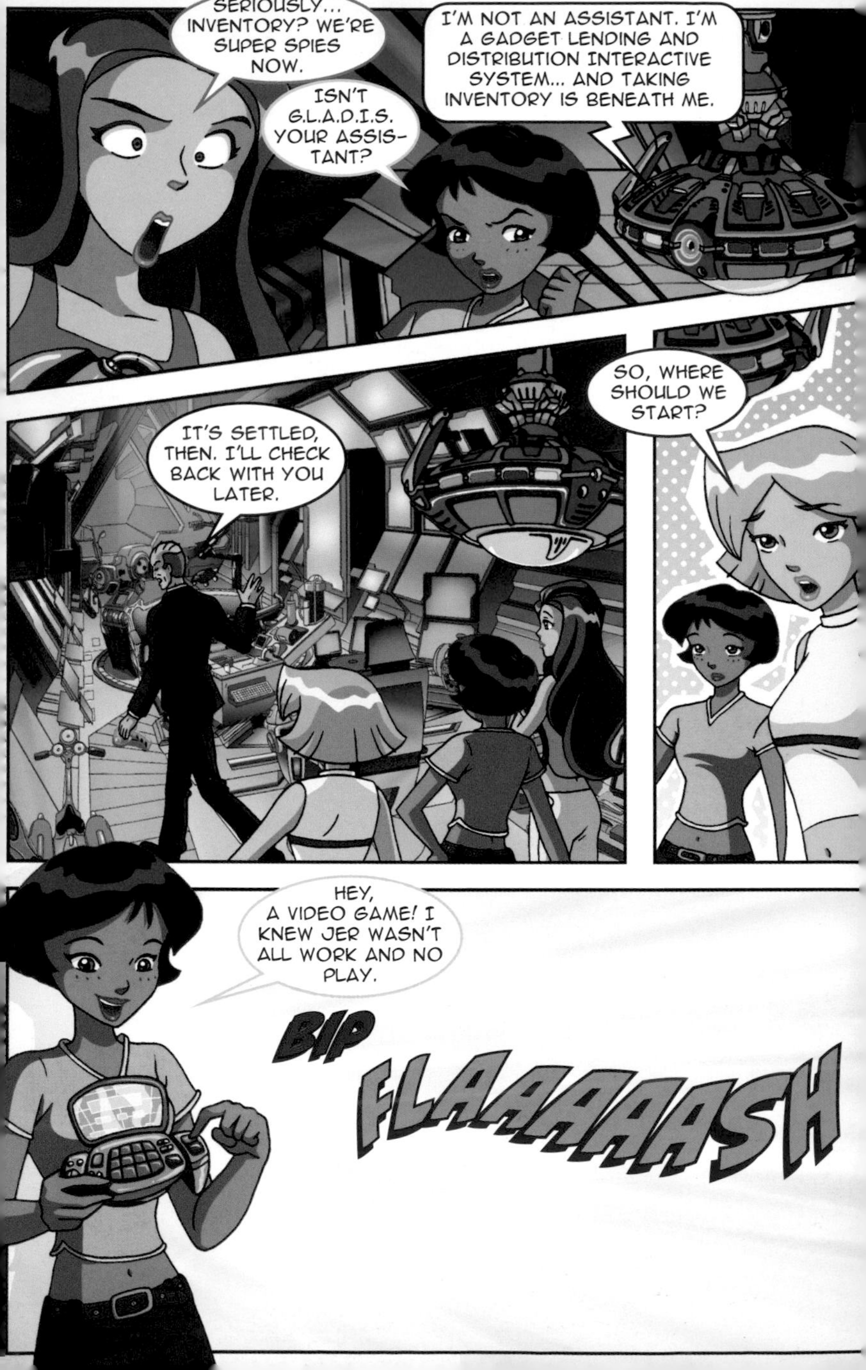
SERIOUSLY... INVENTORY? WE'RE SUPER SPIES NOW.
ISN'T G.L.A.D.I.S. YOUR ASSIS-TANT?
I'M NOT AN ASSISTANT. I'M A GADGET LENDING AND DISTRIBUTION INTERACTIVE SYSTEM... AND TAKING INVENTORY IS BENEATH ME.
IT'S SETTLED, THEN. I'LL CHECK BACK WITH YOU LATER.
SO, WHERE SHOULD WE START?
HEY, A VIDEO GAME! I KNEW JER WASN'T ALL WORK AND NO PLAY.
BIP
FLAAAAAASH

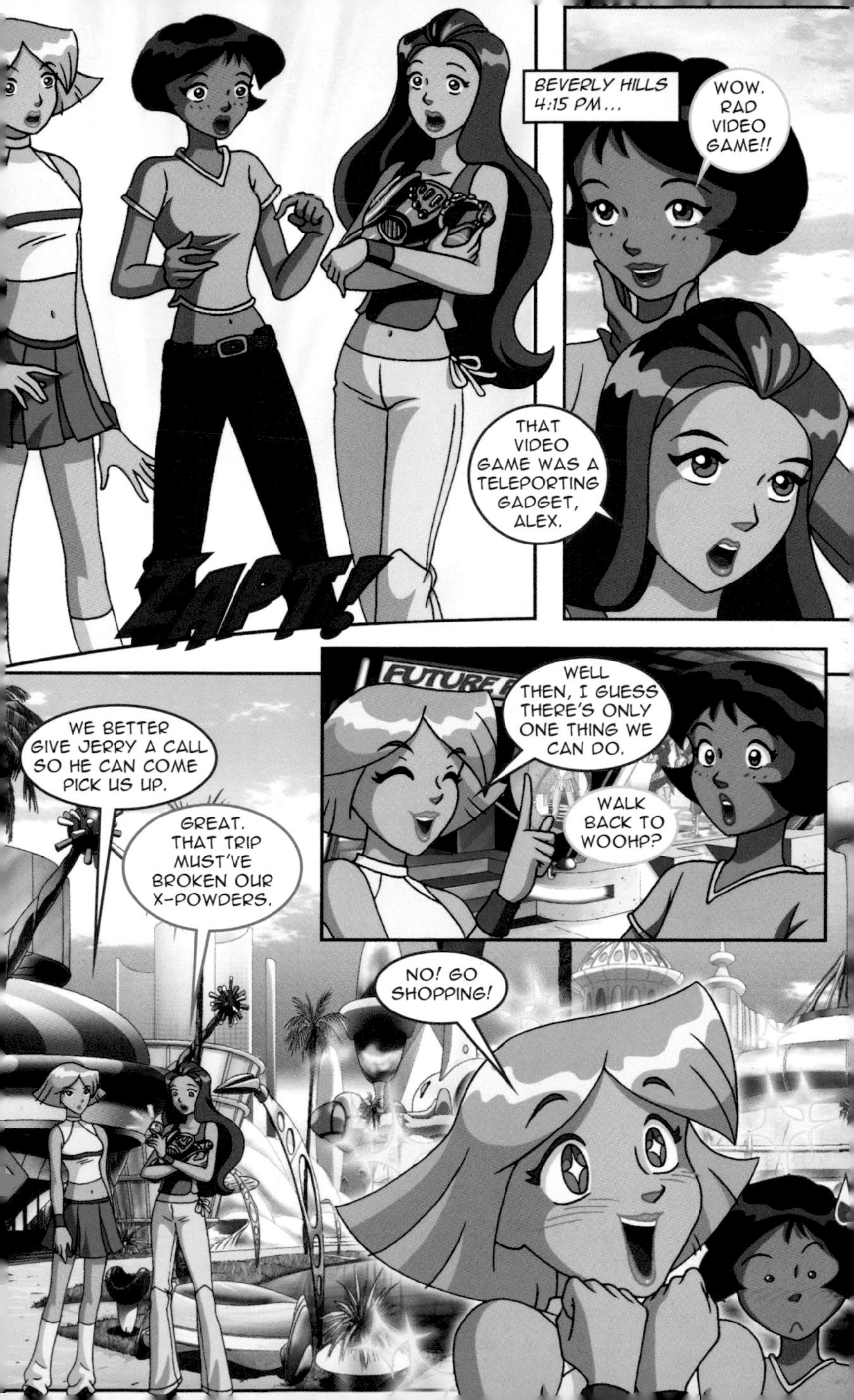
ZAPT!
BEVERLY HILLS 4:15 PM...
WOW. RAD VIDEO GAME!!
THAT VIDEO GAME WAS A TELEPORTING GADGET, ALEX.
WE BETTER GIVE JERRY A CALL SO HE CAN COME PICK US UP.
GREAT. THAT TRIP MUST'VE BROKEN OUR X-POWDERS.
WELL THEN, I GUESS THERE'S ONLY ONE THING WE CAN DO.
WALK BACK TO WOOHP?
NO! GO SHOPPING!

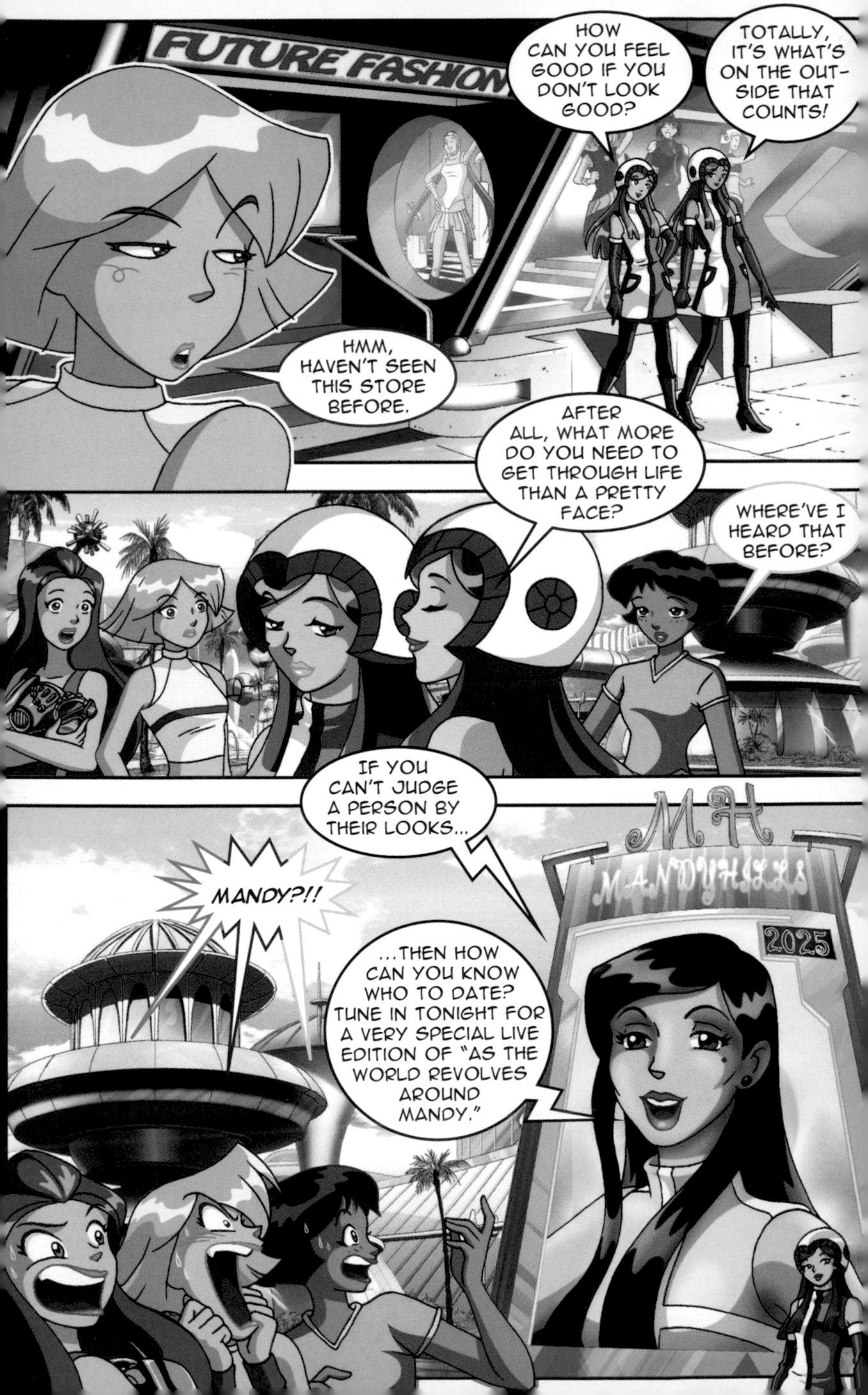

FUTURE FASHION
HMM, HAVEN'T SEEN THIS STORE BEFORE.
HOW CAN YOU FEEL GOOD IF YOU DON'T LOOK GOOD?
TOTALLY, IT'S WHAT'S ON THE OUT-SIDE THAT COUNTS!
AFTER ALL, WHAT MORE DO YOU NEED TO GET THROUGH LIFE THAN A PRETTY FACE?
WHERE'VE I HEARD THAT BEFORE?
IF YOU CAN'T JUDGE A PERSON BY THEIR LOOKS...
MH
MANDYHILLS
MANDY?!!
2025
...THEN HOW CAN YOU KNOW WHO TO DATE? TUNE IN TONIGHT FOR A VERY SPECIAL LIVE EDITION OF "AS THE WORLD REVOLVES AROUND MANDY."

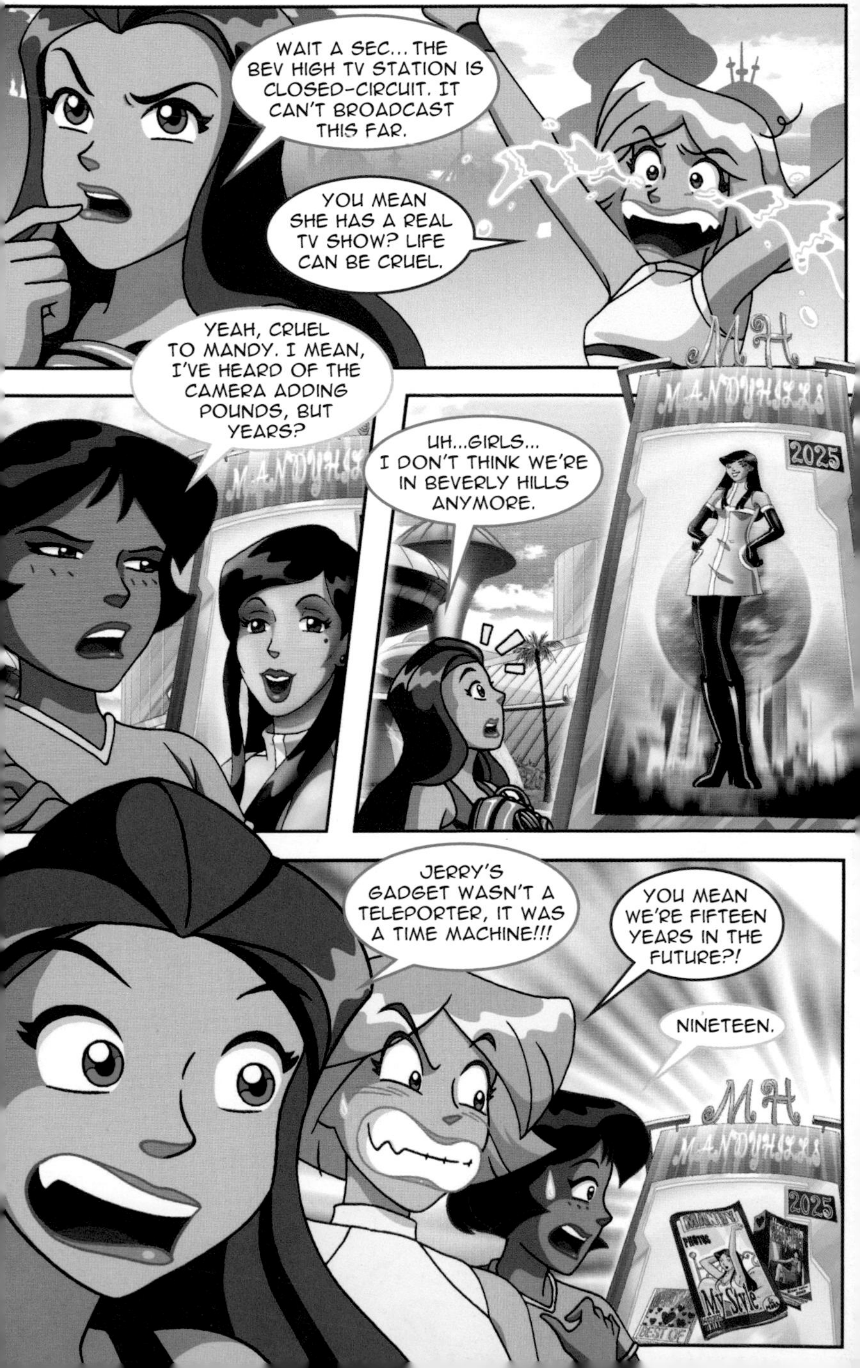
WAIT A SEC... THE BEV HIGH TV STATION IS CLOSED-CIRCUIT. IT CAN'T BROADCAST THIS FAR.
YOU MEAN SHE HAS A REAL TV SHOW? LIFE CAN BE CRUEL.
YEAH, CRUEL TO MANDY. I MEAN, I'VE HEARD OF THE CAMERA ADDING POUNDS, BUT YEARS?
UH...GIRLS... I DON'T THINK WE'RE IN BEVERLY HILLS ANYMORE.
MH
MANDYHILLS
2025
JERRY'S GADGET WASN'T A TELEPORTER, IT WAS A TIME MACHINE!!!
YOU MEAN WE'RE FIFTEEN YEARS IN THE FUTURE?!
NINETEEN.
MH
MANDYHILLS
2025
My Style

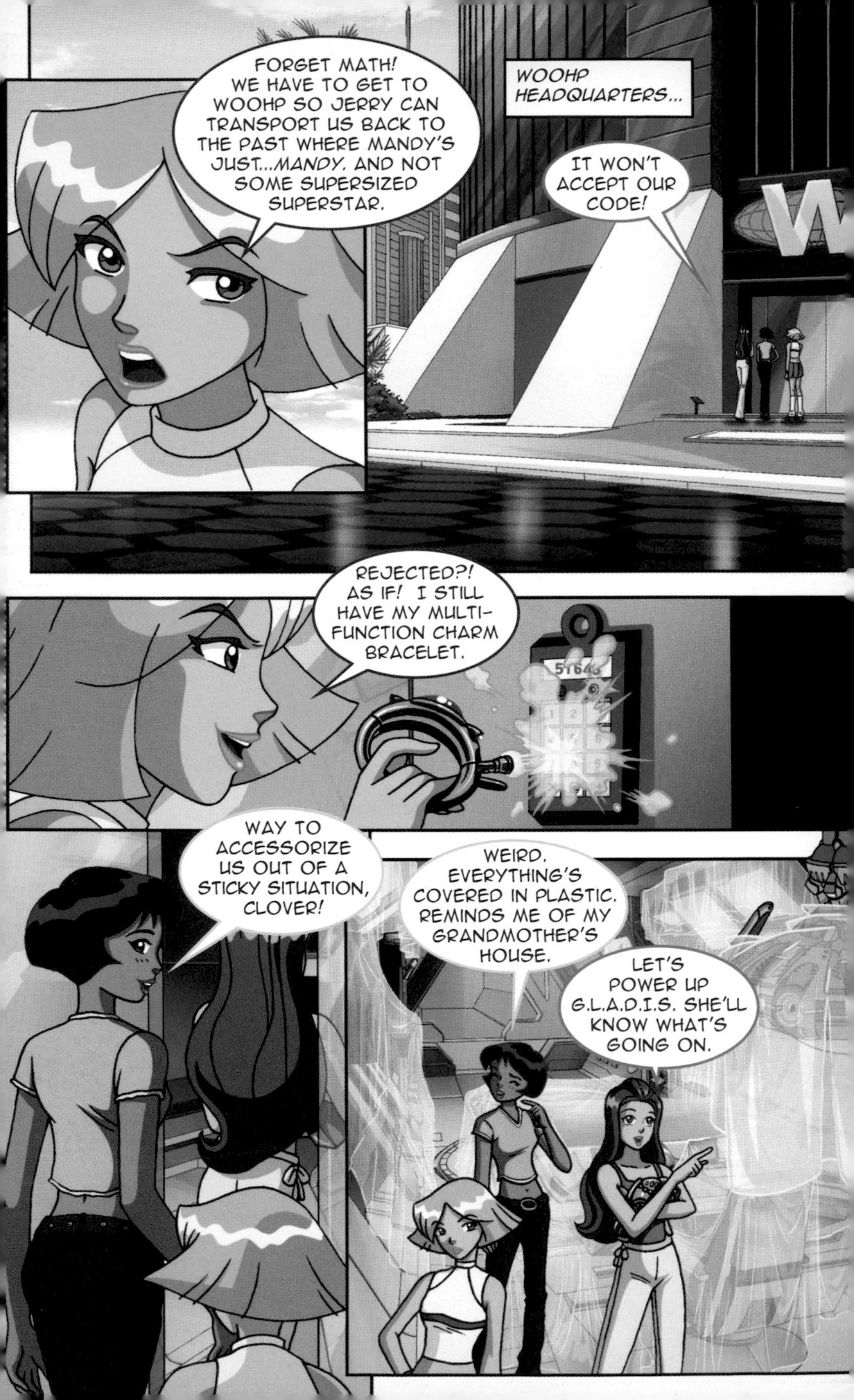
FORGET MATH! WE HAVE TO GET TO WOOHP SO JERRY CAN TRANSPORT US BACK TO THE PAST WHERE MANDY'S JUST...*MANDY*, AND NOT SOME SUPERSIZED SUPERSTAR.
WOOHP HEADQUARTERS...
IT WON'T ACCEPT OUR CODE!
REJECTED?! AS IF! I STILL HAVE MY MULTI-FUNCTION CHARM BRACELET.
WAY TO ACCESSORIZE US OUT OF A STICKY SITUATION, CLOVER!
WEIRD. EVERYTHING'S COVERED IN PLASTIC. REMINDS ME OF MY GRANDMOTHER'S HOUSE.
LET'S POWER UP G.L.A.D.I.S. SHE'LL KNOW WHAT'S GOING ON.

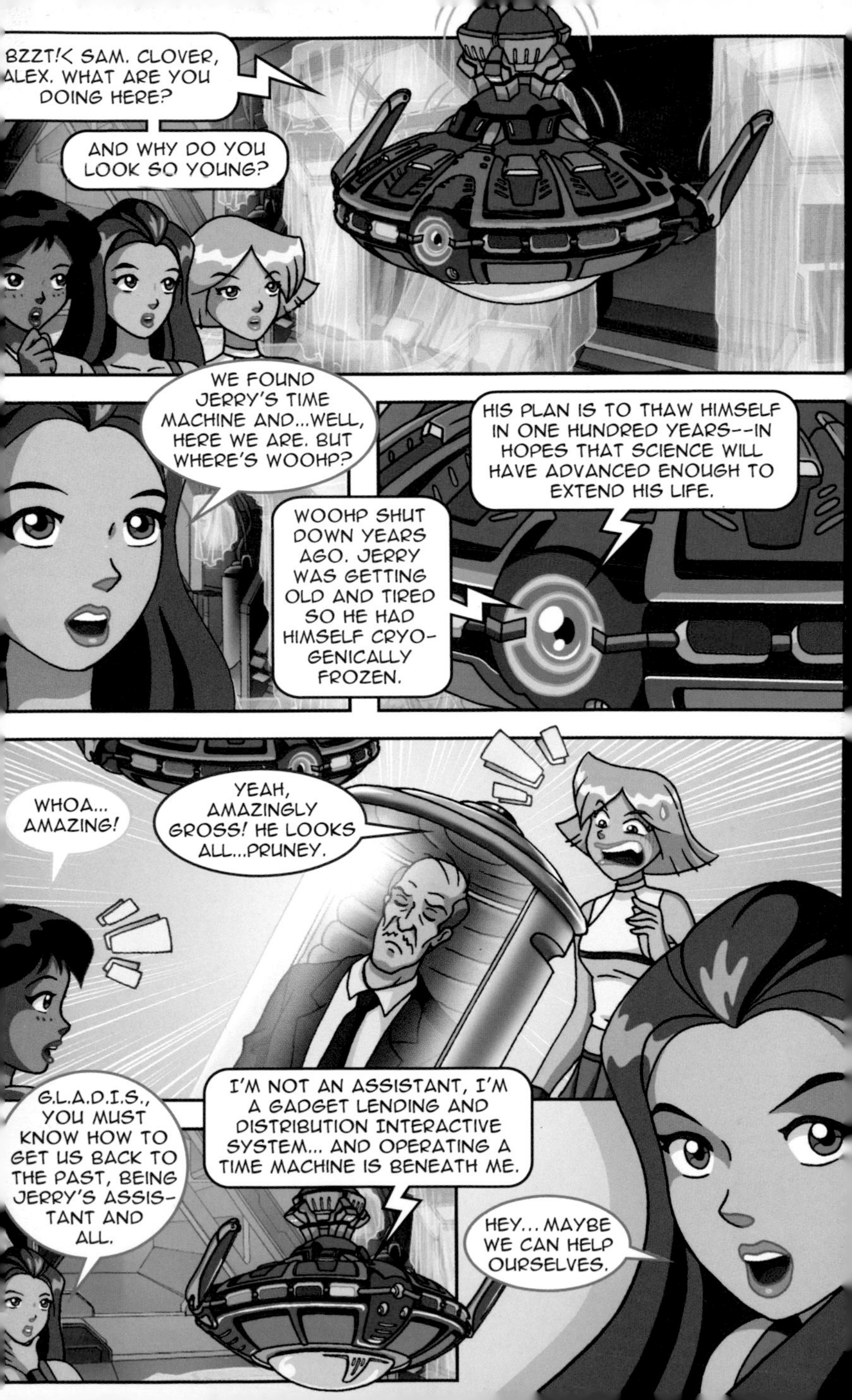
BZZT!< SAM. CLOVER, ALEX. WHAT ARE YOU DOING HERE?
AND WHY DO YOU LOOK SO YOUNG?
WE FOUND JERRY'S TIME MACHINE AND...WELL, HERE WE ARE. BUT WHERE'S WOOHP?
WOOHP SHUT DOWN YEARS AGO. JERRY WAS GETTING OLD AND TIRED SO HE HAD HIMSELF CRYO-GENICALLY FROZEN.
HIS PLAN IS TO THAW HIMSELF IN ONE HUNDRED YEARS--IN HOPES THAT SCIENCE WILL HAVE ADVANCED ENOUGH TO EXTEND HIS LIFE.
WHOA... AMAZING!
YEAH, AMAZINGLY GROSS! HE LOOKS ALL...PRUNEY.
G.L.A.D.I.S., YOU MUST KNOW HOW TO GET US BACK TO THE PAST, BEING JERRY'S ASSIS-TANT AND ALL.
I'M NOT AN ASSISTANT, I'M A GADGET LENDING AND DISTRIBUTION INTERACTIVE SYSTEM... AND OPERATING A TIME MACHINE IS BENEATH ME.
HEY... MAYBE WE CAN HELP OURSELVES.

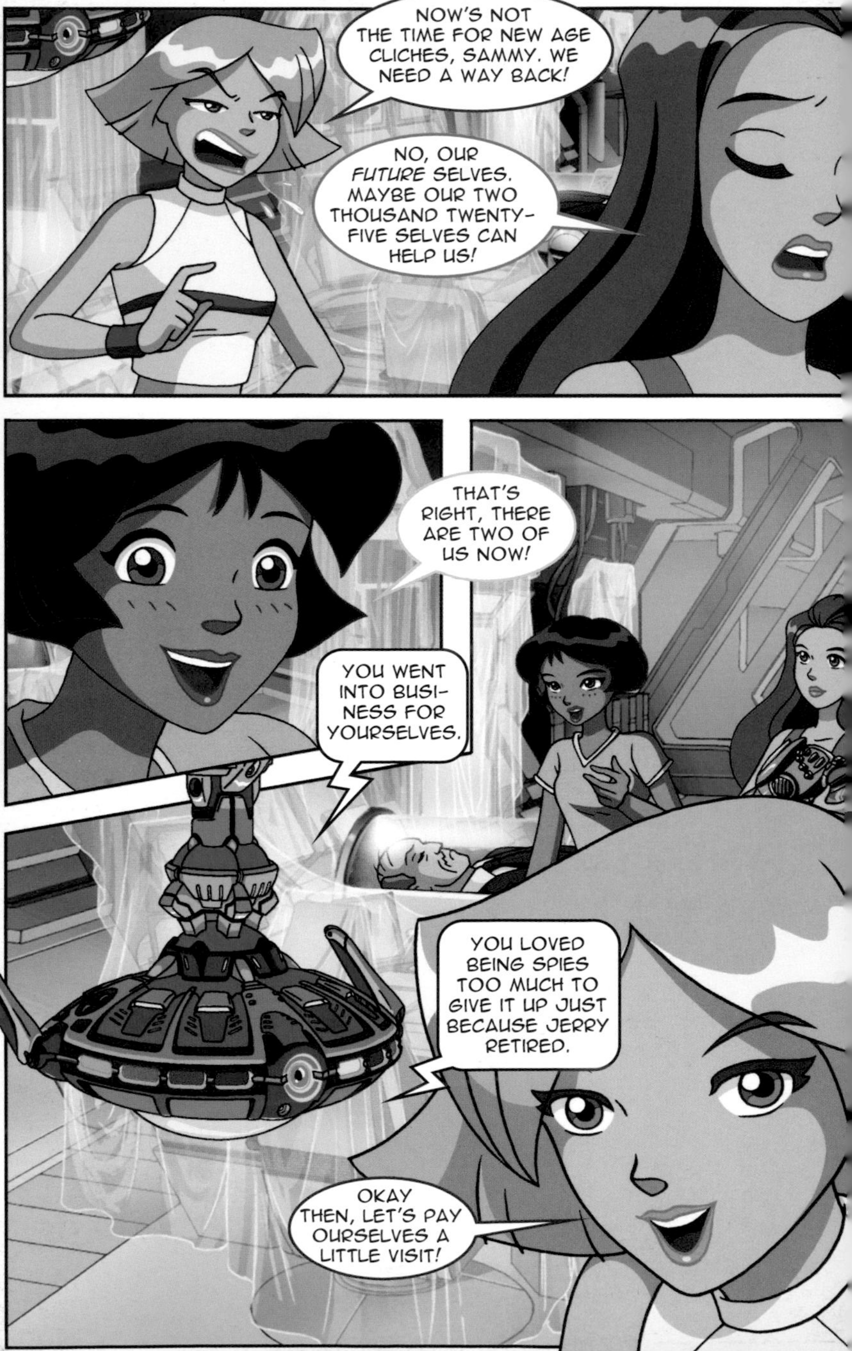
NOW'S NOT THE TIME FOR NEW AGE CLICHES, SAMMY. WE NEED A WAY BACK!
NO, OUR *FUTURE* SELVES. MAYBE OUR TWO THOUSAND TWENTY-FIVE SELVES CAN HELP US!
THAT'S RIGHT, THERE ARE TWO OF US NOW!
YOU WENT INTO BUSI-NESS FOR YOURSELVES.
YOU LOVED BEING SPIES TOO MUCH TO GIVE IT UP JUST BECAUSE JERRY RETIRED.
OKAY THEN, LET'S PAY OURSELVES A LITTLE VISIT!

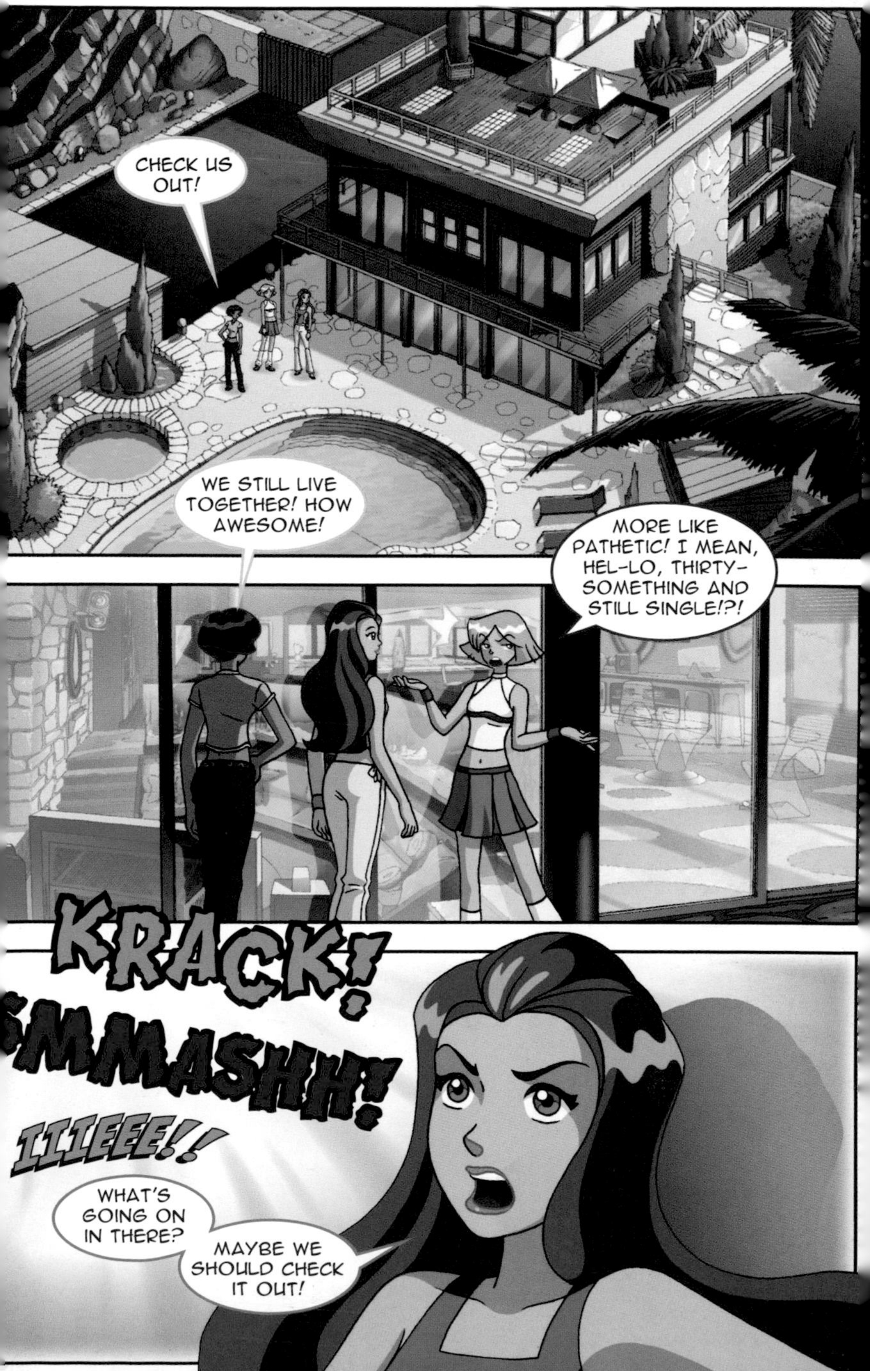
CHECK US OUT!
WE STILL LIVE TOGETHER! HOW AWESOME!
MORE LIKE PATHETIC! I MEAN, HEL-LO, THIRTY-SOMETHING AND STILL SINGLE!?!
KRACK!
SMMASHH!
IIIEEE!!
WHAT'S GOING ON IN THERE?
MAYBE WE SHOULD CHECK IT OUT!

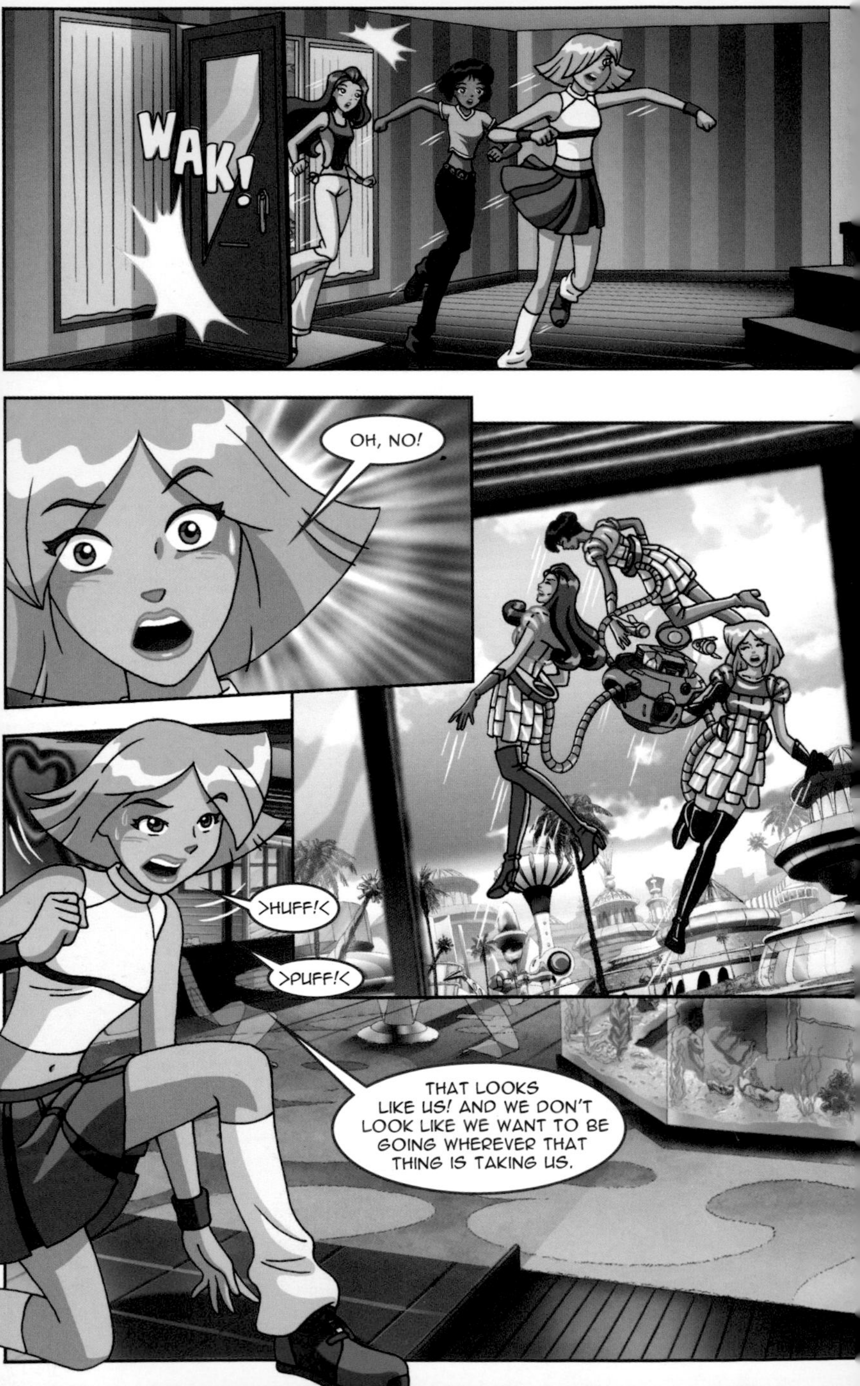
WAK!
OH, NO!
>HUFF!<
>PUFF!<
THAT LOOKS LIKE US! AND WE DON'T LOOK LIKE WE WANT TO BE GOING WHEREVER THAT THING IS TAKING US.

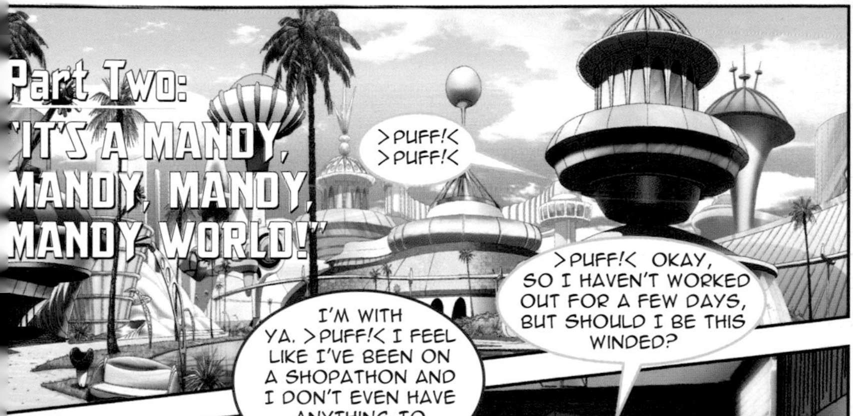
Part Two:
"IT'S A MANDY, MANDY, MANDY, MANDY WORLD!"
>PUFF!< >PUFF!<

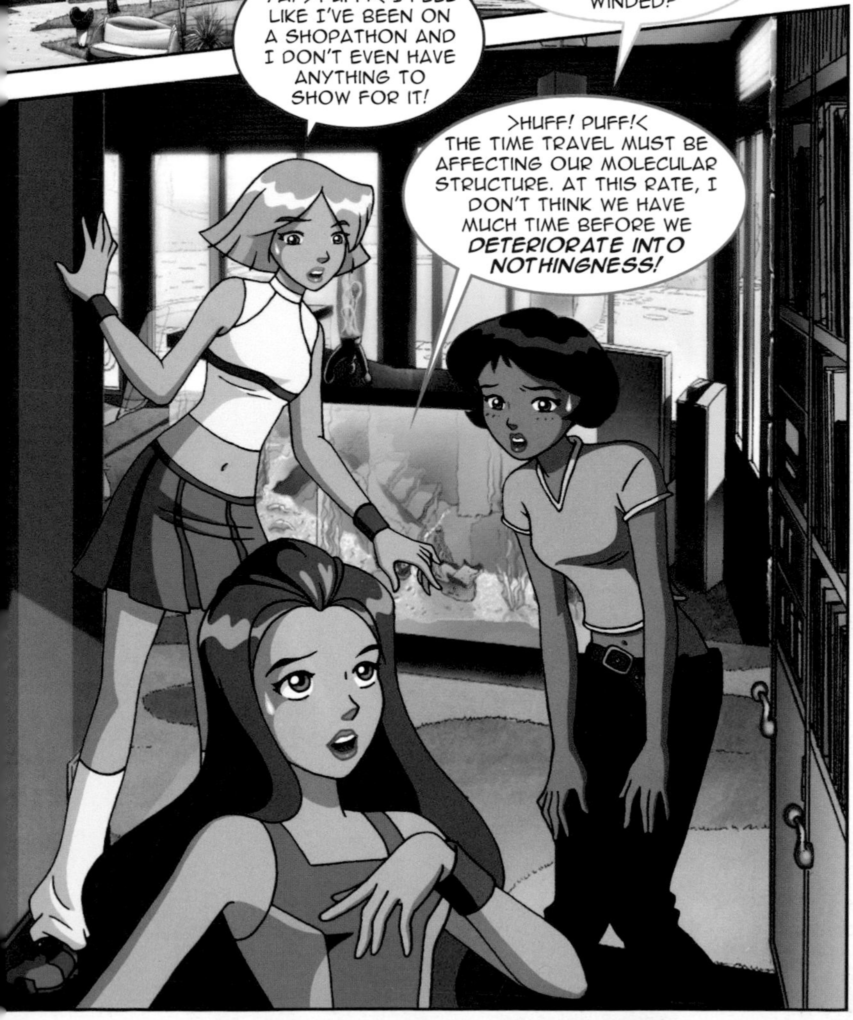
I'M WITH YA. >PUFF!< I FEEL LIKE I'VE BEEN ON A SHOPATHON AND I DON'T EVEN HAVE ANYTHING TO SHOW FOR IT!
>PUFF!< OKAY, SO I HAVEN'T WORKED OUT FOR A FEW DAYS, BUT SHOULD I BE THIS WINDED?
>HUFF! PUFF!< THE TIME TRAVEL MUST BE AFFECTING OUR MOLECULAR STRUCTURE. AT THIS RATE, I DON'T THINK WE HAVE MUCH TIME BEFORE WE DETERIORATE INTO NOTHINGNESS!

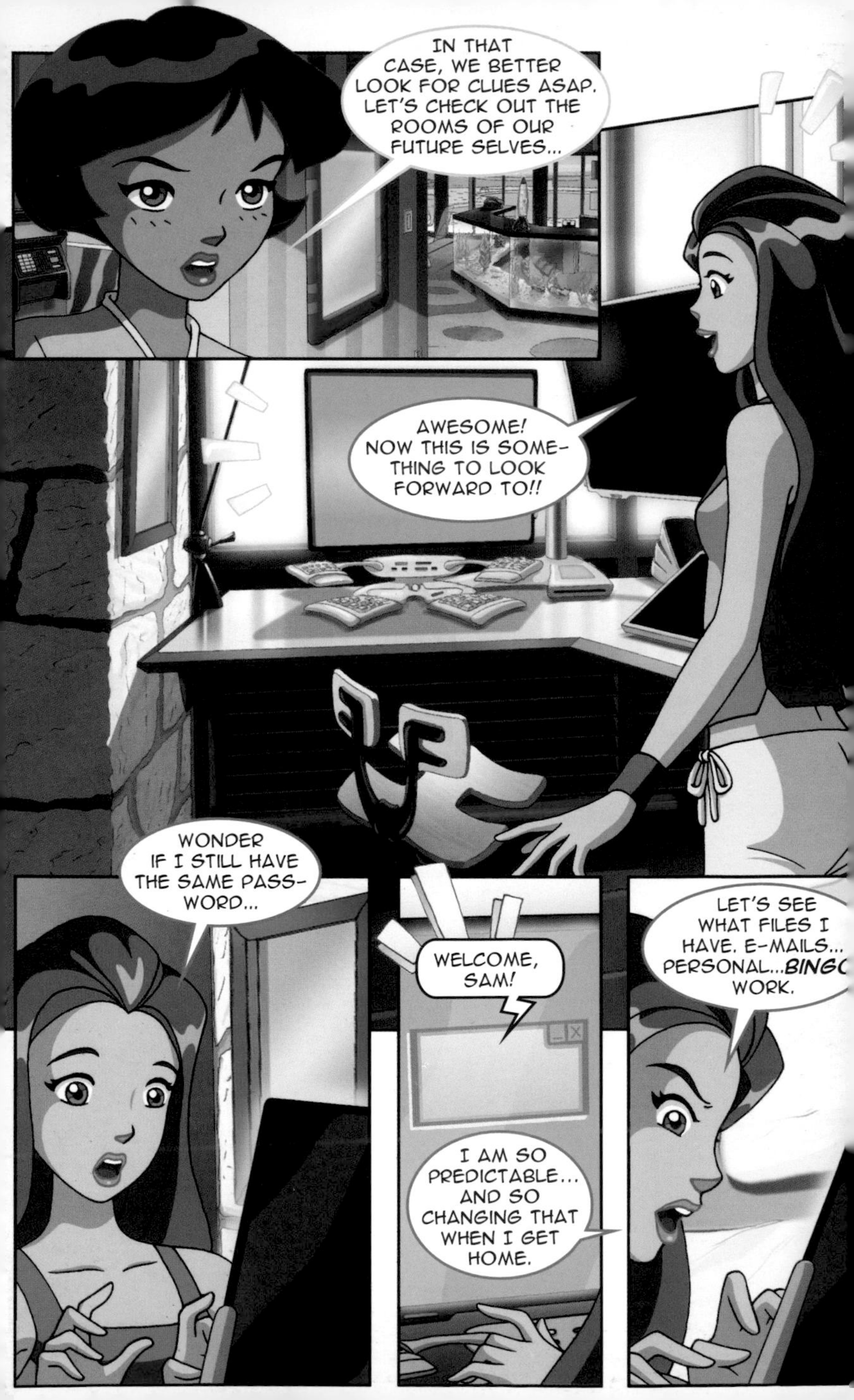
IN THAT CASE, WE BETTER LOOK FOR CLUES ASAP. LET'S CHECK OUT THE ROOMS OF OUR FUTURE SELVES...
AWESOME! NOW THIS IS SOME-THING TO LOOK FORWARD TO!!
WONDER IF I STILL HAVE THE SAME PASS-WORD...
WELCOME, SAM!
I AM SO PREDICTABLE... AND SO CHANGING THAT WHEN I GET HOME.
LET'S SEE WHAT FILES I HAVE. E-MAILS... PERSONAL...BINGO WORK.

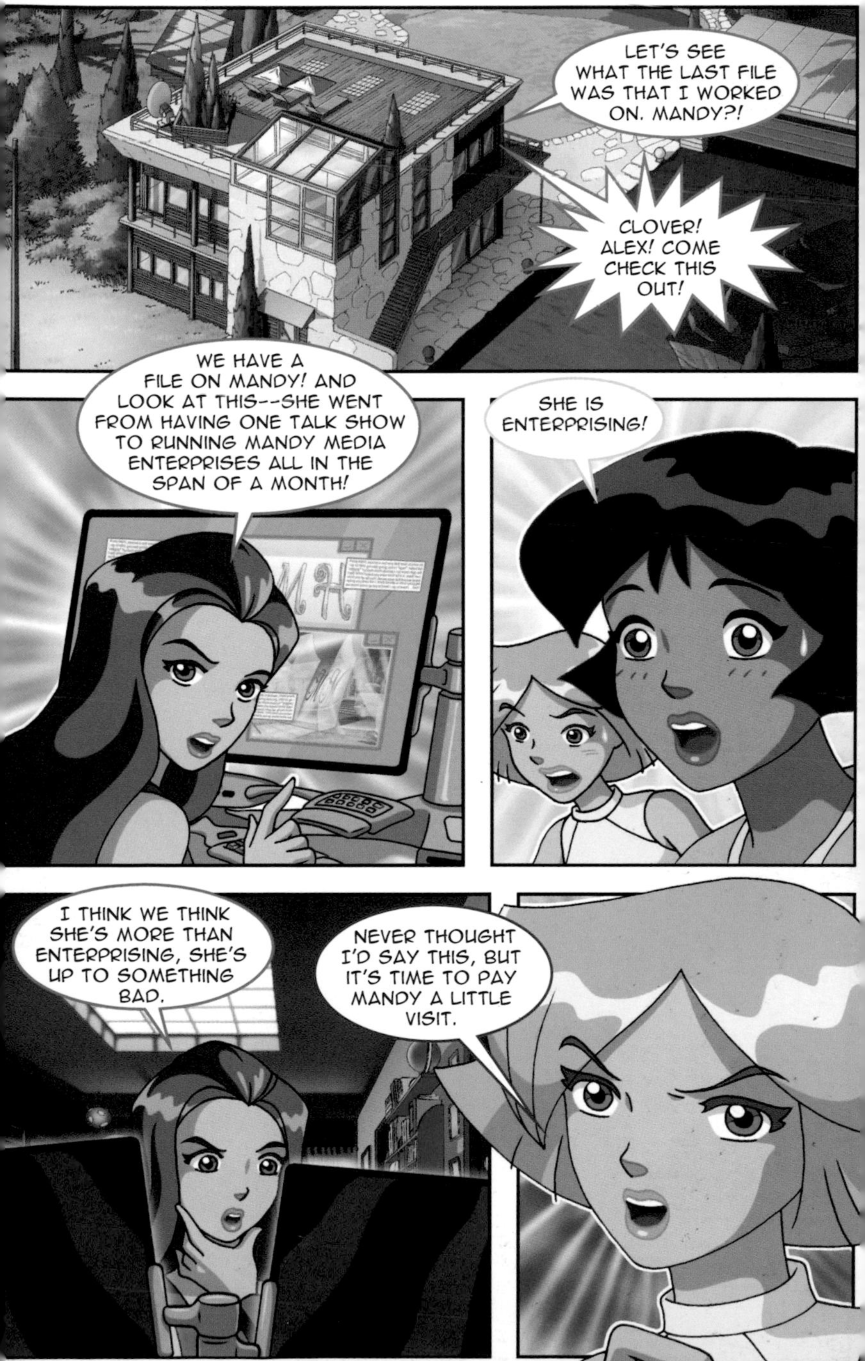
LET'S SEE WHAT THE LAST FILE WAS THAT I WORKED ON. MANDY?!
CLOVER! ALEX! COME CHECK THIS OUT!
WE HAVE A FILE ON MANDY! AND LOOK AT THIS--SHE WENT FROM HAVING ONE TALK SHOW TO RUNNING MANDY MEDIA ENTERPRISES ALL IN THE SPAN OF A MONTH!
SHE IS ENTERPRISING!
I THINK WE THINK SHE'S MORE THAN ENTERPRISING, SHE'S UP TO SOMETHING BAD.
NEVER THOUGHT I'D SAY THIS, BUT IT'S TIME TO PAY MANDY A LITTLE VISIT.

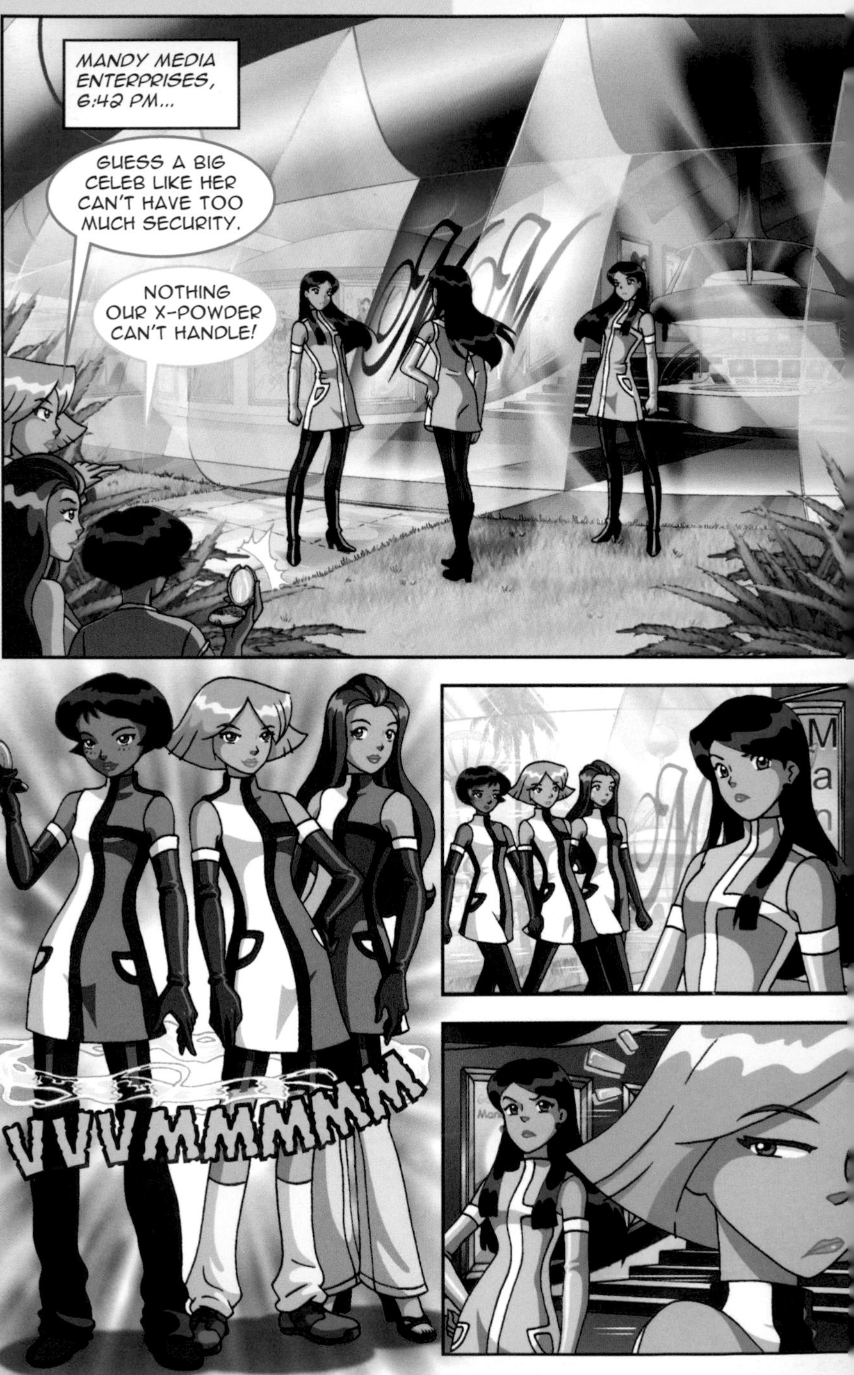
MANDY MEDIA ENTERPRISES, 6:42 PM...
GUESS A BIG CELEB LIKE HER CAN'T HAVE TOO MUCH SECURITY.
NOTHING OUR X-POWDER CAN'T HANDLE!
VVVMMMMMM

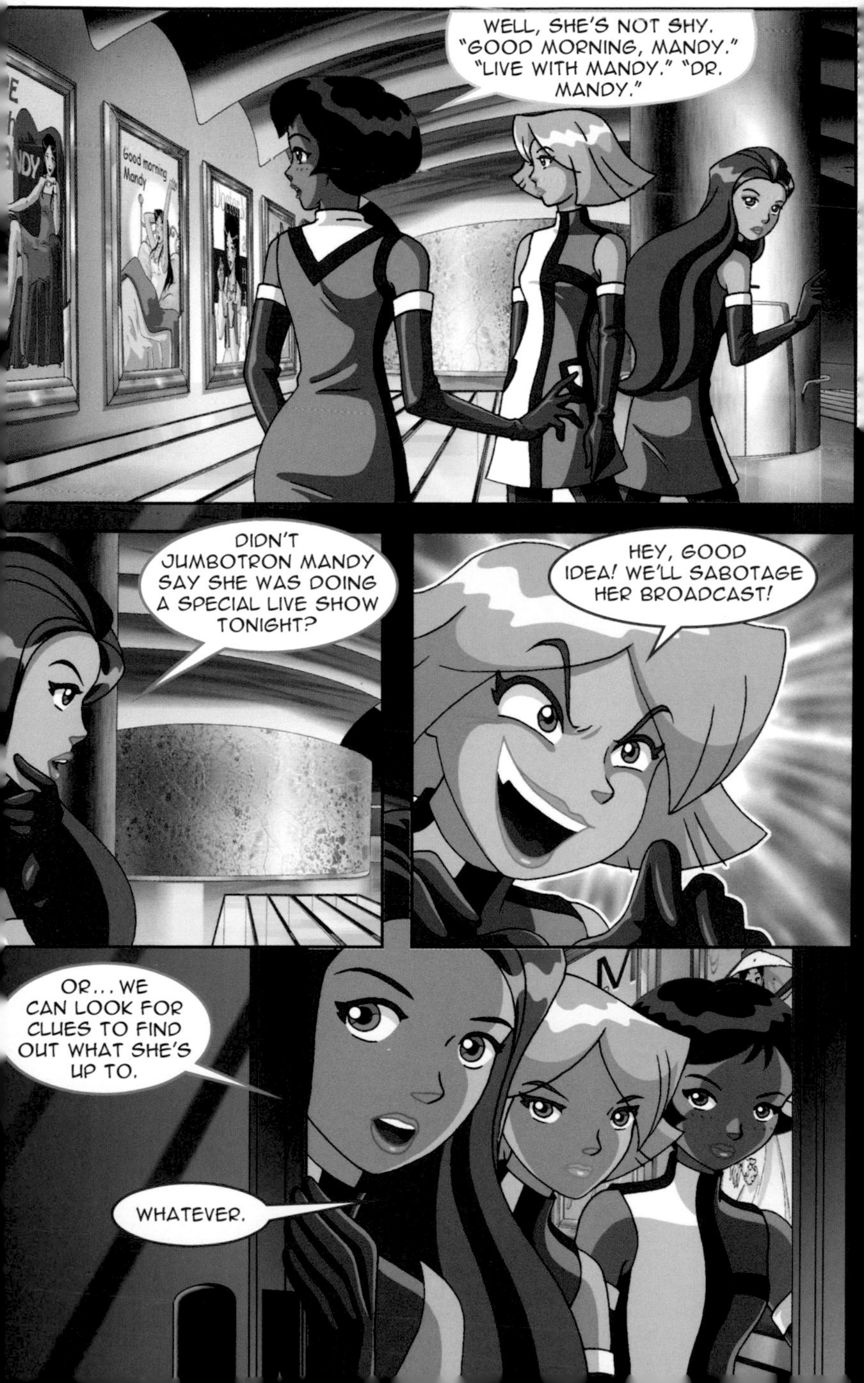
WELL, SHE'S NOT SHY. "GOOD MORNING, MANDY." "LIVE WITH MANDY." "DR. MANDY."
Good morning Mandy
DIDN'T JUMBOTRON MANDY SAY SHE WAS DOING A SPECIAL LIVE SHOW TONIGHT?
HEY, GOOD IDEA! WE'LL SABOTAGE HER BROADCAST!
OR... WE CAN LOOK FOR CLUES TO FIND OUT WHAT SHE'S UP TO.
WHATEVER.

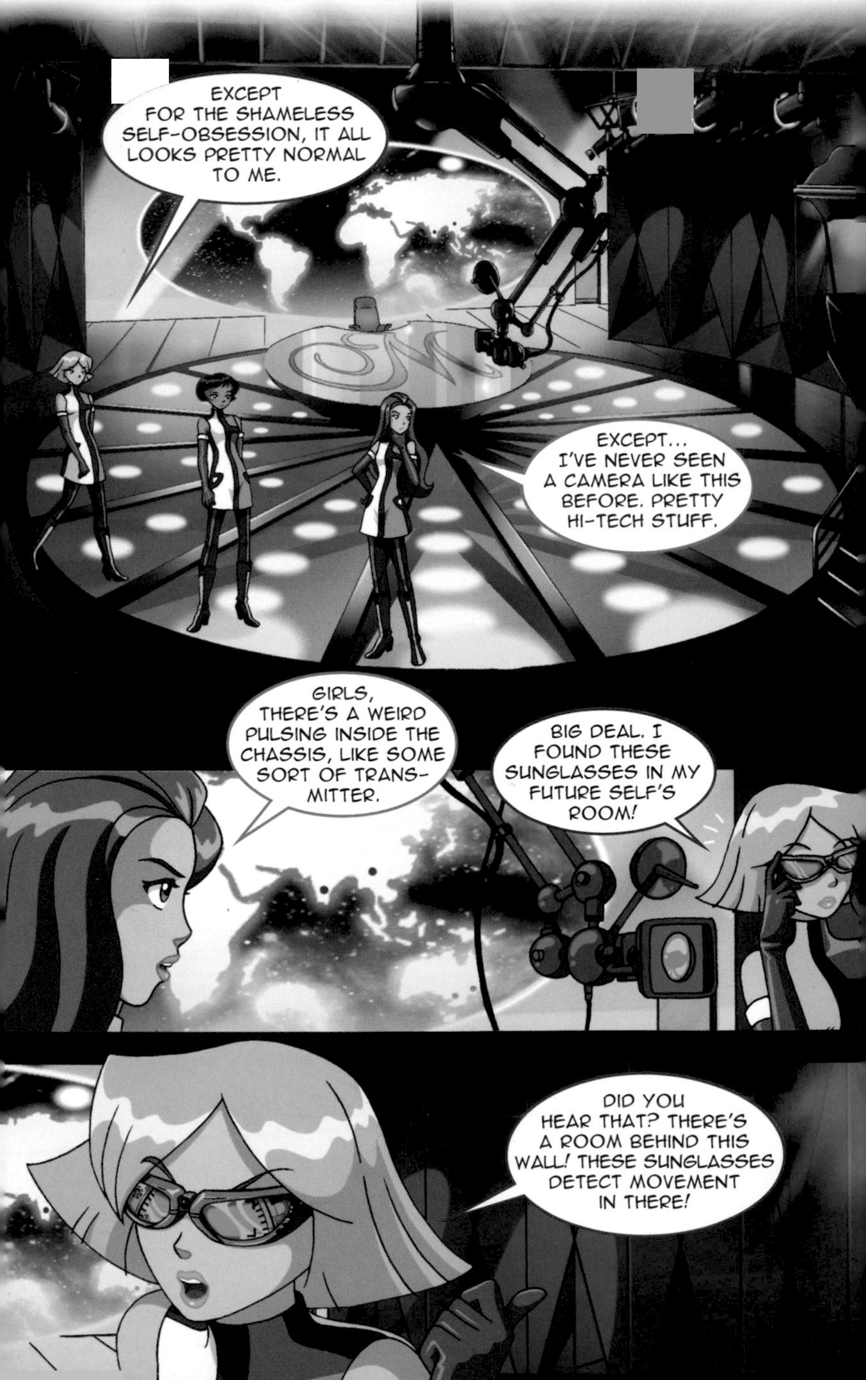
EXCEPT FOR THE SHAMELESS SELF-OBSESSION, IT ALL LOOKS PRETTY NORMAL TO ME.
EXCEPT... I'VE NEVER SEEN A CAMERA LIKE THIS BEFORE. PRETTY HI-TECH STUFF.
GIRLS, THERE'S A WEIRD PULSING INSIDE THE CHASSIS, LIKE SOME SORT OF TRANS-MITTER.
BIG DEAL. I FOUND THESE SUNGLASSES IN MY FUTURE SELF'S ROOM!
DID YOU HEAR THAT? THERE'S A ROOM BEHIND THIS WALL! THESE SUNGLASSES DETECT MOVEMENT IN THERE!

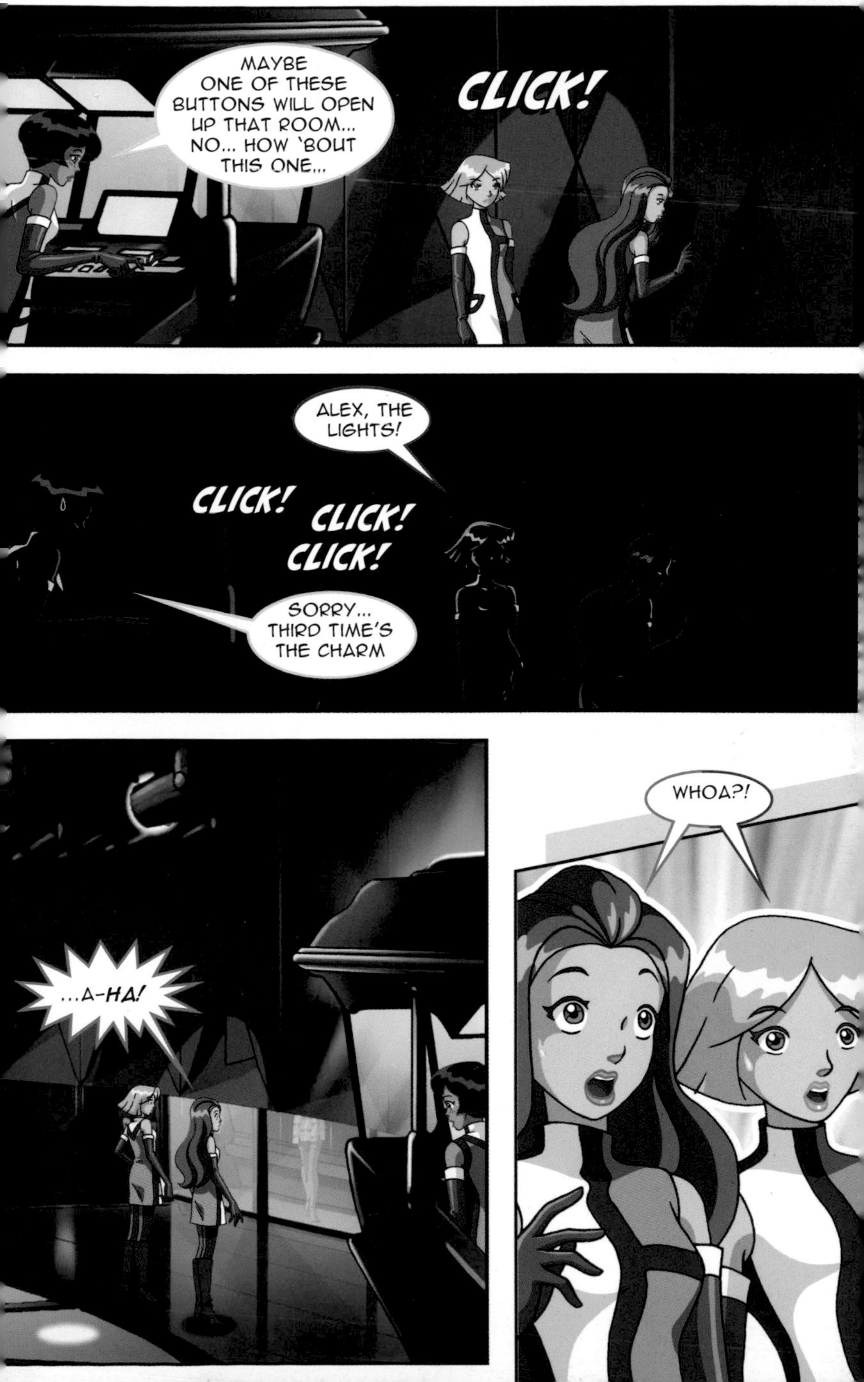
MAYBE ONE OF THESE BUTTONS WILL OPEN UP THAT ROOM... NO... HOW 'BOUT THIS ONE...
CLICK!
ALEX, THE LIGHTS!
CLICK!
CLICK!
CLICK!
SORRY... THIRD TIME'S THE CHARM
...A-HA!
WHOA?!

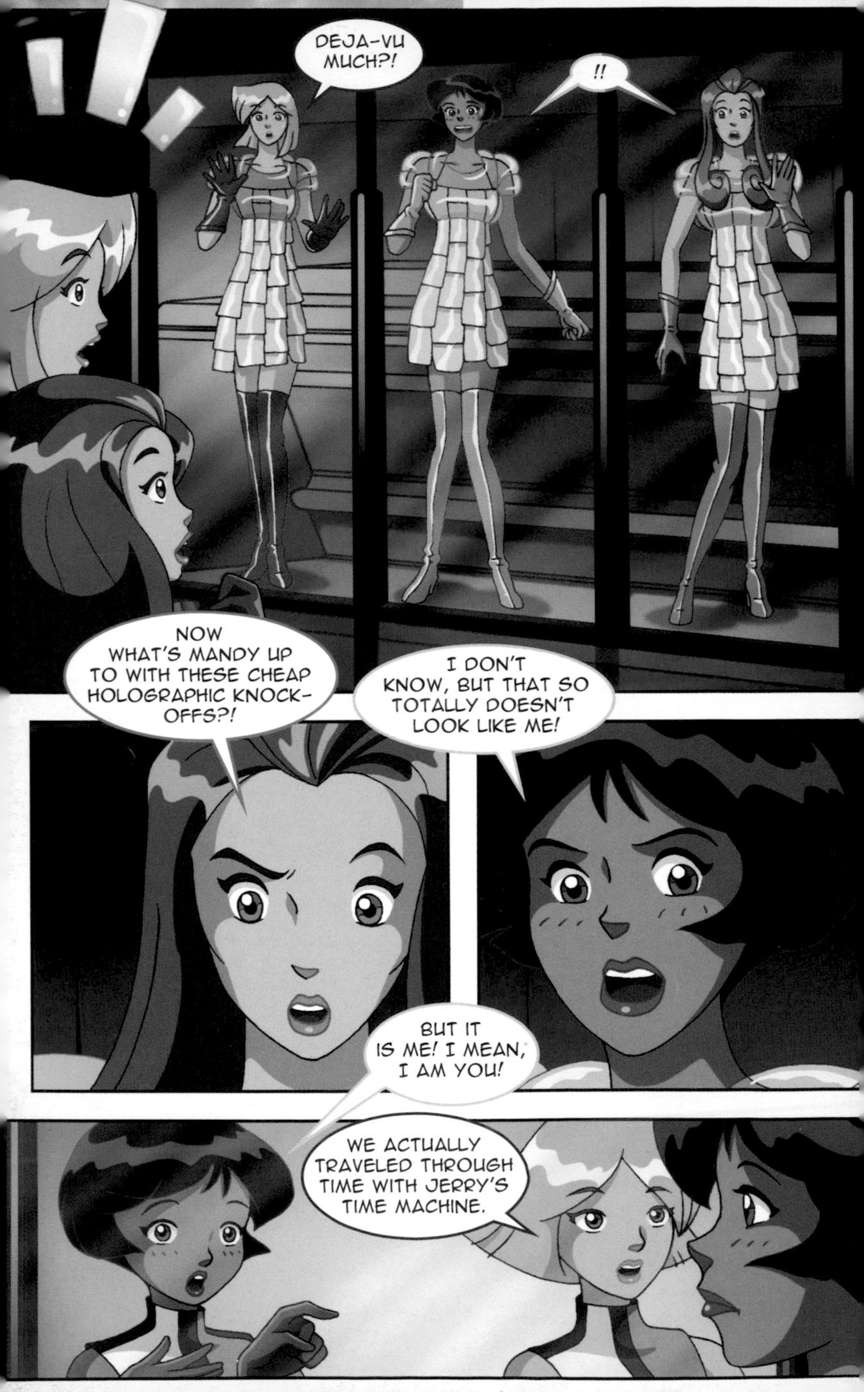
DEJA-VU MUCH?!
!!
NOW WHAT'S MANDY UP TO WITH THESE CHEAP HOLOGRAPHIC KNOCK-OFFS?!
I DON'T KNOW, BUT THAT SO TOTALLY DOESN'T LOOK LIKE ME!
BUT IT IS ME! I MEAN, I AM YOU!
WE ACTUALLY TRAVELED THROUGH TIME WITH JERRY'S TIME MACHINE.

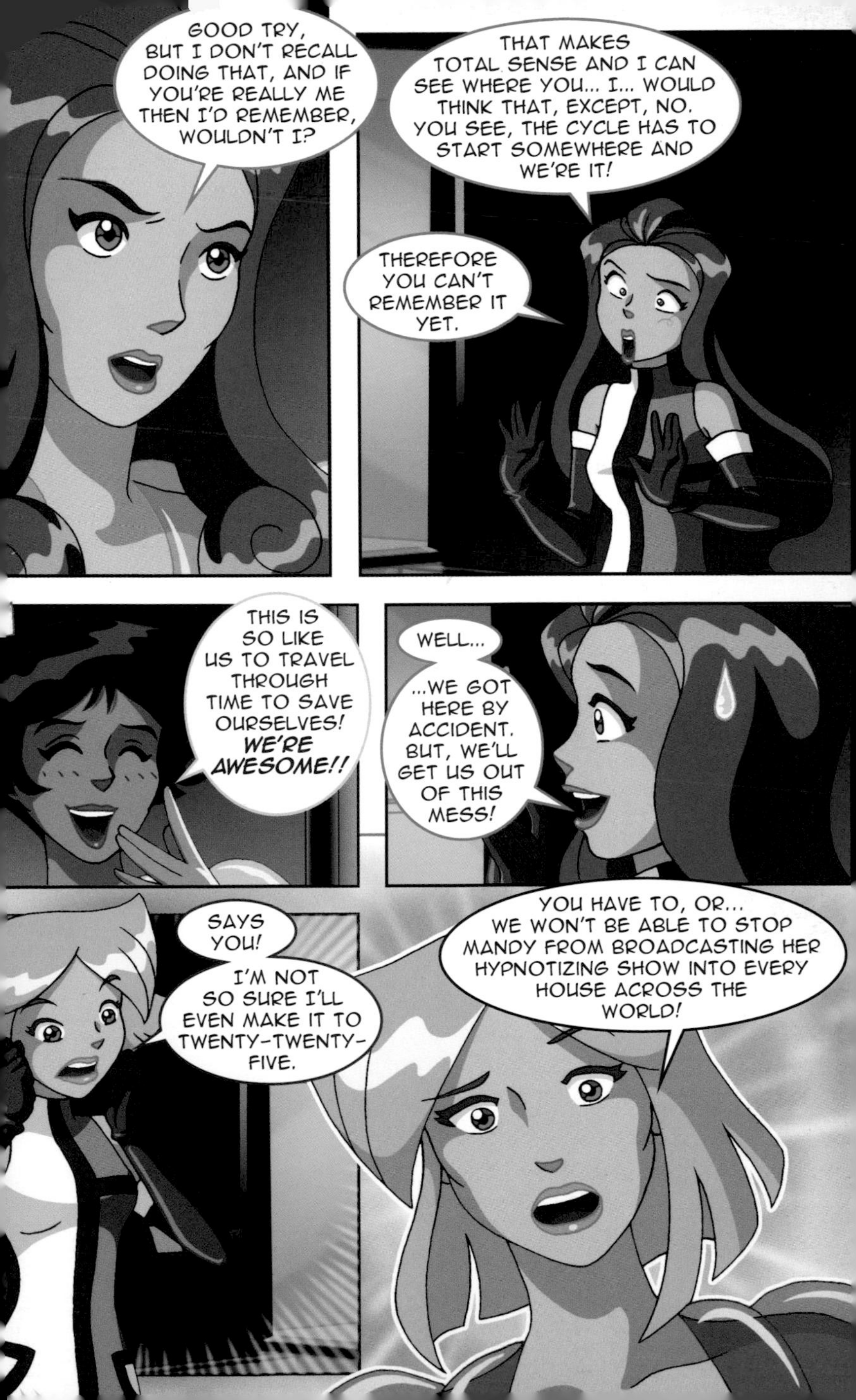
GOOD TRY, BUT I DON'T RECALL DOING THAT, AND IF YOU'RE REALLY ME THEN I'D REMEMBER, WOULDN'T I?
THAT MAKES TOTAL SENSE AND I CAN SEE WHERE YOU... I... WOULD THINK THAT, EXCEPT, NO. YOU SEE, THE CYCLE HAS TO START SOMEWHERE AND WE'RE IT!
THEREFORE YOU CAN'T REMEMBER IT YET.
THIS IS SO LIKE US TO TRAVEL THROUGH TIME TO SAVE OURSELVES! ***WE'RE AWESOME!!***
WELL...
...WE GOT HERE BY ACCIDENT. BUT, WE'LL GET US OUT OF THIS MESS!
SAYS YOU!
I'M NOT SO SURE I'LL EVEN MAKE IT TO TWENTY-TWENTY-FIVE.
YOU HAVE TO, OR... WE WON'T BE ABLE TO STOP MANDY FROM BROADCASTING HER HYPNOTIZING SHOW INTO EVERY HOUSE ACROSS THE WORLD!

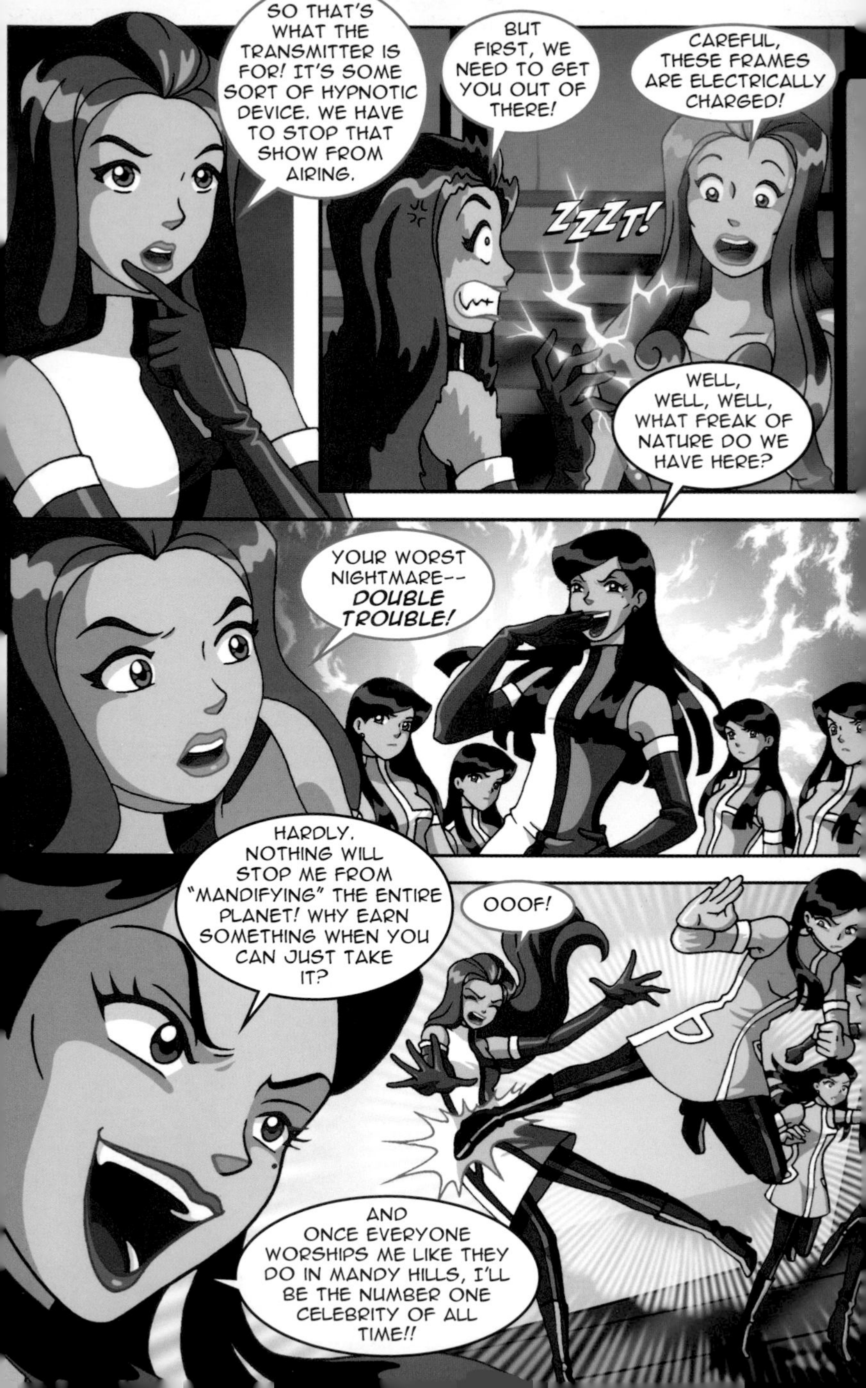
SO THAT'S WHAT THE TRANSMITTER IS FOR! IT'S SOME SORT OF HYPNOTIC DEVICE. WE HAVE TO STOP THAT SHOW FROM AIRING.
BUT FIRST, WE NEED TO GET YOU OUT OF THERE!
CAREFUL, THESE FRAMES ARE ELECTRICALLY CHARGED!
ZZZT!
WELL, WELL, WELL, WHAT FREAK OF NATURE DO WE HAVE HERE?
YOUR WORST NIGHTMARE-- *DOUBLE TROUBLE!*
HARDLY. NOTHING WILL STOP ME FROM "MANDIFYING" THE ENTIRE PLANET! WHY EARN SOMETHING WHEN YOU CAN JUST TAKE IT?
OOOF!
AND ONCE EVERYONE WORSHIPS ME LIKE THEY DO IN MANDY HILLS, I'LL BE THE NUMBER ONE CELEBRITY OF ALL TIME!!

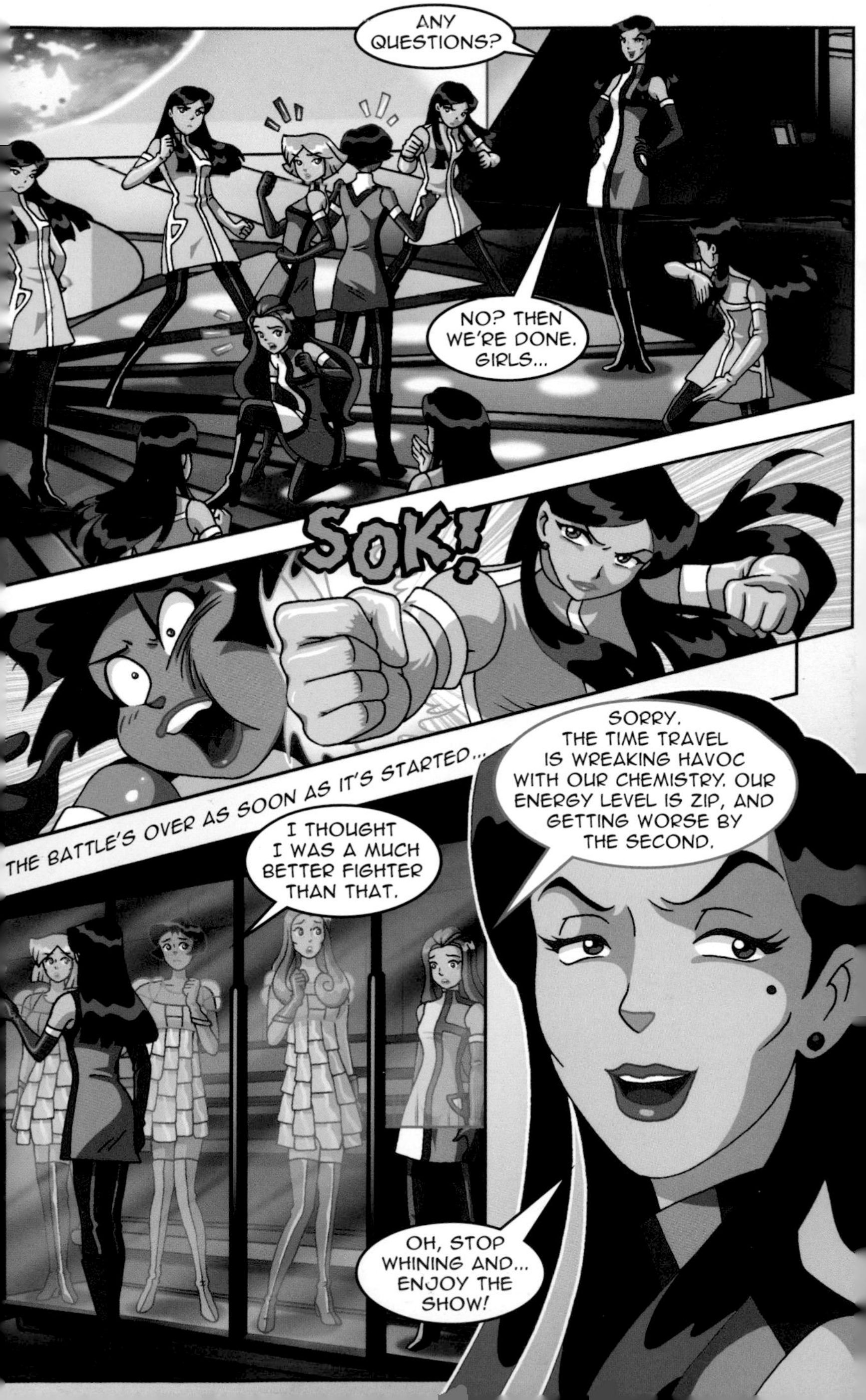
ANY QUESTIONS?
NO? THEN WE'RE DONE. GIRLS...
SOK!
THE BATTLE'S OVER AS SOON AS IT'S STARTED...
I THOUGHT I WAS A MUCH BETTER FIGHTER THAN THAT.
SORRY. THE TIME TRAVEL IS WREAKING HAVOC WITH OUR CHEMISTRY. OUR ENERGY LEVEL IS ZIP, AND GETTING WORSE BY THE SECOND.
OH, STOP WHINING AND... ENJOY THE SHOW!

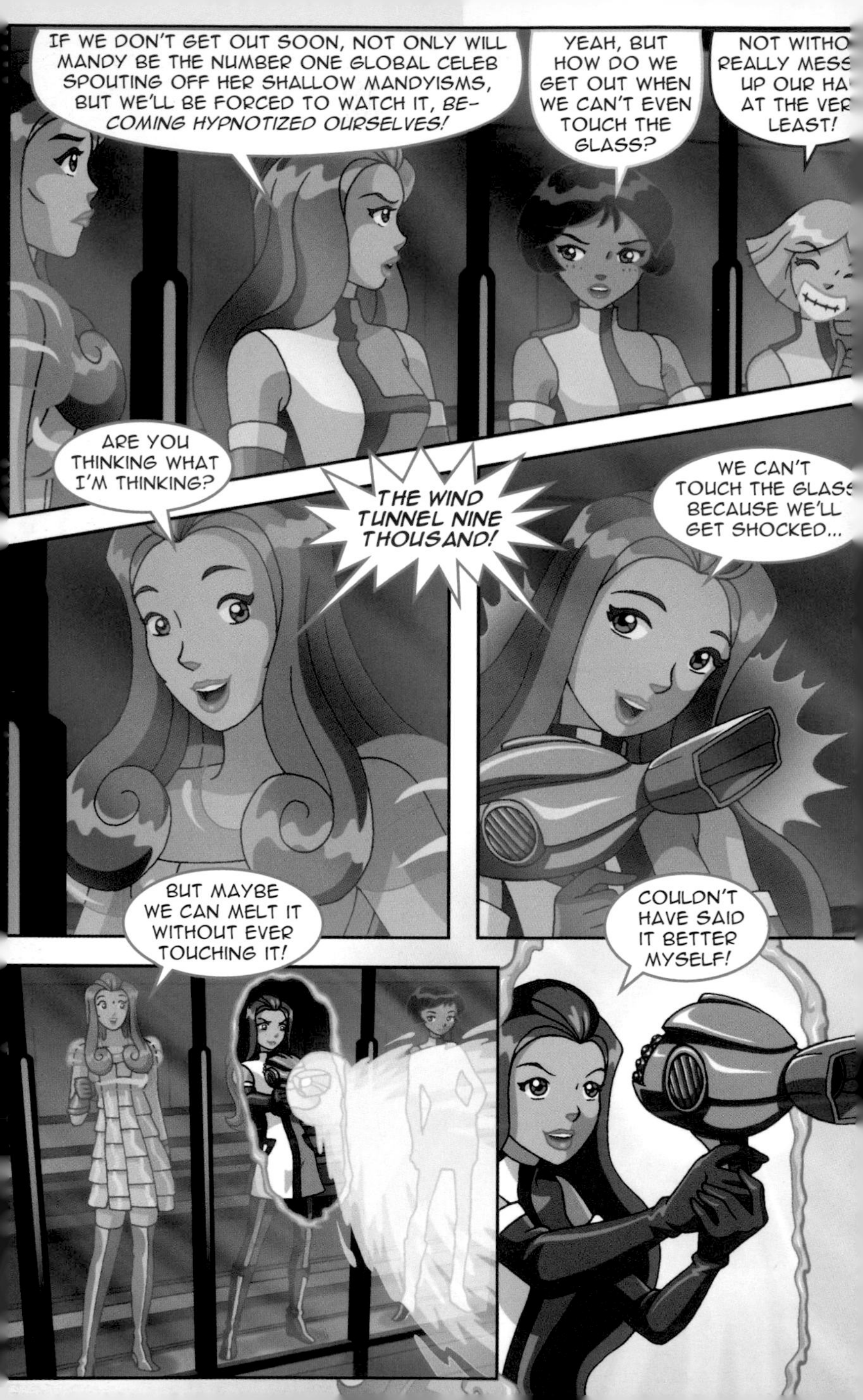
IF WE DON'T GET OUT SOON, NOT ONLY WILL MANDY BE THE NUMBER ONE GLOBAL CELEB SPOUTING OFF HER SHALLOW MANDYISMS, BUT WE'LL BE FORCED TO WATCH IT, BE-COMING HYPNOTIZED OURSELVES!
YEAH, BUT HOW DO WE GET OUT WHEN WE CAN'T EVEN TOUCH THE GLASS?
NOT WITHO REALLY MESS UP OUR HA AT THE VER LEAST!
ARE YOU THINKING WHAT I'M THINKING?
THE WIND TUNNEL NINE THOUSAND!
WE CAN'T TOUCH THE GLASS BECAUSE WE'LL GET SHOCKED...
BUT MAYBE WE CAN MELT IT WITHOUT EVER TOUCHING IT!
COULDN'T HAVE SAID IT BETTER MYSELF!

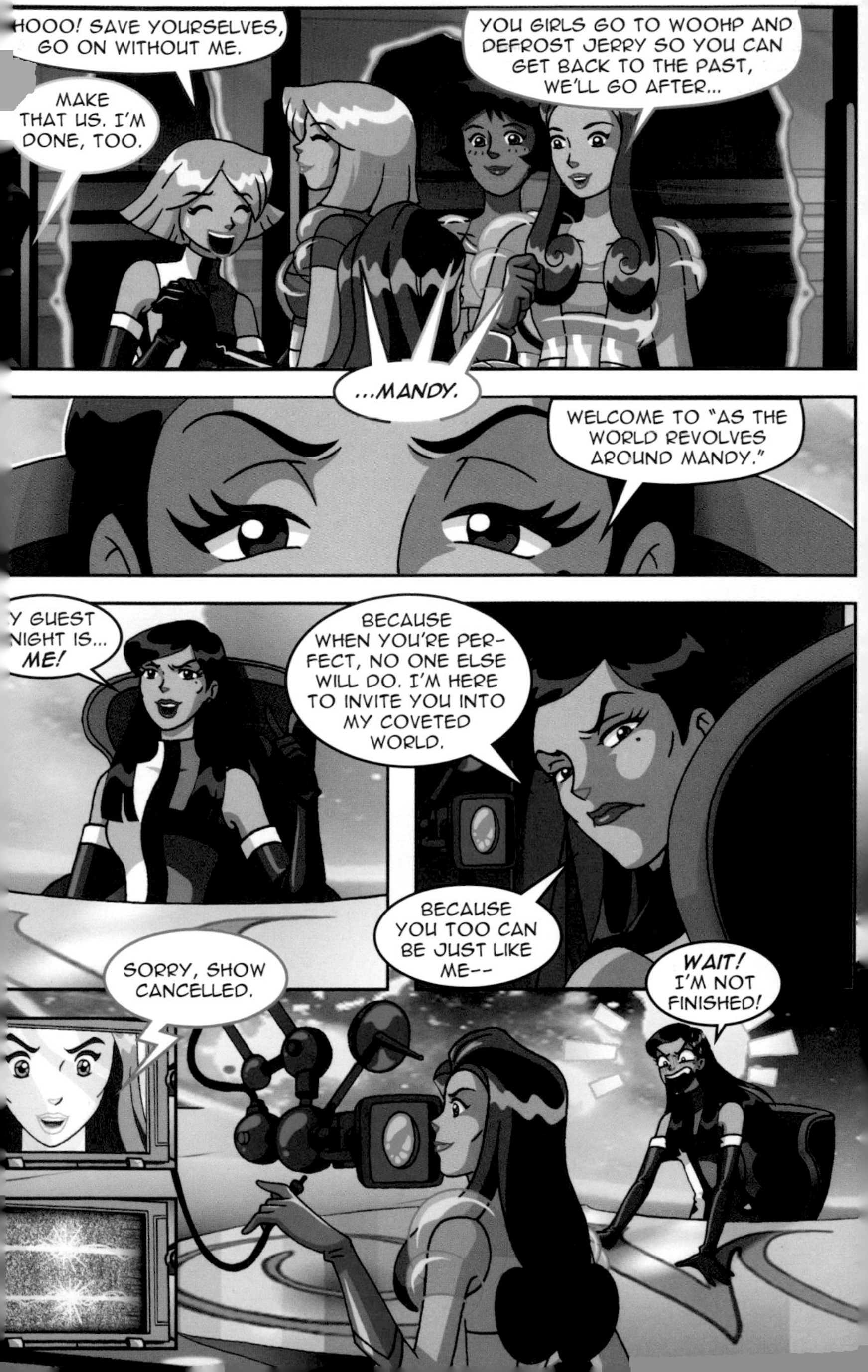

HOOO! SAVE YOURSELVES, GO ON WITHOUT ME.
MAKE THAT US. I'M DONE, TOO.
YOU GIRLS GO TO WOOHP AND DEFROST JERRY SO YOU CAN GET BACK TO THE PAST, WE'LL GO AFTER...
...MANDY.
WELCOME TO "AS THE WORLD REVOLVES AROUND MANDY."
Y GUEST NIGHT IS... ME!
BECAUSE WHEN YOU'RE PER-FECT, NO ONE ELSE WILL DO. I'M HERE TO INVITE YOU INTO MY COVETED WORLD.
BECAUSE YOU TOO CAN BE JUST LIKE ME--
SORRY, SHOW CANCELLED.
WAIT! I'M NOT FINISHED!

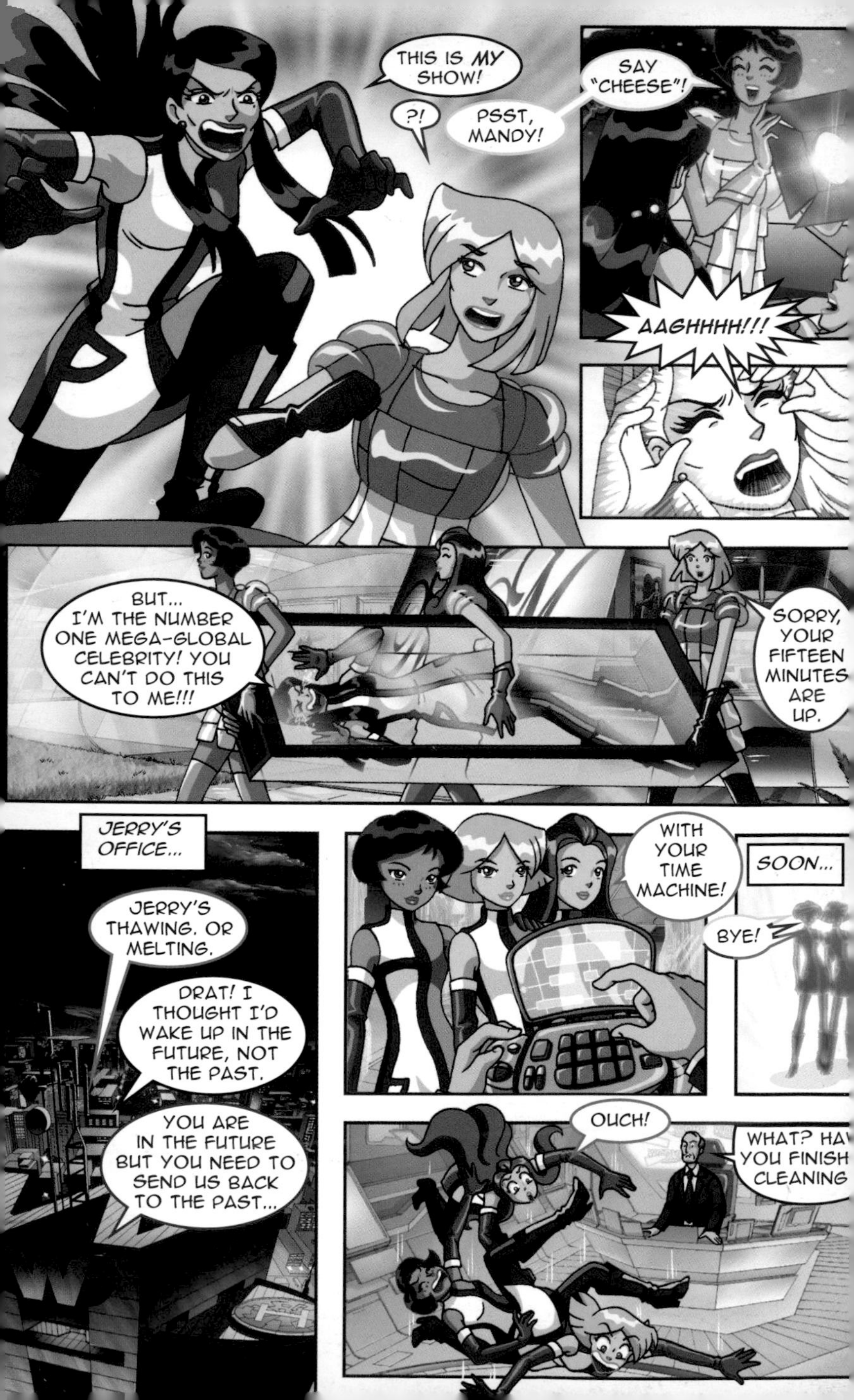
THIS IS *MY* SHOW!
?!
PSST, MANDY!
SAY "CHEESE"!
AAGHHHH!!!
BUT... I'M THE NUMBER ONE MEGA-GLOBAL CELEBRITY! YOU CAN'T DO THIS TO ME!!!
SORRY, YOUR FIFTEEN MINUTES ARE UP.
JERRY'S OFFICE...
JERRY'S THAWING. OR MELTING.
DRAT! I THOUGHT I'D WAKE UP IN THE FUTURE, NOT THE PAST.
YOU ARE IN THE FUTURE BUT YOU NEED TO SEND US BACK TO THE PAST...
WITH YOUR TIME MACHINE!
SOON...
BYE!
OUCH!
WHAT? HA
YOU FINISH
CLEANING

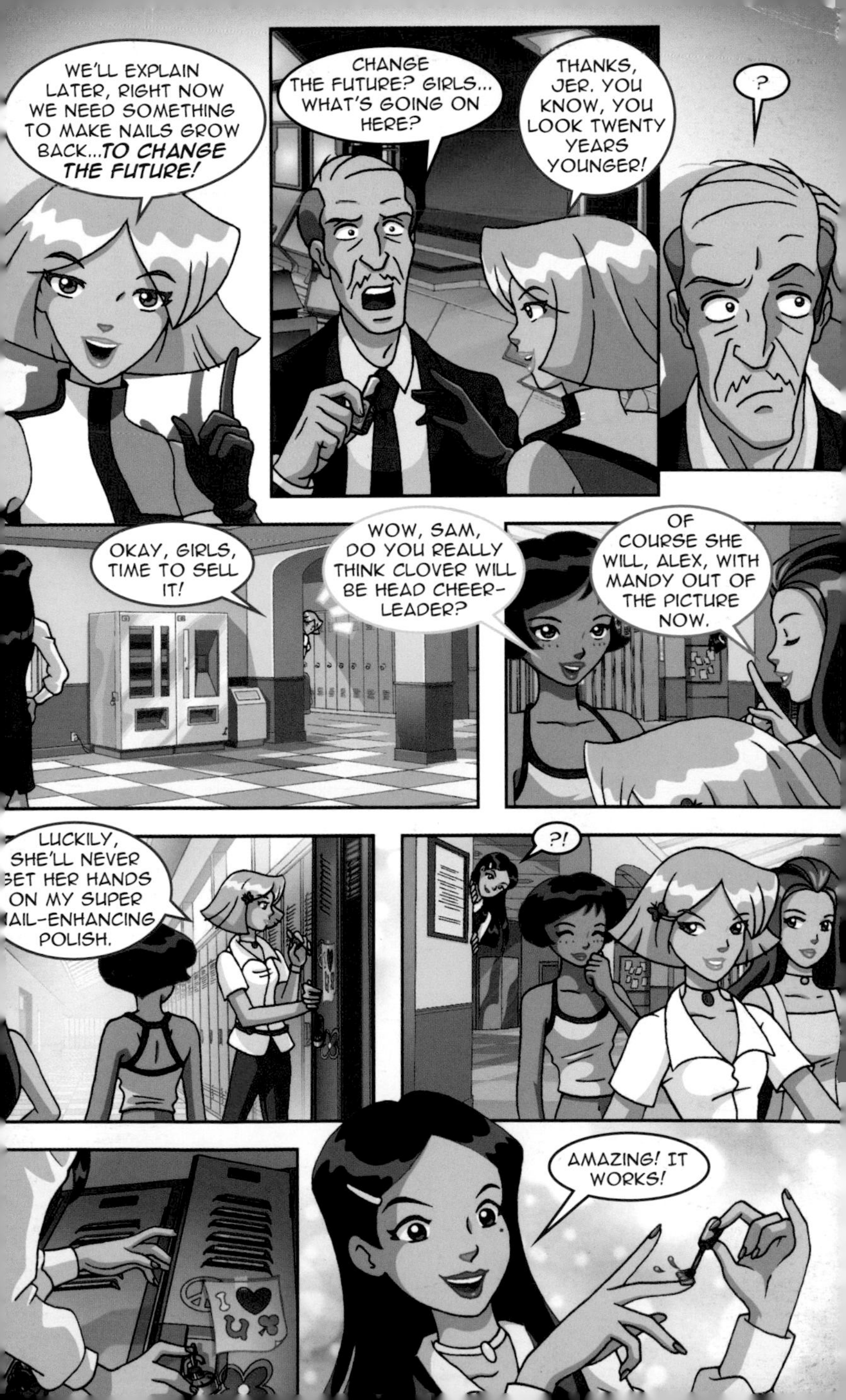
WE'LL EXPLAIN LATER, RIGHT NOW WE NEED SOMETHING TO MAKE NAILS GROW BACK...*TO CHANGE THE FUTURE!*
CHANGE THE FUTURE? GIRLS... WHAT'S GOING ON HERE?
THANKS, JER. YOU KNOW, YOU LOOK TWENTY YEARS YOUNGER!
?
OKAY, GIRLS, TIME TO SELL IT!
WOW, SAM, DO YOU REALLY THINK CLOVER WILL BE HEAD CHEER-LEADER?
OF COURSE SHE WILL, ALEX, WITH MANDY OUT OF THE PICTURE NOW.
LUCKILY, SHE'LL NEVER GET HER HANDS ON MY SUPER NAIL-ENHANCING POLISH.
?!
AMAZING! IT WORKS!

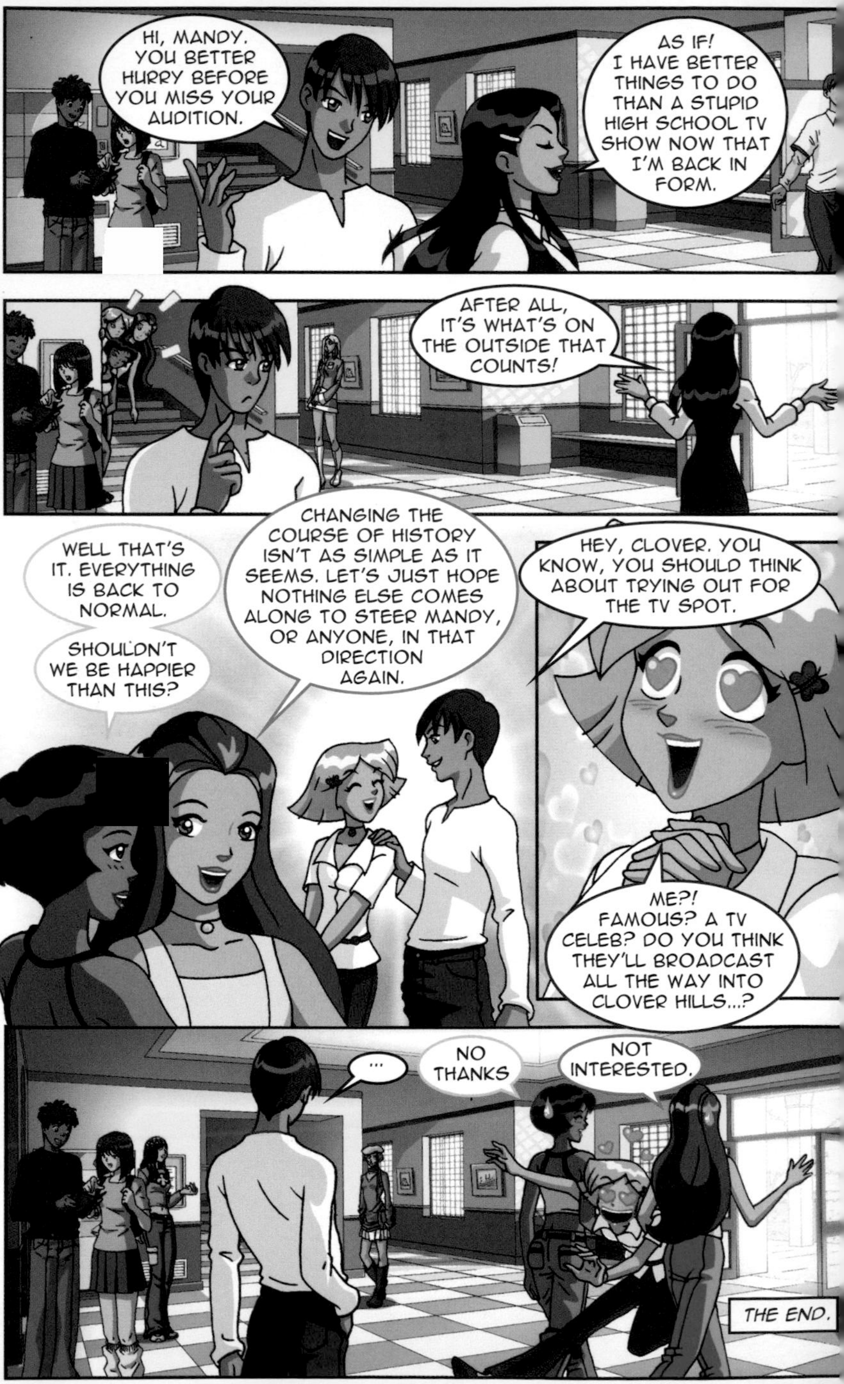
HI, MANDY. YOU BETTER HURRY BEFORE YOU MISS YOUR AUDITION.
AS IF! I HAVE BETTER THINGS TO DO THAN A STUPID HIGH SCHOOL TV SHOW NOW THAT I'M BACK IN FORM.
AFTER ALL, IT'S WHAT'S ON THE OUTSIDE THAT COUNTS!
WELL THAT'S IT. EVERYTHING IS BACK TO NORMAL.
SHOULDN'T WE BE HAPPIER THAN THIS?
CHANGING THE COURSE OF HISTORY ISN'T AS SIMPLE AS IT SEEMS. LET'S JUST HOPE NOTHING ELSE COMES ALONG TO STEER MANDY, OR ANYONE, IN THAT DIRECTION AGAIN.
HEY, CLOVER. YOU KNOW, YOU SHOULD THINK ABOUT TRYING OUT FOR THE TV SPOT.
ME?! FAMOUS? A TV CELEB? DO YOU THINK THEY'LL BROADCAST ALL THE WAY INTO CLOVER HILLS...?
...
NO THANKS
NOT INTERESTED.
THE END.

WATCH OUT FOR PAPERCUTZ™
The publisher of graphic novels created just for YOU!

Find out more about the big brains behind Papercutz on page 82.

TOTALLY SPIES! is now a part of the Papercutz line of super-stars! Discover new secrets about your favorite secret agents on page 84.

Papercutz is also proud to present a special graphic novel, THE LIFE OF POPE JOHN PAUL II ...*IN COMICS*! For more details about this major event in graphic novel publishing proceed to page 86.

There's big news in store for NANCY DREW, GIRL DETECTIVE! The star of the best-selling series of Papercutz graphic novels is heading for Hollywood! We've got the inside story starting on page 89.

THE HARDY BOYS have been on a wild and crazy ride since their very first Papercutz graphic novel. Check out where they've been and where they're going on page 92.

Fans have suggested that the "Z" in Papercutz stands for ZORRO! See for yourself the amazing cast of characters Zorro has encountered in his series of Papercutz graphic novels starting on page 95.

Meet TERRY NANTIER and JIM SALICRUP
– the comics-loving guys that started

PAPERCUTZ

This is the amazing tale of two men, born days apart, who have devoted their lives to comics. Terry Nantier is a pioneer in the world of graphic novels, who for over thirty years has published work by the greatest artists and writers in the world – Will Eisner, Milton Caniff, P. Craig Russell, Lewis Trondheim, and many more. His partner in this new project, Jim Salicrup, started in comics when he was a wee lad of fifteen years old, and went on to become one of the most successful editors in the field, editing top titles such as the X-Men, the X-Files, the Fantastic Four, Dracula, and many more, including Spider-Man # 1 – the best-selling Spider-Man comic of all time.

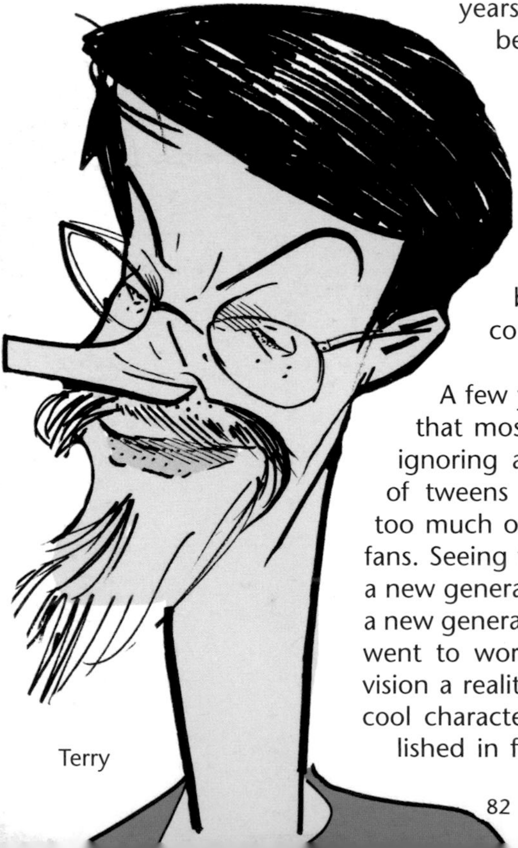

Terry

A few years ago, Terry observed that most comics publishers were ignoring a vast potential audience of tweens and teens and focusing too much on older long-time comics fans. Seeing this opportunity to create a new generation of graphic novels for a new generation of fans, Terry and Jim went to work at once to make their vision a reality. The plan was simple—cool characters, in great stories, published in full-color in a digest-sized format. The best parts of traditional American comics would be combined with the most exciting elements of Japanese comics (called manga).

But what should they call this new comics company? Sylvia Nantier, Terry's brilliant daughter, suggested the name, and *Papercutz* was born.

In 2005 the debut Papercutz graphic novels were published – NANCY DREW, GIRL DETECTIVE and THE HARDY BOYS, with new books following every three months. And right from the start, fans loved the Papercutz approach — the first NANCY DREW, GIRL DETECTIVE graphic novel went into three big printings in its first year!

To stay on top of everything that's coming your way from Papercutz, we've created this special bonus feature. Everything you see presented in these pages is available now at your favorite booksellers. To get even more up-to-date news, be sure to visit www.papercutz.com.

Terry and Jim want to thank each and every one of you for picking up this Papercutz graphic novel. Don't be shy— let us know what you think. After all, we're working hard to produce stories that are not only fun and entertaining – but also respect your intelligence. Send your comments to our Editor-in-Chief: salicrup@papercutz.com

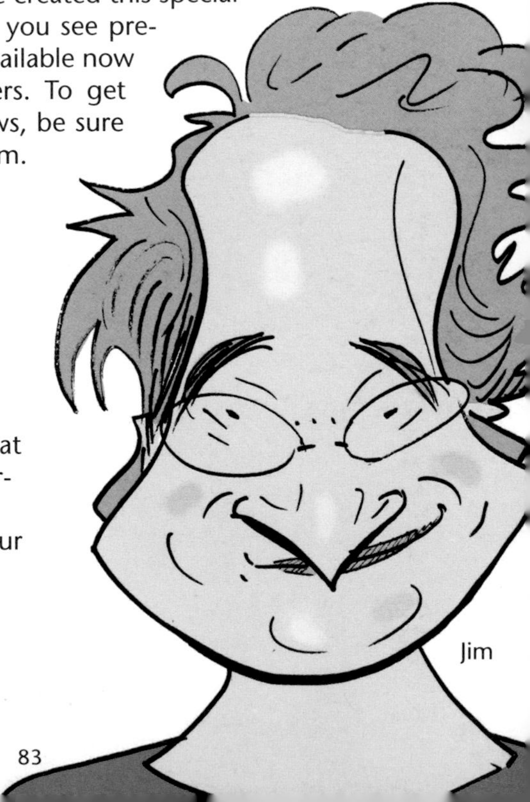
Jim

Caricatures by Steve Brodner.

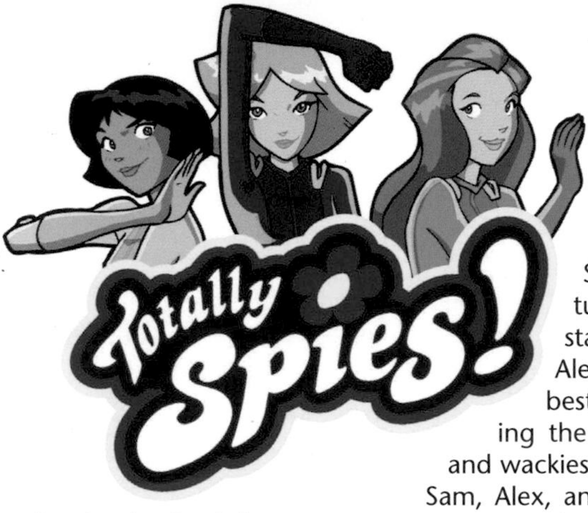
Totally Spies!

They're here! TV's sens tional secret agents c Cartoon Network a now starring in the own series of full-col graphic novels fro Papercutz! Each Totally Spies! graphic novel fe tures two big adventur starring Clover, Sam, an Alex doing what they c best—having fun while foi ing the schemes of the wilde and wackiest criminal masterminds! Sam, Alex, and Clover are three Hig School girls who fight crime on an international scale as undercover agen for the World Organization of Human Protection – WOOHP! Stressfu Sure. Exciting? Totally.

CONFIDENTIAL PERSONALITY PROFILES

Codename: CLOVER

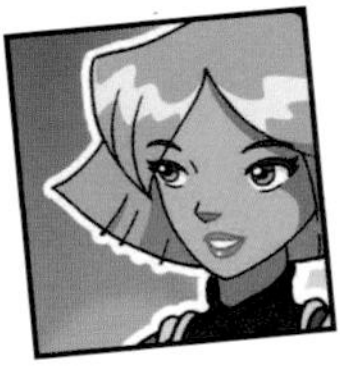

TOP SECRET

Clover is a shopaholic who is always ready for action. Clover acts on impulse rather than reflection — and she can't stop falling in love!

Athletic, agile, and strong, Clover is definitely gutsy and never thinks twice about getting into the thick of the action. She is always ready to teach the bad guys a lesson, even when she has absolutely no chance of defeating them.

Codename: SAM

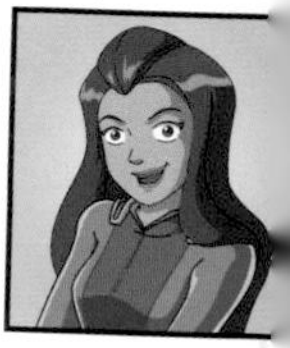

TOP SECRET

The most mature member of the team, Sam is rational and logical.

A star pupil, Sam is capable of finding solutions to problems that require a cool head and extra brainpower. She's the one who knows how to keep things in perspective and always defuses conflicts in a practical way—whether in the classroom or out in the field.

Codename:
ALEX

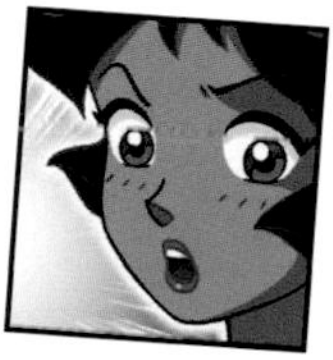

lex, the youngest member of the eam, is also the most affectionate. he admires her older friends, am and Clover, enormously and determined to place their relaonships above all else.

eing the youngest, Alex is also a gullible. She's frequently fooled the baddies... as well as by her ends! Fortunately, Alex is very od-natured and never turns it o a big deal.

odename:
MANDY

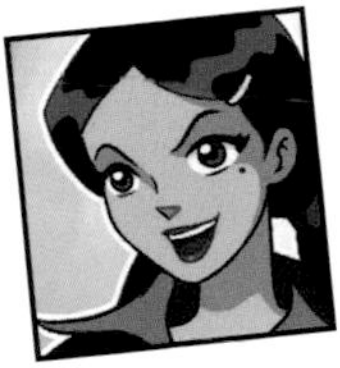

Mandy is Alex, Sam, and Clover's worst nightmare. She is in the same class as our three heroines. Overly self-assured, pretentious, and opinionated, Mandy is a real pest. Whether she's trying to get involved with the girls' private lives or desperately trying to outdo them in order to look cool, Mandy is always around the corner just waiting to cause the girls trouble.

Codename:
JERRY

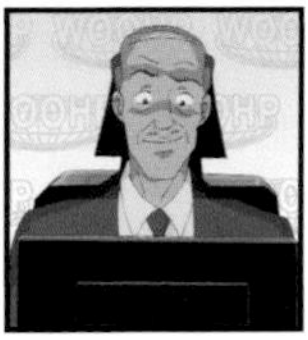

As the head of the World Organization Of Human Protection, Jerry thinks nothing of whisking the girls away from their daily lives to send them off in hot pursuit of a crazy villain halfway around the world!

Both a mentor and an instructor, Jerry is a second father to the girls. He's always there to congratulate them at the end of a successful mission.

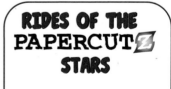

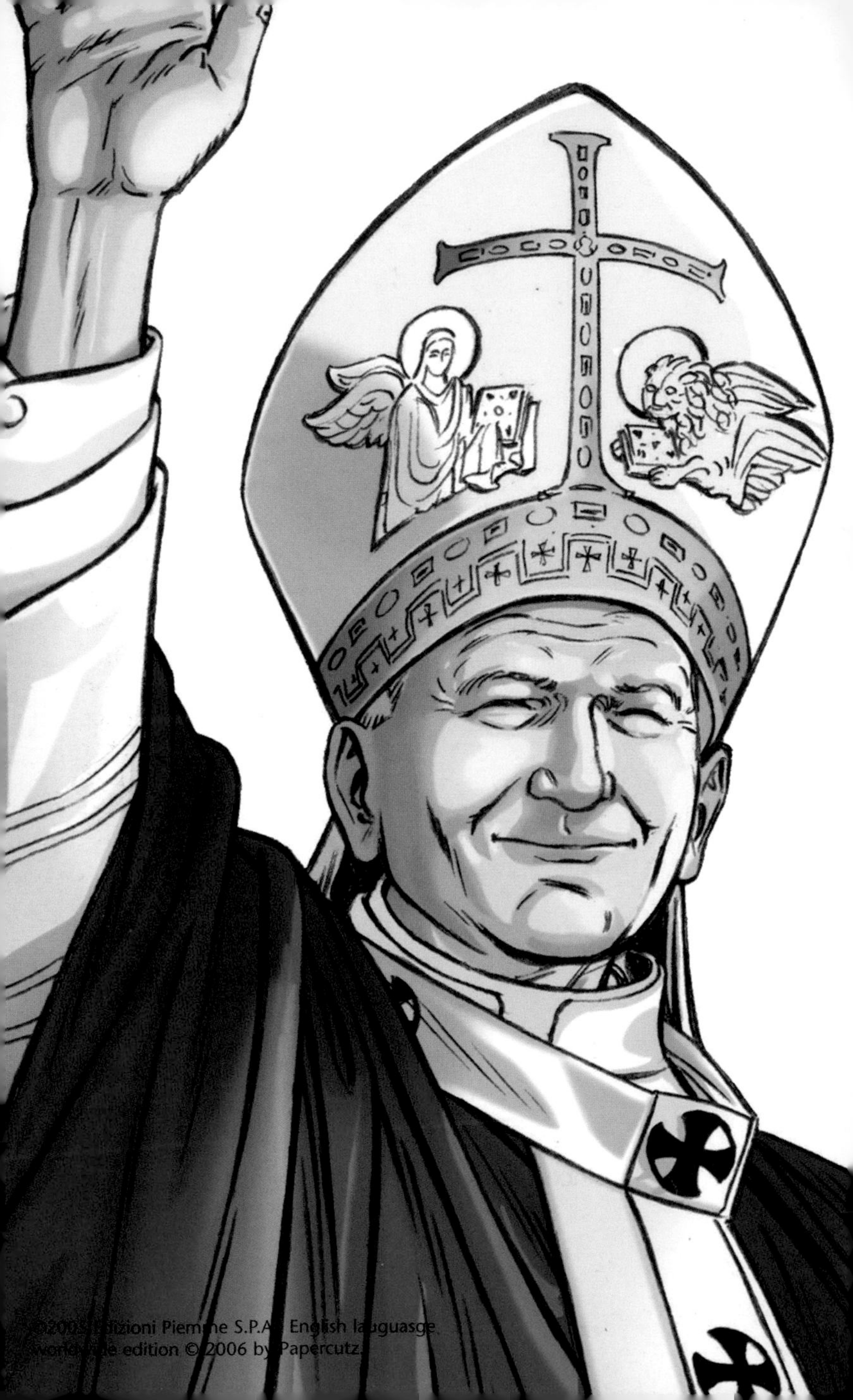

THE LIFE OF POPE JOHN PAUL II ...IN COMICS!

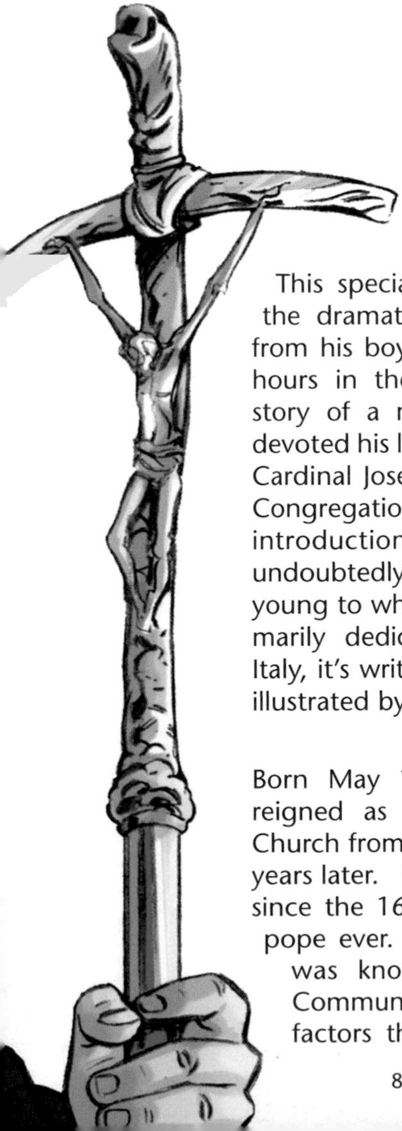

This special Papercutz graphic novel tells the dramatic story of Karol Wojtyla's life, from his boyhood in Poland to his sad final hours in the Vatican. It's the inspirational story of a man who loved humanity and devoted his life to his beliefs. As His Eminence Cardinal Jose Saraiva Martins, prefect of the Congregation for Saints' Causes writes in his introduction, the Pope's "message was undoubtedly understood foremost by the young to whom (this graphic novel is) ...primarily dedicated." Originally published in Italy, it's written by Alessandro Mainardi and illustrated by Werner Maresta.

Born May 18, 1920, Karol Jozef Wojtyla reigned as pope of the Roman Catholic Church from 1978 until his death, almost 27 years later. He was the first non-Italian pope since the 16th century and the only Polish pope ever. In his early years as pope, he was known for speaking out against Communism, and considered one of the factors that helped bring about its fall.

Even in his final years he was unafraid to speak out, and criticized contemporary greed in the forms of consumerism and out-of-control capitalism.

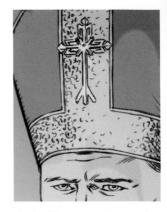

During his reign, the pope visited over 100 countries, more than any previous pope. While he was Pope the influence of the Church expanded in the Third World.

Pope John Paul II was well-loved worldwide, attracting the largest crowds in history. Attracting crowds of over one million people in a single venue and over four

million people at the World Youth Day in Manila.

On April 2, 2005, at 9:37 PM local time, Pope John Paul II died after struggling with Parkinson's Disease, amongst other diseases, for many years. Millions of people flocked to Rome to pay their respects to the body and for his funeral.

This special Papercutz graphic novel is published at the larger 6" x 9" size, in full-color, as a jacketed hardcover, available at booksellers everywhere.

RIDES OF THE PAPERCUTZ STARS

The bulletproof Popemobile was created to protect John Paul II.

NANCY DREW
GOES HOLLYWOOD!

Production commenced in Los Angeles on the live-action mystery adventure movie *Nancy Drew*, starring Emma Roberts (Nickelodeon's *Unfabulous*), Josh Flitter (*The Greatest Game Ever Played*), Max Thieriot (*The Pacifier*) and Tate Donovan (*Good Night, and Good Luck, The O.C.*) as Nancy's dad, Carson Drew. The movie is directed by Andrew Fleming.

In a published interview, Emma has revealed that she's "rather nervous because so many generations have read the books and I have big shoes to fill. But I'm really excited and it's going to be a lot of fun"

Nancy Drew is set to appear at the theater near you in August 2007, from Warner Bros. Pictures, a Warner Bros. Entertainment Company.

NANCY DREW Graphic Novel Episode Guide

Here's a great way to keep track of the Papercutz Nancy Drew, Girl Detective graphic novels...

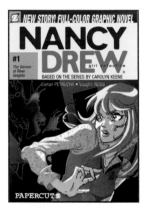

NEW STORY! FULL-COLOR GRAPHIC NOVEL
NANCY DREW
#1
The Demon of River Heights
girl detective
BASED ON THE SERIES BY CAROLYN KEENE
PAPERCUTZ

Nancy Drew graphic novel #1
"The Demon of River Heights"
Stefan Petrucha, writer, and Sho Murase, artist
Join Nancy, along with Bess and George, as they search for missing student filmmakers and discover the deadly secret behind the local urban legend known as "The Demon of River Heights."

Nancy Drew graphic novel #2
"Writ In Stone"
Stefan Petrucha, writer, and Sho Murase, artist
It's double trouble for Nancy and her friends, when an ancient artifact and a little boy are both suddenly missing. Nancy's determined to recover both the artifact and little Owen, but someone's out to stop her – *permanently!*

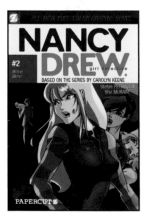

NANCY DREW
#2
girl detective
BASED ON THE SERIES BY CAROLYN KEENE
PAPERCUTZ

Nancy Drew graphic novel #3
"The Haunted Dollhouse"
Stefan Petrucha, writer, and Sho Murase, artist
River Heights is celebrating "Nostalgia Week," and everyone in town is dressing up like it's 1930. But the fun is soon interrupted when the dolls in Emma Blavatsky's antique dollhouse seem to come alive and start depicting strange crimes that soon come true in real life. When Nancy stakes out the dollhouse, she witnesses a doll version of herself murdered!

Nancy Drew graphic novel #4
"The Girl Who Wasn't There"
Stefan Petrucha, writer, and Sho Murase, artist
Nancy receives a desperate call for help from Kalpana, her new friend in India. Soon, Nancy, along with Bess and George, are in New Delhi, looking for Kalpana, where not even Sahadev, a powerful crime lord, can scare Nancy off the case!

Nancy Drew graphic novel #5
"The Fake Heir"
Stefan Petrucha, writer, and Vaughn Ross, artist
Nancy Drew may have lost her ability to solve a mystery! It's totally embarrassing for Nancy to confront the very much alive Mr. Druthers — the man she claimed was murdered by his wife.

ALL-NEW STORY FULL-COLOR GRAPHIC NOVEL
NANCY DREW
girl detective
BASED ON THE SERIES BY CAROLYN KEENE
Stefan PETRUCHA
Sho MURASE
PAPERCUTZ

NANCY DREW
girl detective
#4
The Girl Who Wasn't There
BASED ON THE SERIES BY CAROLYN KEENE
Stefan PETRUCHA • Sho MURASE
PAPERCUTZ

NEW STORY! FULL-COLOR GRAPHIC NOVEL
NANCY DREW
girl detective
#5
The Fake Heir
BASED ON THE SERIES BY CAROLYN KEENE
Stefan PETRUCHA
Vaughn ROSS
PAPERCUTZ

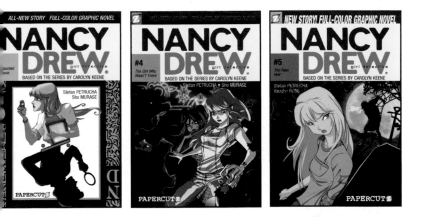

RIDES OF THE PAPERCUTZ STARS

Normally, Nancy Drew drives her gasoline-electric hybrid car, but she drove this roadster during Nostalgia Week.

THE HARDY BOYS ®

Sam, Clover, and Alex, agents of WOOHP (World Organization of Human Protection), who are now battling the forces of LAMOS (League Aiming to Menace and Overthrow Spies), aren't the only spies lurking within the pages of Papercutz graphic novels! There was this guy, who Frank and Joe Hardy rescued in Hardy Boys graphic novel # 3...

NOT TO APPEAR UNGRATEFUL, BUT I WAS EXPECTING SOMEONE FROM HER MAJESTY'S SECRET SERVICE.

MY BROTHER AND I ARE WITH A.T.A.C. BUT WE WERE TRAINING WITH MI 6 THIS WEEKEND -- WE WERE IN THE AREA.

The Hardy Boys ® Simon & Schuster

And, of course, Frank and Joe Hardy are now themselves undercover brothers working for ATAC (American Teens Against Crime), the secret organization created by their dad, Fenton Hardy.

Recently, Papercutz Editor-in-Chief, Jim Salicrup had the pleasure of meeting Robert Vaughn, who played TV super-spy, Napoleon Solo on the classic The Man From U.N.C.L.E. (United Network Command for Law and Enforce-ment). Here the Man From Uncle checks out Hardy Boys graphic novel # 1, as The Man From MoCCA (Museum of Comic and Cartoon Art) looks on...

THE HARDY BOYS Graphic Novel Episode Guide

America's favorite undercover brothers star in an all-new, full-color series of Papercutz graphic novels, with all-new comics stories based on the series by Franklin W. Dixon.

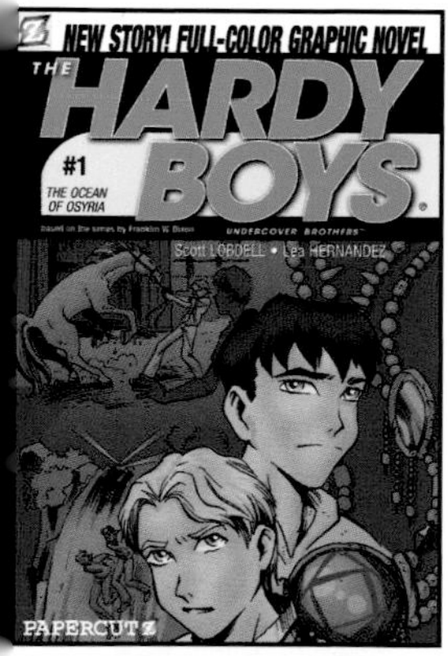
NEW STORY! FULL-COLOR GRAPHIC NOVEL
THE HARDY BOYS
#1
THE OCEAN OF OSYRIA
Scott LOBDELL • Lea HERNANDEZ
PAPERCUTZ

The Hardy Boys graphic novel #1
"The Ocean of Osyria"
Scott Lobdell, writer, and Lea Hernandez, artist
Frank and Joe Hardy, with Callie and Iola, search for a missing Mid-Eastern art treasure — "The Ocean of Osyria" — to free their friend, Chet Morton, who has been falsely accused of stealing it! It's like a blockbuster movie in comics form featuring your favorite teen sleuths!

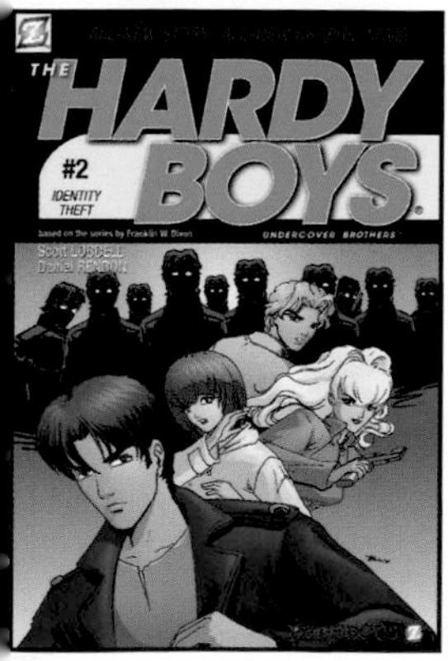
THE HARDY BOYS
#2
IDENTITY THEFT

The Hardy Boys graphic novel #2
"Identity Theft"
Scott Lobdell, writer, Daniel Rendon, artist
Frank and Joe Hardy, are assigned a fantastic case of stolen identity — literally! Joy Gallagher claims another girl is now living her life, with her parents, and in her body! Is she insane? Or can her story actually be true? Featuring a special guest-appearance by Mr. Snuggles!

The Hardy Boys graphic novel #3
"Mad House"
Scott Lobdell, writer, Daniel Rendon, artist
Frank and Joe Hardy go undercover on the hit reality TV series "Mad House," the show in which contestants must live together in a house while cameras record their every move, to solve the mystery of who is harming the contestants— and why?! But things go from bad to worse when the Hardy Boys stumble upon a shocking murder!

The Hardy Boys graphic novel #4
"Malled"
Scott Lobdell, writer, Daniel Rendon, artist
Bayport's much-publicized new mall is about to open, but when suspicious accidents keep happening, ATAC sends Frank and Joe Hardy to investigate! The night before the Mall's Grand Opening, Frank, Joe, and eight others are mysteriously locked in the mall— with a murderer on the loose!

The Hardy Boys graphic novel #5
"Sea You, Sea Me"
Scott Lobdell, writer, Daniel Rendon, artist
The Hardy Boys get caught in a perfect storm! Frank and Joe go undercover aboard "the Silver Lining," an old fishing boat, to find out why teen crew members keep mysteriously vanishing. The number of suspects dwindles when one of the crew turns up dead!

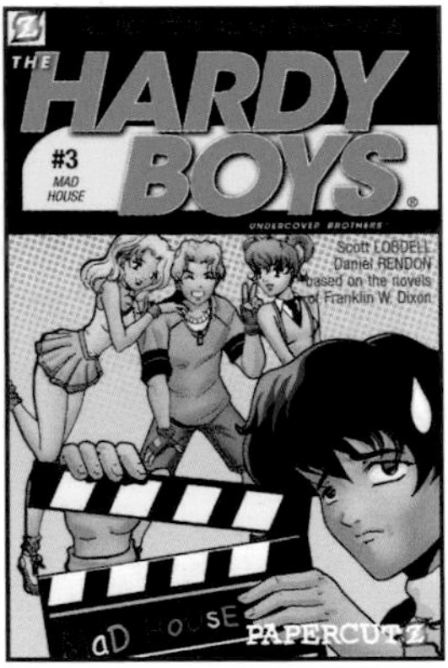
THE HARDY BOYS
#3
MAD HOUSE
Scott LOBDELL
Daniel RENDON
based on the novels of Franklin W. Dixon
PAPERCUTZ

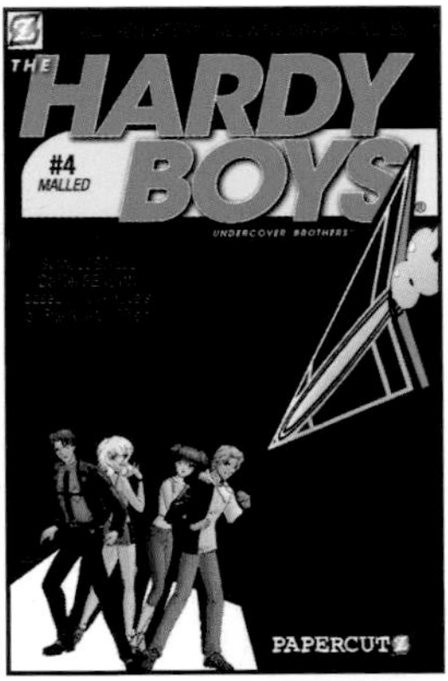
THE HARDY BOYS
#4
MALLED
PAPERCUTZ

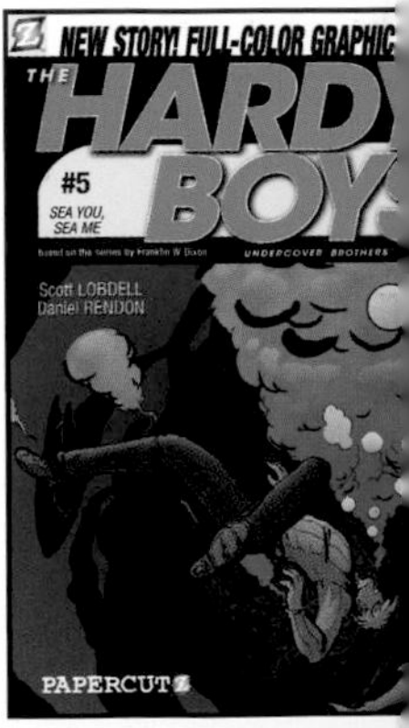
NEW STORY! FULL-COLOR GRAPHIC
THE HARD BOY
#5
SEA YOU, SEA ME
Scott LOBDELL
Daniel RENDON
PAPERCUTZ

RIDES OF THE PAPERCUTZ STARS

Frank and Joe prefer motorcycles to cars.

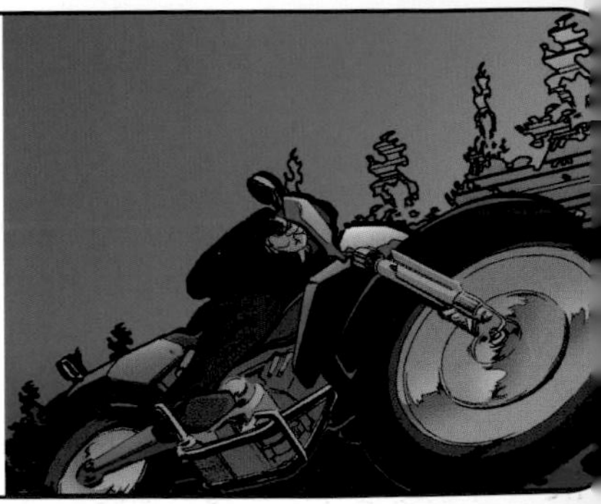

ZORRO

The Papercutz Zorro graphic novels are unlike any other Zorro comics ever published before. The obvious difference is the Japanese comics style look of Sidney Lima's artwork. But the really big difference is that Zorro's new adventures take place outside of the pueblo de Los Angeles. Why would that community's legendary hero ever leave? The answer to that question is this woman:

Eulalia, risked her life to save Zorro from being shot by Commandante Monasterio. Enraged, he struck her across her face with his gun, scarring her, and sentenced her to death. Fortunately, Zorro has returned the favor, and rescued her before she could be executed. Now Zorro and Eulalia are on the run from Monasterio, who is determined to kill them both!

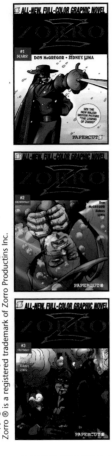

ALL-NEW FULL-COLOR GRAPHIC NOVEL
ZORRO
#1
SCARS!
DON McGREGOR • SIDNEY LIMA
PAPERCUTZ

Zorro graphic novel #1

"Scars!"

Don McGregor, writer and Sidney Lima, artist

Zorro and Eulalia wind up in literally uncharted territory, and actually meet a mapmaker and his wife who are on the run from Lucifer Trapp, a man determined to keep this territory undiscovered at any cost!

ALL-NEW FULL-COLOR GRAPHIC NOVEL
ZORRO
#2
PAPERCUTZ

Zorro graphic novel #2

Don McGregor, writer and Sidney Lima, artist

"Drownings!" takes Zorro and Eulaia even farther away from Los Angeles, as they run into a couple fleeing the deadly Scorched Brothers. But after being with Eulalia day and night for several weeks, can Zorro seriously hope to keep his identity secret from Eulalia? What happens when Zorro is finally unmasked?

ALL-NEW FULL-COLOR GRAPHIC NOVEL
ZORRO
#3
PAPERCUTZ

Zorro graphic novel #3

Don McGregor, writer and Sidney Lima, artist

"Vultures!" proves that wherever Zorro and Eulalia go, they are sure to encounter trouble! Zorro must save Normandie Caniff from becoming the next victim of a con artist called Lockspur. That's not easy to do when you're tied to stakes and being served up as dinner for ravenous vultures!

Will Zorro ever find a safe haven for the woman who saved his life? Or are they destined to be on the run forever?

RIDES OF THE PAPERCUTZ STARS

More than a means of transportation, the great black stallion, Tornado, is Zorro's friend.